# FALLING SKY

# FALLING SKY

## RAJAN KHANNA

an imprint of Prometheus Books
Amherst, NY

Published 2014 by Pyr®, an imprint of Prometheus Books

Cover design by Nicole Sommer-Lecht
Cover illustration © Chris McGrath

Inquiries should be addressed to
Pyr
59 John Glenn Drive
Amherst, New York 14228
VOICE: 716–691–0133
FAX: 716–691–0137
WWW.PYRSF.COM

18  17  16  15  14     5  4  3  2  1

Library of Congress Cataloging-in-Publication Data

Khanna, Rajan, 1974-
    Falling sky / by Rajan Khanna.
        pages  cm
    ISBN 978-1-61614-982-6 (paperback) — ISBN 978-1-61614-983-3 (ebook)
    I. Title.

PS3611.H359F35 2014
813'.6—dc23

2014015842

Printed in the United States of America

*To my mother, Christine Khanna,*
*who always believed in the stories I wanted to tell.*

# CHAPTER ONE

t's when I hit the ground that my skin starts to itch, as if I can catch the Bug from the very earth itself. I know I can't, but I itch anyway, and the sweat starts trickling, which doesn't help.

But there's no time to focus on any of that now because I'm on the ground and there's nothing safe about that. So I heft the rifle in my hands, trying not to hold it too lightly, trying to feel a bit casual with its weight but the kind of casual that makes it easy to shoot.

And then Miranda is next to me. She gives me that half smile, that almost mocking look she always does, and I see the sun reflected in her glasses. Then she's off, moving quickly to the prone form in the nearby clearing, the filthy, long-nailed mess I dropped just minutes ago with a tranq gun.

The fucking Feral.

It's laid out in the grass, head lolling to the side. Not moving. Just the way I like them. Its hair is a tangled mess merging into its beard. Figures. Lone hunters are usually male. It wears a faded collared shirt so matted with dirt and muck that you can't tell what color it might have originally been. Its pants are tatters. And the stench . . . I always wonder how Miranda can stand it.

There's nothing about it that says who he might have been before. Someone's brother? A father? A son?

All swept away by the Bug.

It occurs to me that if my dad were alive, he would be telling me how truly fucked this is. He was the one who taught me to run from the things. To keep to the air. But my dad isn't around. Not anymore. And he'd be one to talk anyway.

As Miranda bends over the Feral, I catch sight of the pistol hanging from her belt in the makeshift holster. I gave her that pistol. Not that I ever want to see her have to use it. Especially not with the ammo supply being what it is. But she has one, and that's at least one smart change I've made.

The others . . . I'm still deciding.

My heart picks up in my chest the closer she gets to him. But that's not the worst part. He's out, and will be out for hours most likely with the dose I hit him with. He's not going to wake up and grab her. No, what I'm afraid of comes next.

Miranda pulls out the syringe.

My breath almost stops.

She's got the gloves on, the mask, and only the skin around her eyes is visible to me—another smart change I've made to the process—but we're talking blood here. Feral blood. And if my dad taught me to run away from Ferals, he taught me to fly away from their blood. Because that's how the Bug is transmitted. By fluids. And if Miranda were to swallow or maybe even inhale just a little of that Bugged-up plasma, well, there'll be one more Feral in the world. And while Miranda pisses me the fuck off on a regular basis, I'd hate to see her go like that.

She has the syringe in his arm, and the blood glugs out into a tube. You'd be surprised at how few test tubes there are in the world. But then again, maybe not.

Just a moment more and we're done, and Miranda will head back to the airship ladder and I'll follow, making sure I give her a wide berth.

I'm getting antsy, feet ready to move, when I hear the first screams. The rifle raises in my hands almost of its own accord as I scan beyond her for the pack. "Miranda," I call.

"Almost there."

"Now," I say. I can see the shapes moving down the next hill, Ferals loping over the grass in tattered clothing. Their howls echo across the space between us. Miranda still isn't up.

Then yelps come from behind me. "Now!" I roar as another pack comes from the other direction, this one larger, and closer.

The rifle kicks back in my hands and gunshots punctuate their screams. I don't worry about where they came from, why I didn't see them. I breathe in, set up a shot, take it. Breathe out. Even after all these years, part of my body wants to jerk the trigger wildly, pepper the whole area with gunfire, but I don't have the ammo for that, and I can't afford to reload. And I've learned to control that part of me. Learned to push it into some dark corner of the soul. Or something.

The rifle bucks. One Feral goes down in a spray of blood that sends a chill through me. Another's face explodes in a wet mess. Miranda runs by me, careful to stay out of my line of fire, and I smell that elusive scent of hers. Then she's climbing up the ladder, and after another two shots I'm right behind her.

I try not to think about the vial of blood she's holding. Try not to think about it falling on me, somehow breaking. I try and I fail.

A Feral reaches the bottom of the ladder, and we're still not up to the ship. I hook my arm around the rope, and do the same for my leg. And I slowly aim and fire down on the thing's head.

Then we're moving up and away, Miranda at the controls of the *Cherub*, and the feel of the wind on my face, meters above the ground, is like a kiss.

Making sure the rifle is secured, I climb the rest of the way to the gondola.

The thing you have to understand for this to all make sense is that Miranda's a little crazy. Back in the Clean, they would have called her idealistic, but back in the Clean idealistic wouldn't have gotten you killed. Or maybe it would. I've never been too good at history.

Miranda's crazy because she thinks she can cure the Bug. Not all by herself, of course. She has a lot of other scientist buddies working on it, too. But they all believe. That one day they can wipe the Bug from the surface of the planet. That one day, even, they can reverse it for all the Ferals down on the ground.

Me, I have my doubts. Which begs the question: why I am even here in the first place? Why sign up with this lot when I just know they're going to fail? Well, I guess sometimes you just have to pick a side. And this is the one that makes me feel the least dirty.

But still, all that blood.

I met Miranda while I was foraging in Old Monterey. She had been bagging Ferals on her own back then. Some ship captain she'd hired had bailed on her, leaving her stranded with a pack of hostile Ferals. I helped get her out.

She offered me a job. Flying her around. Keeping an eye on her while she was in the field.

At first I said no. Like I said, all that blood.

Then Gastown happened, and I saw the path the world was heading down. Miranda's path seemed somehow better. So I changed my answer to yes.

Luckily, Miranda's offers last longer than mine.

Back onboard the *Cherub*, Miranda collapses into my comfy chair. "Thank you," she says, like she always does after one of these jobs, looking up at me from under her glasses, the way that usually makes me feel strong and brave and something of a protector and that usually defuses any anger I might be feeling. I feel the anger slip, but I grab hold of it and pull it right back to me.

"This isn't a game."

She raises her eyebrows. "I know that."

"I don't think you do."

"I needed to get the whole sample." She sets her jaw. "You know how this works."

"I made my rules clear when you hired me for this job," I say. "You hired me to keep you safe. I can't do that when you don't listen to me."

"I do—"

"If you lose a sample, it sets us back a bit, I'm aware. But if you get infected, this whole thing is screwed."

"Ben—"

"So next time you listen to me or I walk."

Silence. She bites her lip. I feel the heat flush my face. My hand is white around the barrel of the rifle.

Then she says, "We all know you prefer to fly."

I walk over to the controls, disgusted with her. But I can't argue with her statement. She's right there.

The controls of the *Cherub* help to set me right. It's where I belong, after all. It's what I'm good at. I power up the engine, turning her back to Apple Pi.

It's a stupid name, of course. But leave it up to a bunch of scientists to name something, and they'll come up with something Latin or something cute. Apple, after the fruit of the tree of knowledge. And the one that fell on Newton's head. Pi after the constant. And a groaner of a pun. I try not to say it too much.

Apple Pi makes me itchy, too. The place, I mean. It's also on the ground.

My stomach yawns and I reach over for the hunk of sausage I left on the console. It's one of the few perks of the job. It's what attracted me to Miranda's proposal in the first place. The boffins are better at feeding me than I am. That's what I call Miranda's lot—I read it in a book once and, well, it stuck. The salty, peppery meat—pigeon, I think it is—goes down easy and helps to patch up my mood.

The food thing was something of a surprise. I mean I wouldn't have pegged scientists for being good with food. But in the kind of communes Miranda grew up in, they learned this shit. How to salt and preserve meat. How to grow vegetables and fruits without fields. I guess it all makes a kind of sense. Keeping food is really all about bacteria. There's enough of them that know about biology that they had it sussed.

The end result is that I eat better than most, and that's one of the things that keeps me coming back. The others . . . well, like I said, I'm still deciding.

I push the engines to a comfortable clip, suddenly wanting to get back to the Core. That's what I call Apple Pi. It sits better with me. Partially because it's the center of everything in the boffins' activities, but also because of the apple thing. There's not much to sink your teeth into in the core of an apple, but it does contain the seeds. Whether those seeds will actually grow anything, though, that's always a gamble.

I may have just eaten, but I feel the need to eat more, almost as if that will justify everything. Why I put up with all this mucking about with Ferals. Why I carry their blood on my ship. Why I put up with Miranda.

Right now she's making notations in her battered notebook. I once took a peek inside and couldn't tell anything other than some of the scrawl was letters and some of it was numbers. She has abysmal penmanship.

Mine is much better, but then Dad drilled that into me. Insisted on me learning reading and writing. It doesn't always come in handy here in the Sick, but it made him happy. And it helps when I come across any old books, which isn't often but happens occasionally. And really, Ferals don't read, so it makes me feel somewhat more human.

Yep, full speed back to the Core and I can divest myself of Miranda, at least for a little bit, and get some clear air. And food. With those and a good pistol at your side, you don't need much else.

Well, those things and a good ship to fly. I've gone days without food. But the *Cherub* has always been there for me. Has always lifted me to safety. Has always been my home. She may not be much to look at, not with the way she's been fixed up and jury-rigged over the years, but she's as much family to me as my father was. She's safety, and freedom and, dare I say, love.

That's why, as the Core comes into sight, I realize that it will never truly feel right to me.

It will never feel like home.

The Core's lab is proof of one of many reasons I love airships.

Let's say that you live above the wreckage of North American civilization. Let's say that below you, on the ground, live a horde of deadly Ferals who could pass you the Bug with just a drop of bodily fluids. But they're little more than animals. They just sleep, eat, and fuck. Well, and hunt. Never forget that.

Let's say that in that wreckage lie a lot of useful pieces of equipment. Lab benches, spectrometers, centrifuges, maybe even a working computer or two. Sure, most of the glass is likely to be broken up from Ferals or from earthquakes or just from time. But a Feral can't do much to a hunk of machinery and has no cause to. No, that stuff can still be used. Only you can't use it on the ground.

Let's say you have an airship. . . . You get the idea.

'Course a whole lot of stuff like that will weigh you down, so you can't keep it in the sky. You need a place to put it down, a place to lay it all out, hook it up. Use it. That means the ground again. And I haven't been able to solve that particular problem. So that brings us back to Apple Pi and the lab that stretches out around me.

The place is a mess, the benches covered with towers of notebooks and papers, beakers, tubes, machines, and more. The boffins aren't meticulous about their working environment.

What the boffins are meticulous about is their science. The experiments. The search for their cure. Each data point is marked down. Checked. Double-checked. Glass is obsessively cleaned, machines tested, to eliminate any random variables from their equations. It's what I aspire to at times—eliminating chance from the equation, keeping things regular and right. But I know, too, that you can never get rid of chaos. And it will always dog your steps, even in the sky.

Sergei nods at me as I walk over to where he works on his project. Sergei is our fuel man. He has already developed several new biofuels, all of which work, with varying degrees of success, in the *Cherub*'s engines. Sergei is a big fucking reason why I stick around. I mean, he has the personality of soggy paper, but the man is a wiz with fuel. Because of course we need to fuel our ships.

And of course to fuel the ships we need to power other things. And electricity isn't wired up the way it was in the Clean. Or so my father told me.

Sergei removes his captain's hat, a battered old relic that Miranda tells me has nautical origins. I've never asked him where he got it. He wipes his damp head with his sleeve. "How did the latest batch work?"

"It worked. But it wasn't necessarily clean. Dirtier than the last three batches, I'd say."

He nods, thoughtful. "I'll play with the ratios."

"I have three jugs left," I say. "I'll need more soon."

He nods again, then gets back to work, jiggling the wires to some batteries.

Power.

The boffins have used a variety of ways to get it, to power their centrifuges and electronic scales. Chemical batteries and solar panels are the most common methods. But panels are hard to repair and they tend to use most of them on the airships. A couple of old bicycles have been rigged to generate electricity through mechanical means. Cosgrove keeps talking about building a windmill, only they haven't been able, or focused enough perhaps, to make it happen. 'Course something like that broadcasts a signal to the world around you that you're a sitting duck, so not having one is fine by me.

Crazy Osaka is fond of telling us all how he once powered an entire lab on oranges. How he and a bunch of his colleagues stripped out an orange grove and hooked them all up to his equipment. The other boffins smile and chuckle when they hear this. Me, I almost punched the man in the face. All that food. All that energy that could have gone into human bodies, going instead into inert machinery. Well, let's just say I found that offensive.

I bypass the lab and head to the room that I like to call the Depot. It's really just a closet with some supplies in it, but it's where we keep the ammo and so I think it fits.

If you ask me what the three most valuable things are in the Sick, my answer would be simple. Food. Fuel. Guns and ammo. The last helps you get the first two. Or helps you keep them. The boffins have done pretty well on the first two, but the third is something they can't make. So it's up to me to barter for them. We have a decent stockpile due to my efforts, but if you want my opinion, it's never big enough.

I grab some more bullets for my dad's revolver. It's not always easy to find ammunition for the gun, but then again a lot of people out there seem to prefer 9mm when it comes to pistols, so that helps. I grab some more rifle ammo, too.

As I'm closing the door, I run into Clay. Or, to be more accurate, he runs into me.

"More ammo?" he says.

I flash him a humorless smile. "That's what happens when you shoot a gun. You need to replace the bullets. Want me to show you?"

He looks at what I'm carrying. "Some would say maybe you're a little trigger-happy."

I grit my teeth. Step forward. "Well this 'some' would have to be particularly fucking naive. I've been hired to protect you people. Sometimes that involves shooting down the Feral about to bite your throat out."

I'm somewhat impressed when he stands his ground. But that only makes me want to hit him all the more.

"You're right," he says. "Your breed is necessary for the time being. But there will come a time when you won't be. When we find the cure, what will you do then?"

I laugh. "Go away, Clay. I'm tired of looking at you."

Clay shrugs in a way that's entitled and snide. "Be seeing you," he says.

I head for the *Cherub* wanting nothing more than to be aboard my ship, in the air where I belong. As I'm all too often reminded, the ground is full of ugliness.

Clay joined the group only a few months ago, another scientist moth attracted to the flame of the Cure. He's into the same things Miranda is—virology, cell biology, biochemistry. They have similar backgrounds, the children of scientists. And Clay is a believer. He holds on to the idea of a cure the same way a preacher holds on to God. Only, as he'd no doubt tell you in that sanctimonious drone of his, he's a rational man. A man of Science. Thing is, he still believes in a fairy tale.

I rummage in the *Cherub*'s storeroom and come up with a bottle of moonshine that some of the boffins distilled for some celebration. Louis Pasteur's birthday or something. I take a swig. It's harsh and it burns as it goes down, but it's warming and I can feel the alcohol spreading out in my system, helping to blot out the anger and frustration.

What the hell am I doing here?

It's a question I've been asking myself ever since accepting Miranda's offer.

Then I think of Gastown and the way it was overrun, and I think having something to look after, something to protect, can help save a man. The Core has clean water, clean food, and fuel. And they make enough for me to barter for ammo. My needs are met, and all I have to do in return is risk my life down on the ground from time to time, risking exposure to the Bug.

Fuck.

I take another swig of the moonshine and settle down against the console.

We are all Life's bitches, until Death steals us away.

# CHAPTER TWO

**M**iranda's knock on the gondola hatch wakes me from the light slumber I fell into. I wipe my mouth and go over to open it. I always know when it's her—she always uses the same pattern of knocking. When you're a forager, out on your own, you learn to pay attention to sounds.

She climbs up into the gondola and falls back into one of the chairs. She sniffs. "Drinking?"

"Just a little nightcap."

She nods, as if she understands. "Have any left?"

I raise my eyebrows and reach for the bottle, pass it to her.

She takes a big swig from it but swallows it down easily, a slight flush of her light-brown skin the only reaction. "We need to go out again," she says.

"What?"

"We need to go back. To the last location."

I reach for the canteen of filtered water and take a gulp. "Why?"

She pushes back the wavy brown hair from her face. "Because I need to find that Feral. The one I drew the blood from." She looks at my face. "There's something in it."

"Yes. It's called the Bug."

"Something else."

My eyes narrow. "What kind of something else?"

She takes another slug from the bottle. "I'm not really sure. A mutation maybe? But the virus seems to react differently in him, and I need more plasma to look at. I need to maybe do a physical examination. It's by no means sure, but this specimen could exponentially increase our knowledge of the virus and help us find a cure."

I rub my hands over my face willing her not to say it.

"Ben . . ."

"Don't say it."

"We need to capture it. Alive."

I shake my head; I can't stop myself. Craziness. I keep telling myself she's really not all that fucked in the head, and then she opens her mouth and—

"Are you fucking crazy?"

"Ben—"

"No." I start pacing. "No. I thought you were crazy when you wanted to transport blood. And you are. And yet I found a way to accept that. To deal with it. But now you want to capture a Feral, knock it out, and what—bring it on my ship? No. No way. Not ever."

"Ben, you know this is important."

"Why? Because you say it is? Because you believe that you'll find a cure? I once knew a woman who believed the Bug was God's judgment, and that one day he would rescue those who were pure from this hellhole of a life. What's to say that your belief is any better than hers?"

"C'mon Ben—"

"No. Fucking no. You. Jesus. You hired me to protect you. To keep you and the others safe during all of this. Well, I can tell you that dealing with a live Feral is not. Fucking. Safe. Especially if you're thinking of. Goddamnit. Thinking of poking it with needles and getting all up close to it. You know how it is. One drop. And that's not even considering what happens if the sedative wears off prematurely. Or if he manages to escape and run wild in the Core. Goddamnit, Miranda."

Miranda stares at me. Silent. Then says, "Are you done?"

"I just might be." It takes a moment for what I'm saying, what I'm really saying, to sink in.

She shakes her head. "You confound me."

"Excuse me?"

"You'll risk your life for trinkets—for scissors and hubcaps—but something real . . ."

My face flushes with heat. "I risk my life so that I can prolong it. I risk it for food. Or I risk it for things I can barter for food. You find me a magical machine that spits out good food on a regular basis and I'll hole up there until my old age. Until then, I aim to keep on living. What you're talking about reeks of going in the opposite direction."

"What I'm talking about is the long view, Ben. What happens when the food runs out? When your sources of barter dry up? If we find a cure—"

"That's a big fucking if, Miranda. And in the meantime, people are going to die. People are going to be infected. And then more. And then more. And I'm not sticking around to have it happen to me."

She leans forward. "There are risks, yes. But what we're trying for . . . it's worth it. Don't you want to help save the world? Isn't that worth putting your neck out for?"

"Not if I lose my head," I say.

She shakes her head again. "You're a selfish coward."

The words sting more than I thought they would. "Fuck you, Miranda. Get off my ship."

"Ben—"

"Now!"

Her scowl breaks for a moment and I see that she's hurt. And for a fraction of that moment, just a tiny little space, I want to reach out to her and tell her I'm sorry. But I don't, and she hardens up again. A little part of me is proud at that.

She doesn't say anything as she lowers herself to the ladder. And for that I'm grateful.

I finish the rest of the bottle after she goes.

I wake up the next day with a steady pounding in my head and a taste in my mouth like a Feral's ass. The bottle of moonshine is lying on its side next to me, a small, clear puddle around it. And of course today is the day I am leaving. I came to that conclusion last night some time before getting stinking drunk. Miranda's not going to change her mind this time—I know her too well.

Neither am I.

So I have no choice but to leave. Though there's still time before I need to. Time for something to eat. And water.

That's one of the other big things about the Core that makes it valuable. They built a filtration system that produces fresh water. There's a collection of vats that take dew and rainwater from the air, but then there's also the stuff they take from the ground. It's boiled first. Because of the Bug. It still makes me nervous, but there's not one person around who doesn't get used to boiling water if they want to survive. I just take it as truth that boiling kills the Bug.

But the stuff at the Core is some of the best I've had. Maybe even as good as the stuff they used to bottle back in the Clean.

So I pull myself up and pull myself together. I know I look like shit, but what else is new. I think about maybe even grabbing a shower before I go, or what passes for one here—a bucket and some clean water. But they have this stuff that cleans you up real good and that's also something worth taking advantage of before I take off.

I descend the ladder, wincing at the sun as it stabs into my eyes, but my stomach feels okay, which is good because I've flown before while puking into a bucket and it's not something I feel like repeating.

I take a while to clean myself up, brush my teeth (yes, they have that, too), shower, nibble on some dried meat and cheese. After I'm done I feel much more human.

Miranda is nowhere to be found.

Before I head back to the *Cherub*, I stop to see Sergei. He nods at me. I feel like there's already more white in his beard than when I met him. People age quickly in the Sick.

"Miranda said you might be leaving," he said.

I guess Miranda knows me better than I thought. "Well, tell me you expected me to stay this long."

He shrugs. Then extends his hand. "Thanks for all your help."

I take it. "Listen, I've been thinking about this plan." He raises his eyebrows. "I think what you need to do is build a cage. Then stash it in the cargo bay. You could even cover it with old screening material. It would help hold back anything it might fling at you while letting it breathe."

He nods. "That could work. We could rig something up fairly easily."

I nod back. "If I could figure out a way to hang it from the ship and still keep the thing alive, I'd tell you to do that. But I know that's not going to fly with Miranda. Just keep your eyes open and stay sharp. Stay alert for any raiders. You know things have been messy since they took Gastown. Make sure you take enough ammo with you. Best to just grab this Feral, wrap it up, and haul ass back here."

"Okay," he says. "We'll be able to handle it."

I nod again and start to walk away. Then turn back. "And watch that starboard engine. It's been a little shaky, I noticed. Make sure you keep an eye on it."

"Okay, Ben," he says. "Good luck."

"Same to you, Sergei." I mean it, too. Sergei's stiff, but he's a good guy.

I start wandering through the Core before I realize I'm doing it. Then I realize I'm looking for Miranda. *No*, I tell myself. *Not a good idea.*

On my way back to the ship, my pockets full of the Core's food—I mean, I *have* been working for them—I run into Clay again. He cocks his head at me, which just makes me want to punch him. I resist the urge. But only barely.

"So you couldn't hack it," he says, a smirk on his face. And my will-power slips just a bit more. "Well, I can't say that it's a surprise."

"Move out of my way," I say.

"We're going to do it, you know. We're going to change the world. While you're picking among the scraps of the old world, we're going to create a new one."

I think of about thirty things I could say to him, about ten ways I could hurt him. But in the end, I just push past him on the way back to my ship.

"Don't worry," he says at my back. "I'll look after Miranda."

I stop for just a split-second, then curse myself for it. But I force myself not to turn around. Then I continue walking.

All I want is to be in the air. To be in the air and fly away.

So that's exactly what I do.

# CHAPTER THREE

I have to admit as I fly the *Cherub* away that she's handling better than she has in years. Sergei and some of his friends were good mechanics. I'm going to miss having their input. Their tools. Their skills.

*Shut up, Ben. That's all done.*

I scan the horizon from the gondola, then flip on the sound system, an old phonograph Dad installed even before I came along. Records are hard to come by these days. Especially when back in the Clean they'd moved on to anything digital. But Dad used to say that records couldn't fail. And every so often you'd come across a stash in an old house or a store, and from time to time you'd find them at trader stands. We'd lost a lot among the years—from too many scratches or just plain breaking, but there was still a decent stack left on the *Cherub*. I put on George Harrison, one of my old-time favorites, and rock gently to the music as I fly the *Cherub* across the sky.

Truth be told, it feels a little weird to be on my own again. Despite so many years of being alone, it seemed like the last six months had a greater gravity to them, more momentum. It feels weird knowing that I don't have a place to go back to. Even though the *Cherub* was always my home.

On the other hand, it means freedom. I can go where I want, do what I want. Beholden to no one.

Foraging is my life. I'm good at it. I'd stayed alive this long, hadn't I?

I think I might fly down over Southern California, near the coast. The heat would be nice, and the water. I can't remember how long it's been since I've had a swim in the ocean. That's one nice thing about the ocean—no Ferals. They live near the coast sometimes, but they don't swim. At least not out too far. And the Bug can't live in saltwater. That makes the ocean feel safe. Of course last time I took a splash I couldn't stop thinking about what was swimming beneath me. Unseen creatures in the dark. Probably harmless, but then again, maybe not. I figured they were happy about the Bug. It meant a lot less of them dying. It meant a change in the ecosystem. And many would say a change for the better.

But still. The Bug.

Harrison chugs on in the background telling me all things must pass.

I think about Miranda and Sergei and the others. I try not to think about Clay. I think about how their little house, the Core, might as well be made of twigs and branches. I think about how just one wrong move, bringing in a Feral, for example, could topple it.

I think about all that food. All that clean water. All that potential. Wasted. It makes me angry. So I stop. Stop thinking about it. Stop thinking about all of them.

I reach for what's left in the moonshine bottle and slug it back.

I'm resting my head against the console, the moonshine carving out a nice warm hole inside of me, when I hear the shots.

Despite the alcohol, my body is hardwired to react to that sound, and I'm up in an instant, running to the window at the front of the gondola, then to those at the sides. Cameras rigged beneath me show me what's happening. Another dirigible, coming in at me from the port side, to the southeast. Green envelope with silver trim. Medium sized, rigged for cargo but still pretty fast. But why are they firing at me? And why from that distance? They have to know that the shots won't do anything. And it's not like ammo grows on trees.

Then I see the second airship coming down from above. That's the one that's firing. On the other.

I'm ready to push off, to fly the *Cherub* as fast as I can away from these two airships and whatever quarrel they have between them. Then I see that the aggressor is flying the flag of Gastown. The new flag.

My hand pauses.

Gastown. It was a city, built in the sky. A city made up of dozens of airships and balloons all lashed together, with platforms suspended beneath. A city where people lived and worked. A city where they made helium. But Gastown was more than that. It was progress. It was hope. It was a place that created its own economy. It was a place where a forager like me could barter things I found for things I needed.

Which is not to say that I liked the place. They charged a fucking ridiculous tax just to dock there. And they strong-armed people into working for them. If you wanted to stay independent, like me, you got cheated. Fewer jobs. Less payment for what you brought in. It was theirs to do, of course, but it wasn't what I was looking for in the city of the future.

Only it didn't last that long.

That helium was too valuable a commodity. And the skycity of Valhalla, off to the east, didn't have any. And they wanted it. Man, did they want it. So they took it.

But the way they took it . . .

Valhalla got a bunch of their ships and attached hooks to the bottoms of them. Then they went fishing. For Ferals. Each of them hooked a Feral the way you might hook a fish and then dropped those dying, bleeding Ferals on a city full of people.

In a world where you learn that being in the air is safe, no one was prepared for that. It caused widespread chaos. Fear. Panic. Everyone tried to run for safety. Back to their ships, if they had them. Probably to others' if they could steal them. It was like the outbreak of the Bug all over again. People ran. For their ships, for shelter, for their loved ones. And as they did, the Valhalla raiders flew in and fired on them.

In the end, it was so easy for them. Those who didn't leave were picked off by the raiders. Then it just took a little while for them to wait out the Ferals and to clean off the city. By then who was left to take it back?

I know all of this because I was there. And yes, I ran when I saw those Ferals. I got Miranda and Sergei off with me. And I don't feel bad about it. There was nothing I could do except die. And if you couldn't guess already, I don't aim to do that.

So here is a ship flying the flag of Gastown, which is essentially the flag of Valhalla, and with all that's going on, well, it just pisses me the fuck off.

So rather than turn around, I go toward them.

Which is something of a problem because I don't have any weapons on the *Cherub*. And this ship I'm heading toward does. But it's distracted. And I have a one-track mind.

I raise the *Cherub* so that she's above the enemy ship, which will protect me from its side-mounted weapons. Then I maneuver myself so that I'm going to pass right over it.

It's true the *Cherub* doesn't have any weapons—no mounted guns, no harpoons, no rams. Dad never went in for any of those, and I don't either. She's a fast airship and that's usually enough. But I'm not strictly defenseless.

As I pass over the other ship's envelope, it starts to rise, having caught sight of me, but I'm already pulling up myself, and I move to the exit hatch. I keep a variety of large, jagged things aboard the ship—rocks, twisted pieces of metal, and so on. I take one of these, a roughly round but sharp-edged rock and roll it out of the hatch.

As it reaches the edge, gravity takes hold of it and pulls it down with relentless force. The enemy ship has closed some of the distance between us, but there's still enough to allow the stone to punch a hole through the other ship's envelope.

If it was hydrogen in there, I could blow it to hell. But this is a Gastown ship, which means helium. So I have to improvise.

As rare as guns are, bullets are a little easier to come by these days, especially if you save and refill your spent shell casings. But even easier to come by is gunpowder. Don't get me wrong—it's not like it grows on trees, but you can make it if you have the right ingredients. And one easy way is to just collect a lot of urine, something we had plenty of back at the Core. You can also collect bat guano, which a guy I knew way back used to do. The salts from that and a little sulfur and charcoal make gunpowder.

Bullets are a little harder, because you need some metal. But take some gunpowder, drop it into a tube with a fuse in one end, and you have a nice pipe bomb.

I generally keep a few around for emergencies or for dropping down a Feral nest. I light the fuse on one, hoping that the glowing end will withstand the winds at this altitude. Then I carefully fit it into the crossbow the boffins mocked up for me. Then, aiming carefully, I fire.

My heart seems to stop as the tiny projectile arcs through the air between the two ships.

I only have this one shot. Then I'll have passed over the other ship and it will likely bring its weapons to bear on me.

Then, like it's been swallowed, my pipe bomb disappears into the other ship's envelope.

I run for the controls of my baby, and as soon as my hands find them I push away.

Most of the cameras on the *Cherub* are shot despite the boffin's best efforts, but the one on her belly is still intact. Through the screen, the explosion is visible as a flash inside the other ship's envelope and what I swear is a ripple through the semirigid frame. It doesn't destroy the ship, but it rips through enough of its ballonets that it starts to descend, deprived of a good part of its lifting power.

I pull the *Cherub* away in a burst of speed, the other ship doing the same, and soon the enemy dirigible is just a speck behind us.

My radio crackles to life on the public trading channel that most airship captains set their radios to. I pick my handset up.

"Thank you for the save," comes a male voice. Deep, smooth.

"I don't much like bullies," I respond.

There's a crackling pause on the other end. Then he speaks again. "Do you happen to have any medical supplies on your ship?"

I hesitate before answering. I do, supplies carefully cobbled together from the Core, but do I want to tell him that? I size up his ship, its condition. Finally, I say, "Yes. You in need?"

"Afraid so. One of the shots clipped me. We're a little low on supplies. I thought that maybe we could barter you something for them."

I consider this. Giving up some of my medical supplies doesn't appeal to me much. But he's offering barter. Still, I don't much like that "we" he mentioned.

"Follow me," I eventually say. "I'll take us to a meeting place."

I tell myself that I want to meet these people. I want to know what their little altercation was about. I tell myself that I want to see what they have to offer in return for the medical supplies.

But frankly, my love of solitude has atrophied. Which comes as something of a surprise.

I pull the *Cherub* down and ahead of the airship, and it falls behind me.

I lead them to one of my favorite way-places, the US Bank Tower in old Los Angeles. Like most of the tall buildings around, zeps use it as a meeting place. The elevators stopped working decades ago and the stairs have been carefully blocked off. The nice thing about the Bank Tower, too, is that it has a flat top that once was used for helicopters. Makes a convenient meeting spot. Sure, you have to watch for raiders and pirates who often fly by places like that, but nine times out of ten, they make good places to gather.

Okay, maybe eight times out of ten.

We put down, one ship on each side. The *Cherub*'s VTOL engines allow me to lower her right to the edge. It's something I don't do on the ground. Too easy for a stray Feral to run up into the ship. But up in the air . . .

The other ship doesn't have the same feature, but the crew members anchor her to one of the large metal rails on the roof and descend by the ship's ladder.

There are two of them.

And suddenly I'm a little worried.

The man is big, well-wrapped and wearing a ski mask, and armed with a rifle of some sort slung across his back. With him is a woman, judging by her size and the way she walks. But she's wrapped up, too, beneath a hat and scarf and a thick jacket that hides any telltale curves.

He's wary as he eyes me from across the roof. His hand hovers near the automatic on his hip. I can't see it in the holster to tell whether it looks well-maintained or not. It's a ballsy move to meet me up here, but then again he's injured. Or at least he says he is.

It doesn't stop my muscles from tensing up.

He opens the conversation. "Thanks again for your help up there."

I nod at him. "Well, let's just say I'm not overly fond of the folks who were bothering you."

He nods back. "And the supplies?"

"On my ship," I say. "But first tell me what you have to barter."

He nods again. "We have some food—fish."

"Fresh?"

"Salted."

I incline my head. I haven't had fish in ages. And my food from the Core will only last so long. Still, medical supplies. "Anything else?" I say. "I have food."

He looks over at the woman and she shrugs back.

He turns back to me and holds his hands up. "Look, can we talk a bit?" He moves a bit closer and my hand drops nearer to my holster. "Let me show you my arm. I'm going to unwrap it slowly."

My eyes narrow. I shift them from him to his partner and back. He slowly unravels a wrapping from his arm. Beneath I can see the red, the seeping blood. "They got me in the arm," he says.

"Why are you showing me?" I ask.

"Because I want you to know that we're telling the truth. We don't want to jump you, don't want your ship or anything else. Just your supplies."

I nod. "Then we can barter."

"Thing is," he says. "We don't have that much on us. We were just finishing up a, well, a run of sorts when those raiders caught us."

I frown. "If you were finishing up a run, why don't you have barter?"

"It wasn't that kind of run," the woman says.

"Look," the man says. "My name is Diego. This is Rosie."

"I can talk for myself, D," she says. Her voice is hard, her eyes too.

Diego inclines his head.

"I'm Ben," I say.

He nods. "You see, Ben, we weren't out for salvage. We were looking for people. Some . . . partners of ours are looking for good pilots, good ships. So we don't have much to barter with. But . . ."

"I'm listening."

"We may be able to offer you work."

"Now?"

He shakes his head. "No. Not yet. It's . . . delicate."

"Why?"

The woman looks at the man, communicating something. She nods at him.

"Look, Ben," he says. "You helped us out. You stuck your neck out for us when you had no cause to, and you got my respect for that. Both of ours. But the people we're working with, they're trying to protect their interests and need to be able to trust the people working for them."

"Trust doesn't come easily these days," I say.

"No," Rosie says. "But we need as much as we can get."

I chew it over in my head. "So you need pilots and ships, and you need to keep some things secret. Could you be working for a new settlement somewhere?"

Diego squints. "Maybe."

"He's not an idiot, at least," Rosie says to Diego.

There's a comfortable vibe between them. I wonder at their relationship. Maybe his partner? Maybe even his wife. There are some folks who still cling to the old ways. I wonder if they're religious.

"Okay," I say. "So you're offering me the opportunity to work for you after you've decided I'm trustworthy. Call me an idiot, but that appeals to me. Only, what do I need to do to gain your trust?" A voice inside my head is asking me what I'm doing, why I'm signing up to work for a new settlement. I just bailed on one, and I was going to be flying, just me and the *Cherub*. But I find that I don't much like the idea of fending for myself right now. Fuck, I think. I'm losing my edge.

"It would have to be a test run," he says.

I nod. It makes sense. See if I can carry out my end. But trusting someone to keep your secret is a bit harder. Do I really want to be jumping (or flying) through hoops for these people?

"I'm interested," I say. "Let me grab your supplies and we can talk some more."

Diego nods. "Good."

A few minutes later we're crossing the roof, me with the medical supplies, Rosie with the salted fish, Diego holding his bleeding arm. We make the exchange, and Rosie begins work on Diego immediately, washing the blood away with some bottled water and cutting some clean linens. I notice that Diego's skin is brown around the wound but that's all.

"It's not too bad," Rosie says. "As long as we keep it clean."

"Why were they after you in the first place?" I ask.

"I don't know," Diego says. Shrugs his good shoulder. "We were just going about our business and they came after us."

I try to read his eyes. He seems to be telling the truth. "Just a simple raider, then?"

"That's about the whole of it."

"Hmmm. I wonder why Gastown Raiders were out this far?"

"Look, man. I don't know. I told you. We were on our way and they came after us. I don't know much about Gastown. I thought it was a fair place."

"Used to be," I say. "Until raiders took it over."

He nods. "Then that's it. They must be sending out more raiders."

I shake my head. "I don't know. That's not their style. At least not for individual ships."

"There were more," Rosie says, rewrapping Diego's arm. "We passed several ships. One of them pulled away and came after us. It was a bit of a surprise. The others seemed specially rigged for lifting."

I frown. "What do you mean? How?"

Rosie's eyes squint. "They were carrying these hooks beneath them."

Cold runs through me. I remember those hooks. "Which way were they heading? North?" Gastown is north of us. I figure maybe they were just returning home.

Diego shakes his head. "No. They were heading mostly east."

East. I mentally trace a path in that direction. All I can think of is . . . Apple Pi.

"Oh no," I say.

"What?" Diego says.

"I think I know where those ships were going. I have to go. I have to warn them."

"What about the job?" Diego says.

"Later. If I can." I hope I'm wrong. God, I hope . . . "I need to go."

"Wait," he says. He looks at Rosie, then at me. "When you're ready, head out to old San Diego and tune your radio to 23.0. Call and we'll try to send someone to meet you."

I run for the *Cherub*. I get her into the air as quickly as I can and head to the Core at top speed.

# CHAPTER FOUR

Sergei's fuel powers the motors. I hope it's one of his better batches because I'm going to need all the speed I can get.

For a moment I question why I'm going back. I don't know that Gastown even knows about the Core. I just left—why am I so quick to reverse that? But then I think about Gastown, and I think about Miranda, and I know I have to.

My only hope is that the raiders' airships are true to form and favor armor and armament over sleekness and speed.

My pulse hammers in my temples. My hands itch. I want to pull out my revolver and shoot it at something. But there's nothing to shoot at.

Naively, I thought that Valhalla would be content with Gastown. Content with controlling the one major center of human civilization left in the western part of what used to be America. But that doesn't seem to be the case. They're going after any settlement they can find. To drain them of anything useful or valuable. Airborne vampires, feasting on the lifeblood around them.

And they need to be stopped.

*So what are you going to do, Ben? You're only one man.*

I can't go after Valhalla. Hell, that would be suicide. But I can try to warn the people at the Core.

I flip on the radio and dial to the station the Core uses. "Come in. Come in. This is Ben on the *Cherub*. If you're there, respond."

I hope the raiders aren't scanning for signals.

No response. I continue. "You need to get out of there. There's a sizable force of Gastown raiders heading for you. Repeat, you've been discovered, and raiders are coming to take the Core. You need to evacuate immediately. Please respond if you get this."

I click off the mike and listen through the static for a response. Nothing.

Fuck.

After another four attempts my voice is getting hoarse and that's when I see them. A loose formation of four airships. Two are hard-enveloped zeppelins. One is a soft blimp. The other is like the *Cherub*—a semi-rigid with an armored gondola. They're staying together, at the speed of the slowest ship, which helps me. They're in no hurry.

I take the *Cherub* higher and hopefully out of their sight. They might think me a passing ship, but they might decide to take me down. I could try to distract them, try to give the people at the Core time to evacuate, but four ships would tear the *Cherub* apart despite my better maneuverability. And then I'd be no good to anyone. Of course that assumes I'm good to someone now. I'm not so sure of that.

About an hour away from the Core, the ships veer off, two taking the lead, the other two providing cover. It takes a moment for me to digest this. Are they not heading for the Core after all? Was what Diego said wrong? I decide it doesn't matter. Gastown knows about the Core, and they will come for it sooner or later. I continue on, trying not to be too happy about my stroke of luck.

Pushing the engines, I make it in less than an hour, and instead of dropping the ladder like I usually do, I lower the *Cherub* right to the ground on the VTOL engines. Then I race down the ramp and don't even shudder as I touch the ground.

The Core is already bustling with activity, and I guess someone eventually got my radio message. But they're not coordinated. They're chaotic. There's no order. I grab one of the boffins, a guy named Seth. "Where's Sergei?"

He's sweating, his hair in disarray. "He's not here. He went out with Miranda and Clay. To find a test subject."

The Feral.

Which explains the chaos. Sergei and Miranda are the unofficial leaders of the Core. When it comes to science, they argue and bicker for days, but when it comes to running the place, they look to Sergei and Miranda.

And they're not here.

Which leaves it to me. And while I can't run a settlement, I know how to survive. So I start barking orders. Telling people to get the essentials to their ships. Telling them to prioritize the food.

"What about the data?" one woman asks.

"Data is no good to you if you're not around to look at it. Just take what you absolutely need."

While they head off, hopefully to do what I told them to, I head for the ammo stores and cram my pockets and my arms full of as much as I can take. I also sling a rifle around my shoulders and tuck a pistol, an automatic, into my waistband.

I pass the water reservoir on the way back to the common area and I think about how it's going to be lost. I start thinking about maybe rigging something up to the *Cherub*, drawing up one of the tanks, maybe. That water would be useful.

Then I hear the whine of ships approaching. No. It's too soon.

Two come in at first, with lines hanging underneath them. My blood goes cold. Each of the ships has a long cable suspended from it and at the end of those cables are large metal hooks. Pierced and wriggling on the ends of those hooks, like bait, are Ferals. One each. Just like at Gastown. The Core freezes, as if etched into my vision. People are still running around, carrying boxes and equipment. Some have made it to the ships and are pulling up cargo. But too few.

One of the Ferals drops and half-runs, half-stumbles through the open courtyard, spraying blood all around it.

The chaos of before returns, intensified.

Two of the three boffin airships start to move away, running from the Ferals and the raiders and for open air. Panicking.

The *Cherub* is too far away.

I unsling the rifle from around my back and enter that cold, dark place that helps keep me alive. There are only two Ferals, but of course I don't want to get close to them. But I know this place better than they do.

I climb one of the frames the boffins use to hold some of their construction projects. It's not the most stable perch, but it will hold me. I sight down the rifle at the dying Feral. I breathe in, hold it, and pull the trigger.

The bullet misses the Feral's face, but his neck and shoulder explode in a shower of blood that I hope doesn't hit anyone. But it puts him down, he falls like a sack of rocks, and we're down to one of them.

I scan to find the other one but don't see it. A voice in my head screams at me. *Run for your ship, you idiot! You're not even wearing your scarf.*

I think the Ferals might be able to climb this frame.

I look around at the remaining boffin ship, wondering if I could get to that, take it around to the *Cherub*, when one of the raiders with a gondola-mounted machine gun rakes the ship and the whole thing erupts in a blossom of fire.

A moment later I'm tossed to the ground. Hard. And thought disappears under a wave of silence and shock.

My hand closes on nothing, the rifle fallen from my hand. My eyes refuse to focus. I see movement, but I'm not sure what it is.

*Get up*, the voice in my head says.

I push myself to my knees. I can't see the rifle, but I feel the weight of the automatic in my waistband and I reach for it. A flurry of legs out of the corner of my eye. I turn to face it. Almost fire. But it's one of the boffins. She's bleeding. Her face twisted in fear. And I don't know if she's been infected. And there's nothing I can do for her.

The raider ships start to descend. They'll be in the Core soon. And I can't stop them.

I run for the *Cherub*, knowing that it's the only thing that can keep me safe. It's the only thing I can depend on.

My ears are filled with an insistent ringing, and sounds are still beyond me.

I throw open the door to the inner corridor, the automatic out, my finger pressed up against the trigger, as close as I can without actually pulling it.

No movement. The corridor is clean.

I'm halfway to the exit when I see the Feral. It's lying on the floor, blood pooling around it. But it's not dead. It's squirming, weak from the loss of blood, its eyes wild. I don't need to kill it. Nature will do that for it. But I can't risk it lashing out at me or shaking a drop of blood at me, so I stop and fire three bullets into its head, knowing that the gunshots will likely alert any raiders nearby.

I move as fast as I can, while skirting the Feral blood, pressing myself against the wall, feeling it scrape against my cheek.

Then I'm at the door, then out of it, and I look up to see the *Cherub*.

Flying away.

# CHAPTER FIVE

I see the *Cherub* flying away without me, and my fists clench and I want to raise the gun and shoot at everyone and everything. My ship. My home. Gone.

And I have no way to get to it.

And there are raiders in the Core. And if they find me they will kill me. Or worse.

And I need to get away.

And I'm mad at myself because my rage is fighting against my survival instincts. The instincts win. Because I can rage all I want if I survive this.

My mind races. I need to get away. I need to move quickly. And I need to avoid running into Ferals. All this noise is liable to attract any that are hungry.

I think about the only other vehicle in the Core. I run for the Ferrari.

I keep the automatic down at my side, ready to raise it and fire at any raiders that come across my path. I get near the dead Feral and leap over it, desperate to get past it. My foot comes down at the edge of the blood slick. *Too close.* And I slip. And slam into the floor and my skin is crawling as I imagine the Feral blood all over me.

But when I turn myself around, I've missed it. All except my boot, and I can deal with that later. I push away the fear. Push away the anxiety. And get back to my feet.

The door at the end of the hallway opens.

I raise the automatic.

A man comes through, large, carrying a rifle of some sort. He doesn't look like one of the boffins. I sight down at the central mass of him and pull the trigger three times, mindful that I'm down to three bullets. The bullets throw him back, but I don't stop to see if he's down for good. Instead I'm running through a different door into the place the boffins call the Garage.

The "Ferrari" is a modified jeep the boffins—Sergei and a few of the others—have been converting for use on rough terrain. It's an ugly beast and nothing like a Ferrari at all. Did I mention that their sense of humor is awful? But one of them had this picture from the Clean, this sleek, shiny red car. A Ferrari. And they had it pinned up while they were working on it. Inspiration from a machine that even I had to admit dripped of power and sex (and I'm deeply committed to the *Cherub*).

I used to give them shit for working on it, hell, I thought it was stupid. Why rig a ground car when we had all these airships at our disposal? Why get any closer to the Ferals than you have to? But now I'm grateful for it because I can no longer take to the sky.

I've watched Sergei enough to know how the Ferrari operates. He hooked it up with an ignition button to make it easier to operate. And it's fueled up for the road tests they've been doing on it.

I throw up the door that leads outside, then jump in and toss the automatic on the seat next to me. Slam the door shut. And hit the button.

Nothing.

I slam it again. And again.

With a lurch the engine fires up and coughs a few times. But it catches and I feel it rev beneath me when I hit the pedal. Then the cart is bursting forward and I've cleared the doors and hit the top of the hill. The wheels catch fresh earth and then I'm barreling down the hill.

I turn the wheel back toward the Core, hoping I can get one or two other people out with me, but as the Ferrari crests the hill, the building nearest me erupts in fire and I can feel the shockwave from where I sit inside the cart.

Above me the raider ships are swarming. And the *Cherub* is gone.

I slam the steering wheel in anger and turn the wheel back around, racing down the hill. The loss of the Core hollows me out, but the loss of the *Cherub* is a keen, cutting ache. I've lost my parents. Lost my father's Star of David. Lost the *Cherub* that used to be his airship. His home.

My home.

All I have left of Dad, aside from my genes, is his revolver. All I've held on to from him is a weapon.

I push it all away. No time to lose my shit now. Get free, get clear. Then lose your shit.

A problem with the Ferrari, aside from the fact that it's stuck on the ground, is that it's not airtight. It's covered on all sides, but there are gaps. There's open space for the engine, for ventilation. And that's space the Bug can get in. Don't get me wrong; I'd be more than happy to take this thing on a joyride to see how many Ferals I could take out by slamming full speed into them. But all it would take is one drop of blood, sucked up into the cart and onto me for my joyride to end.

And don't tell me I'm paranoid. Not unless you've seen your own father Fade right in front of your eyes. Not until you've seen the reason dim in a loved one's eyes.

But these wheels are all I have right now, and I need to put as much space between me and the raiders.

I think of the boffins who didn't get out in time. I hope the raiders were told to keep them alive. Because they would be useful to anyone. And if the boffins are smart, they'll do what the raiders tell them to do.

But something uncomfortable squirms in my belly. I know that if I were the raiders, if I wasn't sure whether the boffins had come into contact with Feral blood or not, I would kill them all. I'm not happy about that, but it's what they'll probably do.

I have no idea where I'm going. Away is all I can think of. It's not like I can get the *Cherub* back.

I drive until my heart stops pounding. I drive until the acid taste in the back of my mouth has subsided. Then I find a shaded spot beside a hill and park the Ferrari. And slam the wheel a few times.

And I mourn the loss of my airship.

I mourn the loss of my home.

✳  ✳  ✳

People often ask me where the *Cherub* came from. They ask me how I came by her because she's a fine ship and because I'm an independent operator.

I don't always tell these people the truth.

The truth is that the ship belonged to my grandfather. More or less. I told Miranda this when she asked. "Was he a pilot?" she asked.

"No. A mechanic. Back in the Clean. When the Bug hit, and the shit went down, he stole a ship. One of the best and newest his company had." He stole the *Cherub* and saved a bunch of people, and I am so damned proud of him for doing that. But most importantly, he saved his own life and ensured that I would be here today.

He obviously wasn't the only one. Lots of people realized that taking to the sky would be the logical thing to do and they all did it.

So granddad stole it and took it, and his family, up into the air. When he died, my father inherited the ship, patching her up and making additions where necessary. After Mom died, it was me and him in the ship up until the time he Faded. So it's something of a family legacy. Stolen, originally, to be sure, but made our own. A Gold family artifact.

Since it fell to me, I had poured all my time that wasn't spend foraging or eating or defending myself into that ship. Into making her faster and better. Into making her my home. Into making her safe.

Now she's gone.

Not to mention everything that was on the ship. The food. The water. The alcohol. The ammunition and weapons. The memories.

Fuck.

I used to hate gravity when I was younger. Always waiting to pull you to the ground. Yet we sailed through the sky, able to evade it. But it was like a demon waiting below. Just waiting to get its claws on us.

Now it had grabbed me. And there was no escaping it now.

✳   ✳   ✳

It's somewhere during my pity party that I realize that while I may be sheltered from the view of any wandering Ferals, I'm still visible from the air, and I'm sure one of the raiders must have seen me drive away. So I start up the Ferrari again and keep driving, aiming to put as much distance between me and them as I can. Of course an airship could easily outpace me. So I head for nearby trees, hoping they'll shield me.

The fuel gauge is already showing a drop in the tank, and I realize with a sinking sensation that this vehicle isn't going to last long. Not without another supply of Serge's special fuel.

But I get under the cover of the trees and kill the engine to save fuel and I just sit for a while. Safe for the moment within the chassis of the cart.

I think about what my plan should be. I think about driving straight through to the coast. Where I can put my back up against the ocean, maybe take shelter in some cave down by the beach. Lay it up with traps and the like. Go native for a while.

It's not a prospect that fills me with joy.

But getting back into the air is going to be a problem. And there are no rendezvous points nearby.

I think about Diego and Rosie. I won't be able to make it out to them either.

I'm royally fucked is what I am.

Christ.

Exhausted and depressed, I put my head back against the seat and close my eyes. And fall asleep.

I awake with my bladder throbbing. This is a problem that doesn't happen on airships. Your typical airship is equipped with at least a chemical toilet that we use (and then dump) for most basic biological needs.

In the Ferrari I have two choices: open the door and brave the ground, or piss in the car and deal with the aftermath.

It gives me pause.

Normally I would piss in the car with abandon. Happily mark the thing as my own in the most basic, animalistic way. But not only does that remind of the Ferals and the things they do, but I may very well be living in this thing for the near future, and I don't relish the thought of soiling my new home.

So instead I ready my guns and prepare to face the ground. I open the door with the automatic out, moving it slowly, pausing after each push to make sure nothing is going to run for me.

When nothing does, I slide out of the car and scan the area around me.

It's lightly wooded, with nothing moving. I wait a few moments more and when nothing happens, a few more.

And here's the thing about the ground. You start out thinking that the longer you take checking, the safer you'll be. But you end up thinking that the sooner you get your business done, the quicker you can get back to safety.

There's no winning.

Especially when you're out in the open, with only one hand free to protect you.

It's one of the most vulnerable situations I've ever experienced.

I have the gun out, my eyes scanning, as I finish and get everything covered again. Then it's a quick scurry back into the cart and a long exhalation that nothing went wrong.

I know it's silly to think, but I'm glad a Feral didn't get to me with my cock out. I have envisioned myself dying a number of ways. That's not one I'd like to even consider.

So it's off to the coast, then, I think. Park the cart on the beach, with plenty of room to piss, a clear line of sight in front of me, and fresh seafood when I need it. Yes, the coast sounds mighty good right now.

Only my fuel runs out before I get there.

✳    ✳    ✳

I drive as far as I can manage, even letting the car coast down a hill until it butts into a tree (softly, though, as the brakes still work). Then I stay in the car as long as I can. I'm in strange territory, lightly wooded, the kind of place Ferals love to nest in. I have my revolver, a tiny bit of water, and the clothes on my body. And the night comes on cold, the way it sometimes does at this time of year.

Again, I force myself out of the car to relieve myself. I have a new system now. I climb on top of the car, which gets me off the ground and able to see around the area better. It's times like this that I thank God I am a man and can do this easily. I don't even want to imagine squatting somewhere.

It's as I'm scanning the area around the cart that I see the lights up on the hill. It almost makes me spray all over the cart.

Lights. That means people. Ferals can't make fire. I can't imagine they can use electricity. Someone is living nearby. Someone who feels comfortable enough to advertise their presence to the world.

Someone who might have food. Shelter. Fuel. Water.

Someone who might have friends. With guns. And bad attitudes.

This is the world we live in. For every good possibility there are at least three bad.

But I can't stay where I am forever. And I have to move.

I decide to sleep on it, returning to the cart and curling up in a shivering heap. My dreams are filled with horrific images. Ferals on hooks. People running, scared. Blood. Screams.

I'm awake before dawn hits, but when it does, I'm ready to move. Already my stomach is growling and I figure braving the place on the hill is better than slowly starving in the cart.

Moving on the ground is scary. It's been a long time since I've done it this way. Sure, working with Miranda required me to be on the ground, but I always had the *Cherub* at my back—there was always somewhere to retreat to. Now . . .

I try not to think about it.

I move over open ground, which means I'm more likely to be seen, but it also means it's easier for me to see anyone coming at me. Besides, Ferals are just as likely to smell or hear me moving, so evening the score works just fine for me.

The revolver is heavy reassurance in my hand. It's my only security and I'm glad for it. I only wish I had more ammunition. I have six bullets in the gun itself and another thirty bullets in my jacket. And the three in the automatic. Then I'm out. If I get swarmed, those could go in a few minutes.

I pray that I don't get swarmed.

The hill starts off as a gentle slope that grows more wooded as I climb it, but then I break through the trees and the incline gets steeper. It's another frustration—Ferals can climb better than I can. I'll be slower than them, and that's never a good thing.

With all this shit going round in my head, it's like phantom Ferals are already pursuing me.

I try to keep my focus on the top of the hill. And I push my legs as hard as they will go.

I'm sweating as the slope lessens, but I can see the structure where the light must have been coming from. Some kind of house. I quicken my pace.

And then I hear it.

The Feral howl.

I've heard many creatures howl—I've heard the occasional wolf, or mountain lion, or even, once, a pack of wild dogs—but none of those is quite as chilling as a Feral. Animals at least sound natural; they were meant to sound like that. But Ferals—their vocal cords should be used for speech. Their cries have the hint of that. Just enough to be unnerving, but not enough to seem human.

I sometimes have nightmares about them.

I scan the area I think the noise is coming from and see a few dark shadows moving toward me. I crouch and aim my pistol. But then I hear sounds behind me and I turn, quickly, to see another few.

They're surrounding me.

I fire off three quick shots at the closest Ferals, hoping the noise will scare them off, but they keep coming on.

All of them keep coming on.

I can't shoot them all. And I can't outrun them.

So I shoot and I shoot and I shoot again, not thinking, barely breathing, just jamming my finger back on the trigger. The automatic goes dry quickly, so I throw it at them, not thinking, just needing to keep them back.

I'm strangely calm. It's like the world slows and shrinks and it's just me and the revolver, one machine, shooting at the Ferals.

But there are too many of them.

And they're getting closer.

And panic starts to set in as I realize they're going to get me.

And bite me.

And I can't Fade. I won't.

I hold the revolver up to my head. My last friend in the world. My last connection to the past. Give me a kiss, friend, I think.

Then I hear a scream unlike any I've ever heard before. No Feral could scream like that. What possibly could?

And the Ferals' feet are pounding the ground around me, so strong I can feel the hits reverberating through my body.

Something large, some monstrosity that shouldn't exist, bursts through the Ferals and, as if by magic, they fall back from it, their bodies breaking and tearing.

"Get on," a voice says loudly in my ear, and I'm pulled up, toward the beast.

Rationality asserts itself again and I realize that this is some kind of animal, with a rider, and he's trying to get me to safety. And seeing all the blood that's flying around, I think that must be a good idea.

The smell of the animal fills my nostrils and I clamber up clumsily, pulling on the man to help seat me. He takes only a moment to make sure I'm secure, and then he swings about with something long and hard, and it pushes the Ferals back. Many of them dead. Most of them injured.

"Grab tight," the man snarls at me and I grip his body. Then, with the barest hint of a command, we're galloping away, up the hill and away from the Ferals.

I sneak a peek behind us and notice that none of the Ferals are following.

It's only then that I exhale, not even realizing that I'm holding my breath.

In what seems like only moments later, we're at the house on the hill, and, springing some kind of mechanism, a gate opens in the tall metal fence and then swings shut behind us with a clashing sound.

We slow, then stop, and the rider slips easily to the ground. I try to follow him and almost fall off the animal that I now realize must be a horse. My father told me about them, but most of them had been killed for food years ago. I'd seen a few pictures on the covers of old books, but I never imagined how big they were.

The rider helps me to the ground, which I gain practically on my knees, and then removes his helmet.

He's a big man. Burly. With dark hair streaked with gray and a large, bushy mustache. His eyes are dark and serious.

"Thank you," I say, loosening my scarf. "You saved my life."

He frowns. "Whatever were you doing out there alone?"

I grimace. "It's a long story. I was running from some raiders. In a vehicle, but then it ran out of fuel. I saw your lights up here last night and thought I would try to make it here today. The Ferals found me, though, before I found you."

"Then you're incredibly lucky that I came along when I did," he says.

"I don't know how to thank you," I say.

He smiles, then, and the serious look is replaced by one of mirth, lines creasing the corners of his eyes. "I'm Viktor," he says, and holds out his hand.

"Ben," I say, and take it. Now that I have time, I can see he's wrapped well. He knows the drill, then.

"A horse?" I say.

His smile widens. "Not just a horse. This is Rex." He pats the horse's flank. "Last of a fine breed." The smile falters for a bit.

"I thought they were all gone."

"Most are, I would expect. But I take care of Rex."

And he does, taking off the saddle, rubbing the horse down, leading him to a special enclosure.

"The Ferals can't get in here?" I say.

He shakes his head and shouts over his shoulder. "The fence keeps them out. They can't jump it and it's barbed and also electrified."

"Electrified?" I say. "Where do you get the electricity?"

He smiles. "That's a secret." He winks. "Here, you better come inside. It doesn't look like they got you."

"No." I show him my coverings.

"Good. Then come in."

And I do, following him through a thick wooden door into his house. I might as well be walking through an entryway to another time. The house is fully furnished and lit, and doesn't show any of the signs of deterioration or damage most homes have. Viktor beckons to a table. "Have a seat."

The paranoid part of my brain pricks up just then, but I beat it back down. If he had wanted me dead, he could have left me to the Ferals. He risked his life to save me.

But what if he wanted you infection-free, the voice said. To eat. Or fuck. Or god-knows-what?

I still have my revolver, I think. One bullet is still chambered, the one I was going to put in my head.

He returns a moment later and passes me a plastic bottle filled with water.

This is the moment of decision for me. He could have put something in the water. Poison. Drugs. Whatever. But at the moment I'm thirsty and the attack didn't help with that, so I take a sip.

It tastes clean. Which doesn't mean much. But I take another sip.

"This is quite the setup you have here," I say.

He smiles again. "I'm rather happy here."

"And it's just you. Alone out here?"

"I'm hardly alone," he says, and tips back his own water bottle. "I have Rex."

I shake my head. "A real horse. What do you feed him?"

"I have some grain," he says. "But Rex is mostly kept on pasture. He doesn't go out too often. Honestly, keeping him supplied with salt is my hardest problem. I've scavenged every source I could find from the surrounding area. Luckily I found a stash of salt blocks that's lasted for a while."

"And the Ferals don't bother you on Rex?"

"They try," he says. "Sometimes. If they get over their fear of his size. But typically they can only reach my legs and I keep those well-armored."

"But what about him?" I say.

He laughs, a rich, deep sound that fills the room. "Horses can't get the Bug," he says.

"You're sure?"

"Before Rex, I took care of other horses. One of them was bitten by a Feral. Nothing happened."

I nod. "I guess it makes sense. It makes people *into* animals. I suppose it wouldn't be able to do anything *to* an animal." I'd listened to Miranda's crew enough, though, to know that the Bug was unpredictable. Some animals, it could kill. But apparently not horses.

Viktor takes a seat opposite me. "So how did you happen to be out in a vehicle without enough fuel?" he asks.

"Not by choice," I say. "I used to have my own airship."

"A zep?"

I nod. "She was called the *Cherub*. I took her to try to help some friends, but . . . well, someone stole her while I was down on the ground. I took the Ferrari, the vehicle, to escape, but the fuel ran out."

"I'm sorry," he says. "I bet you miss your ship. I sympathize. I can imagine how I would feel if I lost Rex."

"How old is he?" I ask.

"Twenty," Viktor says. "And still in his prime."

"Well, then I wish him a long life," I say. I don't add that the longer Rex lives, the longer that Viktor is likely to.

Viktor raises his bottle. "To a long life." We both take long drafts.

"How did you end up here?" I ask.

He shrugs his large shoulders. "My grandfather owned this farm. Kept horses. When everything went down, his children held on to it." He shrugs again. "I was born into this life. It's all I've known. I've tried to hold on to it."

I nod. It's the same with me, my life—my former life—in the sky. It's all I've known.

"To legacies," I say, and hold up my water.

He raises his, then frowns. "If we're drinking to things, then maybe we should be drinking something else. Hang on." He shuffles out of the room and disappears for a little while.

I think of how lucky I am. To run into someone who isn't a complete lunatic. Someone who has survived being on the ground. Lucky plod.

Truthfully, I'm in awe of him.

He comes back with a jug. "I've been saving this."

"What is it?"

"Elderberry wine," he says, setting it down on the table. His smile grows wider.

"Are you sure you want to open it?" I ask.

"Of course," he says. "I don't normally have occasion to. And I would be hard-pressed to finish this myself." He twists off the cap and pours the dark-red liquid into two mugs. He picks his up and raises it to toast again. I clink his, and then we both take long swallows.

It's fruity, and sweet, with flavors I've never tasted before. It makes me curl my tongue. I've had wine recovered from cellars, but this is something different. But not bad. Very not bad.

Viktor tells me about horses and his farm and how he cares for himself. I get the feeling that he's lonely. Why wouldn't he be, living out here, with no one to talk to?

It makes me question my life in the sky. Before Miranda. It was just me and the *Cherub*. Like Viktor and Rex. But Rex at least is living. Rex has a pulse.

Indignation rises up in me. The *Cherub* is as real to me as Rex is to Viktor. She's as precious to me, as important, as useful in surviving the Sick.

But even before I lost her, it was just me and her.

Is that enough?

We drink through our mugs, and then Viktor pours us more. This continues and continues, the two of us trading stories, until the jug is empty and I can barely see straight.

The rest of the night passes in a haze. At some point I stand up, only to realize that I can barely walk a straight line.

I move to a long, flat couch that has some ratty pillows on it, fall onto it face-first, and know no more.

# CHAPTER SIX

I awake the next day with a pounding headache and a dried-out riverbed in my mouth. That's the problem with alcohol. There's always the temptation to drink your cares away, to escape the harshness of the world with a good tipple, but the repercussions are difficult to deal with. Especially if you're about to deal with Ferals or raiders. Especially if water is something that's at a premium.

Luckily there's still some water left in the bottle from last night, and I finish it in one swig.

The headache resists my crafty measures.

I tell myself I need to start thinking of next steps. Even if Viktor were to invite me to stick around—and really, why would he? I'm just another mouth to feed—what would I do? There's only the one horse. I could help groom him, I suppose. Help gather water and food and tend crops and things. But the thought makes me want to crack open another jug of Viktor's wine and drink until I can't see straight again.

The *Cherub* is gone.

Miranda is gone.

The Core is gone.

What do I do?

As I'm wrestling with such weighty issues, Viktor reappears. His hair is windblown and he's wearing his outside clothing, so I assume he's on his way back in. I ask him about it.

"I wanted to check around," he says. "The local wretches don't usually bother me much. They've learned better. But you must have riled them up enough to try something."

"Sorry."

"Eh, it's okay," he says. "It's not like I didn't hit the point home again for them."

I laugh. "You certainly know your way around Ferals."

"Down here you have to." He says it lightheartedly, but I hear an undercurrent in his tone. I expect he doesn't have too high an opinion about us zeps. To him we're probably living in some fantasy world above the clouds while plods like him try to eke out a living down here on the ground.

I don't know that I can disagree with that opinion. But, given the choice right now, I would take the sky every time.

"I expect you're trying to figure out your next move," he says.

I nod. Then shake my head. "I've only known a life in the sky. I don't know how to do anything down here."

"That's not true," he says. "Sounds like you do a lot of foraging. You know your way around abandoned buildings. That could come in handy, I think."

"You want me to help you forage?"

He takes off his boots and eases his bulk down into a chair. I think suddenly of how I didn't think to check him for any wounds. But he just seems so capable. And all I can remember is being up on Rex and feeling like I was out of reach.

Viktor leans forward and presses his hands together. "I'm limited in my range. Rex can only go so far and he needs steady terrain. He's already thrown two shoes and I'm running short on replacements."

"So what do you want me to do?"

"I was thinking—I have some fuel I've used for the farm. We mostly use solar power, but I have some gas for generators as well. I've scavenged some from the surrounding farms. If we could get your cart up and running . . ."

"We can look farther afield."

He slaps his leg and nods.

It would give me something to do.

"What do you say?" he asks.

"I say, why the hell not? You don't mind me sticking around?"

"Not at all. It will be nice to have someone who can actually talk back to me." Viktor smiles. "Then it's set."

And it is. And I'm happy. But we're going to have to go get the Ferrari. And it might not work with the fuel he's got. And it will put us out in the middle of Feral territory. But it's a place to live. Someplace safe. And something to do. And since I have nothing else I say yes.

My heart is thumping as I sit behind Viktor on Rex's back. The horse doesn't seem inconvenienced by the extra weight. Viktor hits the release and we shoot out of the fence and gallop down the hill.

The pace throws my ass around like a balloon, first up in the air, then down hard against the saddle. Somehow Viktor avoids the worst of it, like he's floating above the horse. I try to imitate how he's sitting, but it doesn't seem to work.

Still, I have to admit there's something exhilarating about speeding down the hillside, the wind blowing in our faces. I've often fantasized about riding at the front of the *Cherub* as she cuts the sky. This is the closest I've gotten.

But still . . . my aching ass.

We're getting near where I left the cart and I'm scanning all around us for Ferals. It's hard moving as fast as we are, but I do my best nonetheless. So far it looks clear. Viktor says the Ferals don't get moving this early in the morning (and I don't blame them).

"It's up ahead," I yell in his ear. Normally I'd worry about yelling so loud, but the sound of the horse's hooves on the ground swallow up what I'm saying.

Then, there it is. The Ferrari. Sitting there against the tree, it looks ugly as hell—all ungainly metal and rubber.

And this is the tricky part.

Strapped to my back is a large can of Viktor's fuel. I now have to dismount and make myself vulnerable as I move to the cart, hoping that no Ferals are hiding around or beneath it.

For a crazy moment, I wonder if any could have gotten inside. So it's with my revolver in hand that I approach the cart.

"I'll keep an eye out," Viktor says. But it doesn't stop me from darting my own around. Then I'm crossing to the cart and the fuel chamber and pouring Viktor's mix inside.

When it's done, I nod back to Viktor and move to the door. With a deep breath, I open it, my pistol out, ready for something to jump out. When nothing does, I cautiously look inside and see that it appears to be empty.

Muttering thanks to my father, like I often do, I climb behind the steering column and press the ignition button. The engine coughs but doesn't start. I punch it again. The same thing.

It's then that I hear Viktor yelling. I know what that means. He's caught sight of Ferals. He's a sitting duck standing still, so he's already off moving, and as I slide over to the other seat to look out the window I see Rex's hooves kicking up dirt and grass as he tears away.

I count to twenty, timing the beats to my heart, which is beating pretty fast at this point. I'm protected in the cart, but not against everything. Even with my racing heart, the count seems to take forever. Then I hit the button again.

This time it catches and the engine roars to life. With a smile as wide as Rex I press on the accelerator and pull away from the Ferrari's hiding place.

There's a thump as I slam into something solid and I wince, but there's no blood splatter on the window as I watch the Feral's grimy body spin away.

Then I'm shooting down the hill and to the west.

Viktor and I had planned this part as well. Whether or not we were discovered, I would continue on to the old country road and down to the farms at its end. Viktor couldn't guarantee that they weren't infested, but he was optimistic there might be some good forage there.

It feels good to be moving again. And as much as I enjoyed riding Rex (well, all of me save my ass), this feels somehow better. To have an engine under my control. It's not the air, of course, but it's definitely closer.

I leave the Ferals far behind me and pull onto the dirt road and open up the cart. Viktor assured me that it's clear at least of vehicles, which is rare enough. I've foraged and flown over enough roads to know how unusual that is.

I wonder how it went down out here when the Sick came down. Were people enjoying their quiet country lives when the Bug hit? When the Ferals caught up to them? Did they flee to the big cities like so many others did? Or were their homes empty? Waiting for a day when they could visit them?

Of course there's no way to tell. So many stories. So much horror.

The Ferrari's wheels handle the rough road easily. That was something that Sergei got right—I think he pulled the wheels off a vehicle they found. But it handles easily.

It's not long before I see a house approaching rapidly. It's a tall one, dilapidated after all this time but still standing. It doesn't look dangerous enough to fall on me, which is important.

I slow the cart down and let it coast to a stop in front of the house, angling my head to scan the structure. One of the difficulties with foraging is finding the right way in, which often, but not always, serves as your way out.

There's a front door that looks mostly rotted away, which means easy access. But doors like that mean that Ferals might have gotten in. Though they also could have entered by the windows that circle the porch. From here the panes look mostly intact, but I can't see all of them.

The second floor looks difficult to get to without special gear. If I had the *Cherub* it would be a piece of cake, but I don't and so that's out of the question.

The third floor is a pipe dream.

I pull up close to the house and circle round until I see another door alongside. This one is a set of double doors with more windows than the other.

I get out of the cart. Here I'm faced with a dilemma. Do I leave the door open or close it? Leaving it open means that I can get back in quickly. But so could a Feral. That would be a nasty surprise. So closed it is.

I creep up to the door and look inside through the panes that are intact. I see furniture, but little else.

"Fuck it," I say and start breaking panes. It's easy to push the door in then and I'm inside. It's some kind of kitchen area, with the stove and other appliances to my left and a small sitting area straight ahead. Plenty of space hidden from view. So I walk in with my revolver out, my eyes scanning, my tread light. I have twenty-five bullets left. That's it. Then I'm defenseless.

The place smells musty, and I know that some of the food here has spoiled. It's not a fresh spoiled smell but something older. It doesn't tell me anything. The food could have gone long ago and there still could be Ferals about. I move into the kitchen, my gun preceding my every move. Nothing's there. So I set about rooting through the cupboards, trying not to be too loud, keeping my eyes moving, first on a cupboard, then all around me, then another cupboard, and so on.

I turn up a few cans early in the search. Cans can be tricky—they might be intact and still turn up rancid or give you bad stomachaches—but they're still valuable. I stuff them into my bag. The next few drawers and cupboards turn up some dry goods. They're likely full of bugs, but I stuff them in the bag anyway. I'll have time to check later.

The next set of cabinets turns up a prize. Liquor. If I were on the *Cherub* I would have a hard choice with this. A good drink is always a good thing to have around, but I could also barter quite a bit for this. Vodka. And . . . yes, deeper in the back there's a smaller bottle. Tequila.

The house is a veritable gold mine. Viktor's idea had been sound. By the time I clear the kitchen, my search has been Feral-free and I've added a stash of rice and some dried corn kernels to the mix. I could walk way right now and be happy.

But I'm feeling a bit more confident, and I want to give the rest of the house a search.

It's tech-lite, the way a lot of these country homes are. Dad used to tell me that people preferred these homes without too many modern distractions. People who lived in the cities often used these places to get away. I had to take his word on that. I never knew a world with distractions other than finding a way to survive. But I've read about them. It's like reading about wizards and sorcerers.

I find a couple of tech boxes whose uses aren't clear to me. I strip what I can from them and pile them into the bag.

Then it's up the stairs.

Again, this is a bit trickier. Just because no Ferals came at me before doesn't mean there isn't a whole nest up here, enjoying the slightly elevated temperature, waiting for a tasty morsel to drop in on them.

So it's revolver out, my finger ready to fire away.

I realize this place is bigger than it appears. Lots of rooms. Which can be trouble. But I take them one by one. Swinging the gun into the entrance, switching between the room and the hallway.

It also appears to be clean. There's not much up here. Some old furniture. Some books. I pick up a few. These are for me. Entertainment isn't easy to find in the Sick, and it looks like I'm going to have a lot of time on the ground to fill.

At last I crest the third floor. It's just one room up here. A huge room.

With a window looking down on the fields below and some kind of stove or heating unit crafted to look like an antique.

There's nothing here for me, either. But still I stop for a moment and admire the view, trying to imagine what it would be like for someone to live here.

After just standing for a while, I decide it's time to leave. I could check out another of the houses, but my haul is substantial enough and I don't need to right now. Besides, I'll have plenty of time to clear these old houses. At least until the fuel stops lasting. I might as well take it a little slow.

I drop my finds into the back of the Ferrari and gun her up. The sound of the engine seems louder now that my heart isn't jackhammering in my chest. Then I'm heading back to the hill and toward Viktor's farm.

My smile is wide as I make my way back.

I park the car near the fence's gate and scramble with my haul inside and into the house. Happy, almost beaming, I remove all my treasures and line them up on Viktor's table, waiting for his arrival.

I also crack open the liquor and take a quick celebratory swig.

I expected Viktor to be here when I got back, but he must have decided to do something else. In a way it's better like this. I can surprise him when he gets back.

I slide into a chair gripping one of the Westerns I took from the house. I haven't read many of them, but every time I come across one I feel drawn to it. Something about that time, people living in a wild, dangerous frontier. It reminds me of now. Only those were society's growing pains. Now we're living in its death throes.

I'm into the second chapter when I hear a horrific squeal outside. I run to the window and through it I see Rex rearing in front of the gate. I wonder what's going on, then it hits me. Maybe the horse is hurt. Maybe Viktor's hurt. Maybe that's why they aren't already inside the fence.

I'm out the door and halfway to the gate when I realize that Viktor isn't on Rex's back.

I hit the gate release and the horse comes galloping in, running around the open yard and tossing his head. He looks wild. Huge. I'm afraid to go near him.

I wonder if he would attack me. My hand hovers near my revolver.

It's as I'm thinking about how to subdue him that he seems to calm down and approaches me slowly. I reach my hand out the way Viktor showed me, though my other hand still remains near the pistol.

Rex walks closer and nuzzles my hand.

Where the fuck is Viktor?

I slowly walk around Rex and then I see it. The large dark stain on the horse's brown flank. Sticky.

Blood.

I back away. I don't know whose blood this is. It could be Viktor's, of course. Or it could be Feral blood. I know that it doesn't appear to be the horse's blood. He doesn't appear to be injured from what I can see, though I'm certainly not getting too close to that blood.

What the fuck happened?

I feel like I should get on Rex and go out looking, but I barely know how to ride and again, there's that blood. So instead I leave Rex and go out to the Ferrari. I drive down the hill, around where we saw the Ferals. I drive in the direction I saw him leaving that morning. I go around and around until I'm not sure which direction I'm facing.

There's no sign of Viktor.

That doesn't mean anything, I think. He could still be out there. Maybe he just fell off Rex and is now making his way back to the house. Slowly. Carefully.

So I return to the house myself. Rex is now calm, away from the outside world. I manage, somehow, to undo the straps on the saddle and remove (or rather topple) it from him, being careful not to get close to the blood, even wrapping my gloves in additional cloth. Then I leave the horse to wander.

I return to the house and sit there, worrying. Wondering. So I pick up the book and start to read. Have to pass the time somehow. I keep listening, though. For any sign of Viktor. For a shout. A groan. Anything.

But nothing comes, so I read instead, hoping that cowboys will distract me.

I fall asleep with the book on top of me.

I dream of gunslingers and horses and revolvers and gunfights. The book I was reading is about a sheriff in the Old West, a lawman, trying to bring order to his chaotic town. Only without the Bug to dog his steps.

I wonder if anyone back in the Clean ever longed to live in a time like that. It was rough if the book is any indication. People dying left and right. Disease. Violence. Lawlessness. But you could live the life you wanted. You could have a house. Friends. Neighbors. Family. You could make a living doing something. Running a store. Building things. Training horses. Farming. I find myself longing for even the simplest of lives back then. Something quiet and comfortable. Maybe even a marriage. Growing old and getting fat with a woman beside me.

And if lawlessness or violence did come my way, well, I know how to deal with that.

There's only one real law in the Sick: survive.

When I wake I go back to the Ferrari and take it out again, looking for any sign of Viktor. I know what it's like to get caught outside. Sometimes the best thing to do is to hide, hole up somewhere warm and safe and come out when things get quiet. Stirred-up Ferals tend to stick around. But they didn't have the best memories sometimes. Let them get distracted by something else and you could often make a run for it.

I drive around, hoping that if Viktor is out there he sees me and comes running. Without Rex he'll be easy prey unless I can get him in the Ferrari.

But he doesn't appear. I stay out as long as I can, only returning when my stomach starts howling at me to fill it. I know I'll be better with some food in me, so I go back and go through some of the food I foraged from the house. The canned beans are a little funky but seem to be mostly okay. You tend to develop instincts about this sort of thing. The fish, likewise, seems good if a little salty. I wash them down with some of Viktor's fresh water and a sip of tequila.

That flat, gray voice is starting to speak inside my head again. It's the voice of Reality, the one that always kicks in when I start to stray into wishful thinking. It's saying that Viktor isn't coming back. It's saying that he got caught and he's either dead or Faded and there's nothing I can do to help him. I try not to listen to it.

But I start thinking about what happens if he doesn't come back. What do I do then? I look around at his comfy digs and think, can I really just stay there?

The gray voice says, can you really afford not to? Here I have protection, security, food, water. It's not the Core, but it's close. I have the Ferrari. I can forage through the nearby houses until I amass a suitable stash. And if I end up with some really good salvage, maybe I can barter it to get back in the air. I could sign up with a crew, work my way up to my own ship again.

The thought makes me want to spit because I had my ship. I had my home. But then I think about how I didn't really bleed to get the *Cherub*. Don't get me wrong, I've bled lots. For my ship. For my family. Sometimes even for strangers. But I got lucky growing up on the *Cherub*. Some other zeps out there had to earn their ships, bit by bit. I never had to deal with that. And isn't being in the sky worth it?

You're getting ahead of yourself, the voice says, and I know it's right. For now, I have a place to live, food, and shelter. I'll deal with the rest as it comes.

But first, I go out to look for Viktor one more time. I spend a more time this round on looking for hiding places, under rocks, beneath bushes, things like that. Those are often places that Ferals hide out in, but what can I do?

Nothing. The air smells fresh and wild and I think of Viktor out wounded in it. He couldn't have gone too far, I think. And if he's not back now, something has gone horribly wrong. Odds aren't good, the gray voice says.

But I push it back. He could be hurt, sure, but that doesn't mean he was infected. Maybe he broke his leg falling off Rex. He pulled himself into some crevice somewhere, and he's just trying to figure out a way to get back. I make sure to shut off the Ferrari's engine, strain to listen beyond the bird calls and the rustling of the trees.

Nothing.

The gray voice stirs again and again. I silence it. I wonder why I'm spending so much time on this. But it's fairly simple in the end. Viktor saved me. I want to do the same.

What if you can't? This time the gray voice doesn't go away. It's not like you're good at saving people. Better at getting them killed.

Since I'm already out, I decide to try another house. The one I choose is smaller—less to check—and so I carefully kick in the door and enter with my pistol out.

Nothing moves, but a smell washes over me. Not the stink of Ferals but the smell of death. Something died in here. And relatively recently.

I take in the room quickly. It's a large open space, with a kitchen area ahead of me and a lounging area to my right. I move through the open area to make sure there's nothing hiding and then check out the kitchen.

Unfortunately, any of the dry goods were rotted by a broken-in window and the weather it let in. There are a few bottles of sauces and condiments, but nothing with real nutrition.

There's also a dearth of electronics here. Just a pair of old guitars that have long since rotted through.

A set of stairs leads up to a second level. I take them up.

The scent of death is stronger upstairs. A long corridor winds its way around the top floor with doors leading off it.

I take them one by one, willing myself to be quiet, hoping not to alert anything that might be hiding here. The first room is just a bedroom—bed, bureau, and rocking chair. I open the drawers, but there are only moldy sheets inside.

The next one is the same. And the next. Maybe some kind of boarding house?

The last room reveals the source of the smell. A figure is twisted up on the ground at the foot of the bed. Dessicated and stiff.

It's a Feral. Female. The nakedness doesn't give it away, but the long, dirty nails do. I don't get close to it. The Bug almost certainly died with it, but I don't think I can bring myself to approach.

I can't help but wonder why it came in here. Maybe searching for food, I think, but then why not just leave? Maybe it had been sick with some kind of Feral disease?

It was almost certainly on its own, otherwise other Ferals would have eaten it. Miranda says that in addition to stealing away reason and increasing aggression, the Bug speeds up the victim's metabolism. So they're always hungry. They're as likely to eat each other in extreme cases as they are anything else.

But they prefer other meat, be that animal or human.

I've often wondered what happens when we're all infected. When the human race is dead and there are only Ferals left, will they just feed on each other? Will they hit some kind of equilibrium where enough are being born to keep the others alive?

I can only consider that for so long.

I carefully shut the door and go back down the stairs. This time I look for any closets or storage spaces or anything to indicate a cellar.

I don't find the latter, but I do find a door under the stairs that opens into a storage space. I see what looks like an old music player, which I pull out. And behind that, dusty and covered in cobwebs, is a radio. I clear myself a path and carefully remove it, cradling it in my arms. It looks battered and neglected, but there's a possibility I could coax it back to life.

The trip now worth my while, I bring my prize back out to the Ferrari and load it into the passenger seat. As I'm leaning into it, I hear movement behind me.

I snap back out, bring the revolver around.

Then I freeze.

Across the street, at the edge of the trees, is a bear.

It's on all fours, sniffing, but I'm clearly visible to it.

My finger hesitates over the trigger. I should shoot it now, I think. Before it decides to charge me.

It moves slowly, ponderously, out into the open.

I can't help but think it's a magnificent beast. With a full brown coat and a regal face.

I lower the revolver. Then, carefully, I slip into the passenger seat and shut the door. I slide over to the driver's seat, start up the Ferrari, and, rather quickly, pull away.

In the end I return to the farm and let myself in, hoping to see Viktor there.

But the place is empty.

I pour myself a liberal glass of the tequila. It's warm and it burns and I focus on that sensation for a while, then on the warmth inside of me, and the growing numbness in my belly.

"You're a plod now," I say to myself. "Might as well get used to it."

✳    ✳    ✳

The next morning I awake to an empty house. Viktor still isn't back. I spare a moment to step outside, scan the area for any movement, expecting to see Viktor crawling back to the house. But he's not there.

Instead I head back inside and start to search the farm. If I'm going to be a plod, I need to understand how it works, what I have at my disposal. My scavenger instincts serve me well and I uncover a cellar door carefully hidden behind some boxes. I grab a lantern, light it, and descend beneath the farmhouse.

The space is filled with metal utility shelves. The shelves are filled with an assortment of items, loosely organized. The food stores are rather sparse. Some cans, some dry goods—salt, spices, et cetera. There are numerous jugs of unidentifiable liquids. I open one and smell something alcoholic and sweet.

Another row is filled with battered boxes. One is filled with mostly personal items—an old music box, a mirror, some jewelry—items with only sentimental value. Another contains old photographs. I flip through a few of them. Smiling faces. Old clothes. So much flesh uncovered. A different age. I wonder if they're Viktor's family or just strangers.

The next row contains machinery, or parts of machinery. I spot some car parts, an old lawnmower that remarkably hasn't been stripped, and some unidentifiable pieces.

I dump out a nearby box filled with nuts and bolts and other various bits and pieces (I'll apologize to Viktor if he ever shows), and I take a handful of parts upstairs to where the light is better.

Once back upstairs I lay out the radio. It takes me the better part of a day, but I manage to open it and do a careful check of the interior, clearing out the worst of the dust and muck. There are a few connections that aren't quite working, but I think I should be able to fix it. I might need to find or make myself a soldering iron, but I think I can get it to work.

And then what? That damned voice again. Are you really going to broadcast your position to anyone who might hear you?

I ignore the voice. It's a good question, but first things first. I can fix the radio and then decide what to do with it (if anything). Besides, it will give me something to do.

I spend the rest of the day on the radio, taking a break to go out and see Rex. He follows me into the barn and I manage to figure out what kind of food he eats and dump some into a feed bucket. I leave him munching on it when I return to the radio. I stay up into the night working on it and opening a fresh jug of Viktor's moonshine. What I end up with is strong, more like liquor, though with a fruitiness of its own. I pass out at the table among wires and circuits.

The next day, though, I finish it. The radio is complete. I even found a soldering iron in Viktor's toolbox (though my dad taught me how to make one when I was a kid). I sit and stare at it, my fingers twitching. This is my choice: I can broadcast on a friendly frequency (there's one the boffins usually use) or I can leave well enough alone. Broadcasting means I might possibly reach someone, but . . . well, that person might not be friendly.

I'm a plod now, I think. That means playing it safe. I can't fly away anymore. I'm fixed. Stuck. Stationary.

Put it away, the gray voice says. This is your life now. You have to protect it.

I think back to what I told Miranda before I left the Core. That if I found a place that spit out food on a regular basis, I'd stay. Viktor's farm is the closest to that kind of thing I've ever found. It's well stocked, safe, and close to some good forage.

I think of Miranda and realize that I lied.

I sit up, stab for the "On" switch, depress it. Then I'm transmitting. Not a voice message, but code. Morse code like back in the Clean. A string of numbers. Prime numbers. The boffins love shit like that. It would practically scream at them. But your average raider, even if they could decode it, odds are it wouldn't make a lick of sense to them. So it's safer, if not safe. If any of the boffins hear me, then they should get back in touch. Hopefully it's not a code in advanced mathematics.

This is it. I'm sending my message into the sky. It's up to the sky if I'm worthy enough for this to work.

But I try not to think about that. Try not to want anything. As far as I'm concerned, I'm a plod. This is my new life. As limited as it is.

But inside, deep inside, some part of me hopes.

It's the next day that I hear knocking on the door. I'm halfway to it when I suddenly stop. I'd first thought it was Viktor, but he wouldn't knock at his own door. Even if he was wounded. He'd call for me. Or just let himself in. I pull the pistol out and hold it tightly.

Maybe my message was picked up. But by whom?

The knocking comes louder. And I recognize it. The same pattern I've grown used to.

Miranda.

I lower the revolver and open the door. She stares back at me, her hair stirring in the wind, her glasses reflecting my face back at me.

"Ben! Thank God."

She pulls me close and embraces me. And I feel a surge of feelings bright and warm and comforting push up inside me. For a moment I feel this incredible sense that everything's going to be all right.

Then I push her back. "You got my message?"

She nods. "We didn't know it was you. We thought it might be someone from Apple Pi."

"But how did you find me?"

She smiles. "We triangulated your signal. It took a few hours, but we got a rough position and then when we got close, Sergei spotted the Rover."

Of course, I think. Of course Sergei has some directional radio antennas on his ship, and any one of them could do the calculations to figure out where the signal was.

"I'm glad it was you that picked it up."

She nods. Then her smile fades. "We were looking for survivors. After . . ." She looks down at her clenched hands. "We went to Apple Pi and saw."

I look down, too. "Was there anyone left?"

"Just bodies. The crumpled shell of one of the airships. Wreckage. They took . . . they took everything they could. And just left a mess behind. Why? Why not just take over?"

"Because they don't want to hold the Core. That's not their land. They have Gastown and Valhalla. That's where they're invested. That's where they want to be. They just suck everything else dry to make themselves stronger."

"And the *Cherub*?"

My teeth clamp down. "They took it. It's gone. Fuck, Miranda. My father's ship is gone."

She reaches an arm out and rubs it along my shoulders. Comforting. After everything that's happened, she's comforting me. After I told her to leave my ship. After I ran from the Core. After the loss of all her data, everything she worked so hard to build. She's comforting me. It makes me feel like the world's biggest asshole. But I take it, because at that moment I need it and it's all I can do not to ask her for more.

"Where's your ship?" I ask at last.

"Above us," she says. "With Sergei and Clay."

And then it hits me. I can get back into the air. Without the *Cherub*, of course. But up in the sky. With Miranda. And Sergei. I deliberately ignore all thoughts of Clay.

"But what are you doing here?" Miranda asks. "What is this place?"

I frown. "Someone found me. Helped me." I shake my head. "Saved me."

"Where is this person?" She looks around as if Viktor will materialize and they'll get to meet. And I wish that that were going to happen.

"He went out a few days ago and didn't come back," I say. "I don't think he's going to."

She gives me a look of sympathy. "I'm sorry."

I nod. "Me, too."

"And the horse?" She jerks her thumb back toward the door.

"His . . . his name is Rex." Suddenly I wonder if Rex is the last horse in the area. Hell, he could be the last horse in the world for all I know.

We both stand there in silence. Then Miranda says, "Do you want to come with us?"

I realize she didn't have to ask. I basically told them to fuck themselves. Yet here we are.

"I was all set to stay here," I say. "Live on this farm. Forage for what I could get until the fuel ran out. Make at least some kind of life."

"Do you still want to do that?" she asks.

"No. I want to be in the sky. I want to go with you."

She smiles. Then her face goes serious. "Okay. There's just one thing."

"What?"

"You're not going to like it."

"Tell me."

"The Feral is onboard. Alpha. We rigged up a cage in the cargo area and he's inside it. Inside the *Pasteur*."

I close my eyes. "You kept it?"

"We had to," she says. "Especially now. With most of our data gone, this is all we have."

"And what are you going to do with it? Make it part of the gang? We have nowhere to secure it. No place to study it. Better to let it go and not let it slow us down."

She stares at me hard in the eyes. "Look, Ben. These are the terms. You want to come with us, you suck it up and deal with this. You don't want to do that, then you stay here. Keep the Rover. Do with it what you will. But that's the way things are."

In that moment I love her and hate her at the same time. Hate her for what she's telling me. And love her for how tough she sounds.

Above me, inside Sergei's ship, is the Feral. A drop of its saliva could infect me. And I'm going to have to go with it. On the other hand, Miranda is offering me the sky. She's rescuing me from Gravity. And I realize that's more important to me.

She walks to the ladder leading up to the ship. "You coming?"

I nod. "Yes. But I have a few things to take care of, some things to get. I'll be right behind you."

I return to the house and pack up everything I took from the farmhouse and a few of Viktor's things. It makes me feel dirty, like stealing from a friend, but I know he's dead. That he's not coming back. At least not as a human being.

Then I walk outside. Rex comes trotting up to me. I reach out to him and stroke him lightly on the head where he's thankfully free of blood. He may just be the last horse left in the world. A magnificent animal who deserves to be cared for. Only . . . I'm not the one to do it.

I step back, pull my revolver, and shoot Rex in the head.

He dies quickly. Quicker than he would by starving to death. Or getting some strange horse disease from not being cared for properly.

It's then that I do retch. I bend over, gagging, vomiting all over the ground. The truly sad thing is that in any other situation, I would have cut poor Rex up into little pieces. Packed that meat away for later eating. You don't let that much meat go.

But there's the possibility that he's got the Bug all over him. Viktor assured me that it doesn't affect horses, but it does affect humans. And I can't eat anything with the Bug all over it.

When I'm done, I walk to the ladder and leave the ground behind.

✳  ✳  ✳

Sergei gives me a strong handshake and a pat on the back when he sees me. His face looks tired, haunted. Like he saw his home, his safe place destroyed before his eyes, which he did. I know the feeling. When there's no place to go back to.

Clay nods at me with a look like he just ate something rancid. I suppose in a way he did.

Miranda clears away some things in the gondola to make room for me. The gondola of the *Pasteur* is by no means small, but much of it has traditionally been used for research. Now it's the remaining store of the Core's data and it's covered in papers and small solar-powered devices that I have no names for.

With all that, it's suitable for about two people. Three, in a pinch. Four is pushing it. We'll be jammed up tight against one another. But we're in the air, and I'll take it.

"We lost a lot," Miranda says. "Too much. But I have most of the latest data here. Luckily I brought it with me to review. And we have Subject Alpha. I suppose it could have been worse." She says it nonchalantly, like she just didn't have everything taken away from her. And suddenly I feel like such a baby. But I also worry.

"Have you been in touch with any of the others?" I say. "At least two of the dirigibles got away."

Sergei shakes his head. "We've been listening for them, but nothing. Though with everything that's happened, they may be maintaining radio silence."

"What exactly did happen?" Clay asks. He makes it sound like an accusation. Like I was in on it somehow. But they deserve an answer.

"I was heading west and had a run-in with another airship set upon by raiders. Gastown raiders. I helped them with that particular problem, and they mentioned, after a fashion, that they saw other ships heading in the direction of the Core. I was worried, so I set back to try to warn everyone. I got there ahead of them, but . . ."

"But what?" Clay says.

"They came in soon afterward. With Ferals on hooks." Sergei and Miranda both go pale. They were there on Gastown when the raiders attacked. They saw the horror there.

"At our place?" Miranda says. Her hand curls into a shaking fist.

I nod. "I tried to get to the *Cherub*, but . . ." I rub a hand over my face. "They took it. So I ran for the Ferrari. Took that instead."

"Why didn't you take anyone else with you?" Clay says. "Why didn't you grab any of the data? The equipment?"

I stand up. Take a step toward him. "You weren't there, Clay, so just shut the fuck up. It was chaos. You think I'd know what to grab? Which stack of papers or which hunk of metal was important? And if I had, I'd likely be dead in the Core along with everyone else."

"So you ran," he says.

Pressure builds behind my eyes and I'm moving, bringing my arm up. Then Sergei has his hand on me, pulling me back, and Miranda's up off her seat and stepping between us.

"Ben's right, Clay," she says. "Sergei and I have seen this before. There wasn't anything he could've done. And we just have to deal with the fact that we lost . . . excuse me." She pushes away and moves to the back room of the gondola.

I follow her, pretending Clay isn't there. Because if he's there, I'm going to have to hit him.

Miranda slides to the ground and puts her face in her hands. Then her shoulders shake, and choking noises come from her throat.

I sink down next to her, and it's my turn to put my arm around her. She feels so small next to me. So fragile. I know she's not. I know that inside of her is this core of hard steel. A core I helped to harden. But right now she feels like glass and I want to pull her against me and hold her tight. But I don't. I don't move away either.

"It's all gone," she says.

"It's not all gone. You have some stuff here. The others might have managed to salvage more. And you have that loaded gun in your cargo bay, crazy as you are."

She cracks a thin smile at that, knowing how much it unnerves me. "What do we do now?" she asks.

I shrug. "We'll think of something. We always do."

She looks up at me, her eyes red and wet behind her glasses. "But for how long? How long can we do this? How long can we take all of this?"

I place a hand on the side of her face. "For as long as we have to."

"I don't know if I can."

"I'll help you," I say. And it surprises me. "C'mon. Let's get back in there. Figure out what we're going to do. It will make you feel better." I stand up, help pull her to her feet. She hugs me, clinging to me, and the scent of her, that smell I can't place, is all in my nostrils. And she's warm and solid against me. And my body responds of its own accord and I gasp. We stay like that for a moment. Then we pull away. She gives me a little smile and we return back to the others.

"What now?" Sergei says.

"We should go back. See what we can salvage," Clay says.

"No," I say. "They may be watching the place. And if they're not there now, they will be soon. You can never stay there again. It's too vulnerable."

"Then where are we supposed to go? We have a Feral aboard."

"Oh, I'm aware," I say. "I'm very fucking aware." Then it clicks into place. I smile. "I know where we can go."

# CHAPTER SEVEN

They all look at me.

"Just before the shit went down," I say, "I got word of a new city out there. They're not advertising their presence, of course, but I think I can get us in. We just have to head out to San Diego."

"Not advertising is a good idea considering what's going on," Miranda says.

"Right. But so far they've escaped notice. I ran into a couple of their people before the attack. I think they might let us hole up there. At least temporarily while we consider our next move. We can refresh our supplies, too."

"Well, we'll need to find a place to study Alpha," Miranda says.

"That's going to be the tricky part," I say. "A live Feral? That's not going to be a popular addition to any community."

"We'll just have to see what they say," Sergei says.

"We can't lead with the fucking Feral," I say.

"You want to lie to them?" Clay asks.

"No. But give them one big reason to turn us away and they will. We need to play it more carefully than that. They're going to want to see the thing, see how you have it contained, at the very least."

"That's fine," Miranda says. "He's contained and rigged so that we can test him with minimal exposure."

"Is that all documented?" I ask.

"Not yet," she says.

"Then get it written down. The more we have to show these people, the better."

"If they can read," Clay says.

"Someone will be able to read," I say. "Just do it."

"I'll get on that," Sergei says.

I pause for a moment. Then I say words I didn't think I would hear come from my mouth. "You need to show me."

"What?" Miranda says.

"The Feral."

I don't think Miranda's eyebrows can go higher than they go right now.

"I know, I know," I say. "I don't really want to look at this thing, but if it's staying on this ship, I want to make sure I check out its . . . accommodations."

Miranda stands. "You're sure?"

"No. But I need to do this."

"Let's go, then," she says.

And she takes me into the cargo bay.

✳   ✳   ✳

The *Pasteur*'s cargo bay is a little odd. The *Cherub* was built for carrying things, and her cargo bay is secure and pressurized and you could sleep in there if you wanted to. The *Pasteur*'s cargo bay has been rigged and re-rigged. Sometimes they haul equipment in it. Sometimes it's been a mobile lab. The farther you get from the gondola, the more into the superstructure you get, and the colder it gets as you're nearer the envelope. The boffins seem to like this; they can get into the guts of the ship if they need to, rig machines up to the solar cells, things like that. Once I even saw them run wind power off the outside of the ship into it. At least until it broke down.

All of this means that the Feral is closer to the gondola than I'd like. But if it were to be a bit farther out, it might not survive. Which is fine with me, but not with Miranda. And right now she's calling the shots.

They have their Feral in a cage, rigged with mesh like I'd suggested.

But they were smart enough to rig the tranq gun up to the cage, behind a sliding panel so that they can easily take it down without having to dismantle anything.

"Aren't you worried that you'll have to tranq it too much?"

"That's what the cage is for," Miranda says. "We won't need to until we land. Then we can study him more easily. I can maybe rig up some storage for his blood."

Those words make me light-headed.

"I don't feel good about doing this, keeping him like this, but we need him."

Leave it to Miranda to worry about the well-being of a Feral.

I move closer to the cage. "Well, Alpha," I say. "Let me get a good look at you."

The Feral's hair is long and messy, like most of its kind. It hangs down around its face like a bird's nest pulled to shit. Caught in its hair are leaves and other bits and pieces. I try not to think too hard about what else might be in there.

Its chest is covered with the tattered remnants of what might have been a shirt. It's little more than shredded cloth now, but it remains bound around its shoulders and neck. That's one of the weird things about Ferals. Some of them keep their clothes. Or maybe they're just not very good at getting rid of them.

I wish Alpha had kept more. He's naked below the waist, his skin smeared with dirt, his cock hanging there for all the world to see. As I move up to him, he's playing with himself, falling back on the primitive pleasures of the flesh in a time of stress, perhaps.

When he sees me, however, his attitude changes. He forgets his erection and changes from his prior lax pose into something tense and coiled. His lips roll back from his teeth and he growls at me. My hand drops to my holster out of reflex and I have to will myself to stop from pulling it out and shooting Alpha through the head.

He growls, and slaver flies from his mouth. My body is screaming at me to run. Or to shoot the thing. Or both. But Miranda is behind me and I force myself to stand my ground.

Then I hear Clay's voice. "Is everything to your satisfaction?" he asks, and I can hear the sneer in his tone.

*You can shoot him*, the voice in my head says. *One bullet for Alpha, one for Clay, and all your problems will be solved.* Which is not true. I still wouldn't have the *Cherub* back. And Miranda would hate me. But it's a delightful thought.

"I'd still rather put a bullet through his head," I say.

"His?" Miranda says softly. And I curse under my breath. When did I start thinking of Alpha as a "he" and not an "it"? *Probably around the time you started using his name*, I think.

Alpha starts slamming himself against the cage. I guess he knows a threat when he sees one. The cage holds, though. I note that the places where it's bolted into the floor don't move and it seems secured on all sides. I still tug my scarf up higher on my face.

I intend to turn away, walk back to the gondola, but I don't. Instead I look into Alpha's eyes, try to see if there's any hint in there of humanity. I've never spent this much time looking at a Feral, not unless it was through a scope. I try to see anything that I would recognize as a person. But all I see are red-rimmed eyes and large black pupils. Mindless animosity. He slams himself against the cage, again and again, and my hand falls down to my revolver again, but then he slumps back, panting.

Like an animal.

I'm still prickly, hackles up, and of course now is the time that Clay chooses to come up alongside me and try to usher me forward. His palm falls on my back and I react. Strung out like taut wire, I snap, and in a moment he's on the floor and I have his arm bent at an angle that wouldn't be called normal. He gasps in pain.

"Ben!" Miranda calls.

Awareness of what's happening comes back to me, but I hold the pose a moment longer, meeting Clay's eyes before releasing him.

"Fucking psycho!" Clay yells.

"Touch me again and I'll break your arm," I say low and even. Then I walk out of the room sparing one last look for Miranda as I go.

Back in the gondola I feel my body relaxing, muscles unknotting, tension ebbing into ease.

Sergei smiles at me. "Do you mind taking the controls for me?" he asks. "I want to discuss what we're going to do with Alpha with Miranda and Clay."

I smile back, like sunshine is leaking out of me. "If it will help." I remember now why I like Sergei so much. He can be about as fun as a bucket of mud, but he has a good head on his shoulders.

Also, I remember, buckets of mud can be fun, too. There aren't many toys in the Sick.

I've only piloted the *Pasteur* once before, but its controls are standard for a semirigid ship, and I push her in the direction of San Diego.

Based on the speed of the *Pasteur*, I'm guessing we can get to San Diego in about three hours. It's a kind of mental shorthand, calculating speed and wind and fuel. I try not to think about the fact that the *Cherub* would have gotten us there faster.

Even then, there's the radio call to make and I'm not sure what the deal will be there. Will they require me to fly through a few more hoops before they give us the location? Will I have to meet with Diego?

I push that all out of my mind. It doesn't make sense to worry about it now. I know where I'm going, for at least a few hours, and the rest can be dealt with when we get there. For now I'm back in the air, with a ship beneath me, and I'm at the controls. Life could be a lot worse.

I relax into the rhythm of piloting a ship. Checking weather patterns, keeping an eye on engine readouts. Adjusting course. The *Pasteur*'s instruments, from back in the Clean, are largely intact and Sergei's rigged them to now run solar. Again, she's not the *Cherub*, but she's a decent ship.

Sergei told me once that the *Pasteur* was always a science ship. That she was originally used to follow animal migratory paths. And, if he's to be believed, it was used to track the spread of the Bug when it first hit. Like Miranda, Sergei comes from a scientist family and they passed it down the same way my grandfather passed down the *Cherub*.

Whatever she was used for, she handles just fine and she's enough to restore some part of myself to me. The part that belongs at the controls of an airship, cutting the sky.

Slightly less than three hours later, we arrive, flying over the ruins of San Diego. I tune the radio to the correct frequency and call out, identifying myself as Ben and calling for Diego.

There's no response, so I do it again. And again. And again.

When I turn to look at the others, Clay is shaking his head. "Don't start," I say.

"It's probably—"

"Not now, Clay," Miranda says. She looks at me. "What next, Ben?"

"We wait for a bit. Try again," I say. "The settlement is probably not here; he wouldn't have given that away, so that means he must come in and out."

"What if he doesn't come at all?" Clay asks, his arms crossed against his chest.

"Then we leave."

"And go where?" Clay asks.

I stand up. "I don't fucking know yet. Why don't you—"

"Boys," Miranda says. "This isn't the time. Ben's right. We can wait for a little while, see if anything happens, and if nothing does, we'll figure out a Plan B."

Sergei clears his throat. "We should keep an eye out for other ships."

He's right. If we hover here for too long, we'll be a target. And San Diego, like most cities, is still popular among intrepid foragers.

"We'll take turns," I say. "Broadcast at regular intervals. And I'll take us down into the shadow of some of those buildings. That should buy us some cover."

Everyone agrees.

As we all separate, Miranda pauses, places a hand on my arm. "How long do we wait?"

I shake my head. "Let's see what happens first."

Then I move the *Pasteur* out of the light.

A few hours pass with nothing. I broadcast a few times, then take my turn on lookout. Waiting for a ship to appear. Tense, ready to fly the ship away. The *Pasteur*'s not armed, and she's not as fast as the *Cherub*, so we're vulnerable, especially stationary as we are.

I wonder if maybe I should go foraging down in the city while we're here. I have the stash I took from Viktor's, but we're going to need food and supplies pretty soon, what with four of us. Five, I suppose, counting Alpha. Fuck, I think, we're going to have to give some of our food to that creature.

Frustrated, I slide back into the seat by the radio and broadcast once again.

Then the radio cuts in. "Ben?"

"Yes," I say, smiling. "Diego? Thank God."

"You made it," he says. "Did you get to your friends in time?"

"Yeah, well, that's the problem." I lean against the console. "The place I was working for. It . . . it got hit by those raiders. The whole settlement was wiped out."

A pause on the line. "Man, I'm sorry."

"Yeah, me too." I spare a glance for Miranda, but she's looking away. "Diego, I'm with three others. We're all that's left. We need to find a place to put down and lick our wounds. I know the people you're hooked up with are doing their best to keep things quiet, but if you have any ideas, I'd appreciate hearing about them."

There's silence on the other side of the line. I wonder if Rosie is there. If he's discussing it with her. Then, after a few minutes have passed, I wonder if he's signed off. I wouldn't blame him. He doesn't know us. He doesn't owe us anything. And what I'm feeding him could be a load of shit meant to take advantage of him.

I get back on the line. "I'm not expecting full access. I just . . . if someone could escort us somewhere. You can even come onboard. It's just the one ship. We . . ."

I put down the transmitter. Then pick it up again. "We're desperate."

Still nothing. I turn to the others and shrug. Clay gives me another of those annoying looks that makes me want to hit him. Only I don't have the energy anymore. I feel deflated. I've got no more lift.

The line crackles to life. "Let's meet," Diego says.

✳   ✳   ✳

We meet at the top of another tall building. This time it's just Diego and me, a suitable distance between us. The wind whips around us, carrying the smell of green things. That's one of the few problems with the sky— it doesn't smell that interesting.

"Thanks for coming," I say.

"I still owe you," he says. "You never even took your barter for the medical supplies."

"I was in a hurry," I say.

"Seems so." His hands are in the pockets of his big black coat, and I wonder if he has a weapon concealed there. Or maybe I'm just jumpy.

"What are you asking, Ben?"

"Like I said, I have three others with me. Scientists. Idealists. They're good people." Well, and Clay, but I don't tell him that. "Their home got wiped out. Their friends scattered or got killed. They need a new place to stay."

Diego nods. He's traded in his ski mask for just a gray woolen cap, and his green scarf is low around his neck. He has rich, brown skin and a black beard. He has a good face. A trustworthy face. I know that counts for very little, but I hope he feels the same way about me.

"I understand," he says. "Sounds like a shit situation. Only . . . we don't know your friends. Hell, we don't even know you. You know what it's like. We can't just let anyone in."

"I know. I do. But the boffins, my friends, they're useful. Sergei is a magician when it comes to fuel. Clay and Miranda are top biologists. They're studying the Bug." And here's the part where I put on my master barterer face and fake some enthusiasm. "Diego, they're working on a cure."

He doesn't laugh at this, which is a good sign.

"They're close to a breakthrough. Something they were working on when the raiders hit. This could be huge. But they can't do it in the air. They can't do it running from raiders and foraging for food and fuel. They need a place."

"We do have some scientists back at . . . our place," Diego says.

"Great!" I say. "Show them Miranda's data. I'm sure they'd be impressed.

He runs a hand over the back of his neck. "You think they have a shot?" he asks.

I consider my next words carefully. "I think that if anyone does, it's Miranda. She won't rest until she finds a cure or she dies." Or gets infected, I silently amend. But that's not worth getting into.

Diego grimaces as he tosses things over in his head. "What makes you think you'll be happy there?" he asks. "You know nothing about our settlement."

I nod. "It's true. I thought about that. But like I said, we're desperate. And a place that sends people like you out to scout for them can't be that bad." I shrug. "Sometimes you just have to go with your gut." And if things go pear-shaped, then we'll just have to deal with it then.

He rubs his beard. "If we take you, you won't be able to leave. Not for a while at least. You'll be grounded." I try not to wince at the word, but I'm not sure how successful I am.

I nod. "That seems fair." What else can I say? I no longer have a ship. The *Pasteur* isn't mine. Maybe this way I can work my way back into the air.

He nods again. This time deeper. "Okay," he says.

"Okay? You'll take us?"

"Yes." He smiles at me. He has a good smile, the kind that puts you at ease. The kind that seems genuine. The kind that still seems to know what happiness is. "Sometimes you just have to go with your gut."

# CHAPTER EIGHT

The trick to any settlement in the Sick is to secure it against a Feral incursion. All you need is to have a penned-up group of people exposed to the Bug. All it takes is one person to Fade, and the infection spreads. That's how the world got fucked, after all.

So in the case of Valhalla and Gastown they built the cities in the sky. No chance of Ferals getting up there. And with dirigibles being the preferred mode of transport for a large portion of the remaining population, it made a lot of sense. Until the germ warfare introduced by Valhalla.

But there are other places to hole up. I heard tell once of a converted prison. Seems to make sense, right? Defensible walls, watchtowers, plenty of places to sleep, plenty of storage. Kitchens, probably generators. The whole deal.

Only word got out of the place. And people flocked to it. And why not, right? They were going to start a new settlement. Get civilization working again. Only one of those people had the Bug. Somehow they got through all the precautions. Someone got sloppy or stupid and let them in and that person Faded. And suddenly those walls that were once great at keeping the Ferals out ended up keeping people trapped inside. And as the Bug spread, it overtook the whole place. Now there's a place on forager maps that says "Here there be dragons" where a city once lived.

The Bug just pisses on civilization.

As we wait for Diego and his ship, the *Osprey*, to lead us to the settlement, the atmosphere on the *Pasteur* is light. Sergei's humming some jaunty tune. Clay is out of my hair. And Miranda is . . .

Where is Miranda?

I find her looking at Alpha in his cage.

"I still think we should dump him somewhere over the ocean."

Miranda sighs. She's used to this argument. She turns to me and takes off her glasses. Pinches the bridge of her nose. I notice the glasses have left a red mark. "He's all we have," she says.

"He's really that important?" I ask.

She nods. "He's different. The virus he carried reacts differently to the formulas we've devised. So far we've been testing on the standard virus, but this gives us another way to zero in on the problem. Kind of like triangulating the position of your radio signal."

"You managed to save some of your treatments?"

She nods again. "Some. In the field kit. But others shouldn't be hard to simulate. And if this new settlement has scientists, it might be easier."

"How long do you think you can keep him?"

"As long as he lasts," she says. "As long as he can give us blood." She puts her glasses back on. "I'm not an idiot. We have to be careful. And the more we tranq him, the less he's going to last. But . . ." She turns back to him. "Maybe we can rig something. That lets us draw samples when we need to. I don't know. But he's the closest we've come to a cure in some time. I think that's worth holding on to."

I don't say anything. I just rub a hand on her back. For a moment she leans against me. Then she's back to her notebook and I return to the controls.

"Thanks for this. Again," I say over the transmitter to Diego.

"Like I said, I owed you for the medical supplies."

He's joking, of course. It's worth far more than medical supplies. What he's given me in return is trust. That doesn't come easily in the Sick. This Diego is not your average man.

"So, where are we going?" I ask. Right now we're headed out over the ocean.

"You'll see," he says with a laugh.

And later we do. Sergei is the first to spot it outside the port window. An island. Well enough off the coast to be off the routes of most airships, but close enough that it's within easy reach. The island is not that large.

Larger than Alcatraz, but smaller than some of the other islands up north, the ones that pirates often use as bases and to stash their take. A few, much smaller, satellite islands trail off to the west like ellipses.

Much of the outside of the main island is ringed with jagged rocks, while inside the land has been leveled and buildings stand, places for people to live and work. It's well fortified, from the water at least. But it's vulnerable from the air, which is the reason for all the secrecy. True, there's no real reason for ships to come out this far, there's nothing to find out here. But if some did, the city would be vulnerable. To a few well-placed firebombs. Or Ferals. Which is why I understand their strict practices.

"You have some fancy secrets," I say to Diego.

"Don't I just?" he transmits back.

"Now what?"

"Head for the docking platform. We like to keep our ships close to the ground so they can't be spotted from other ships. They want me to stay up to cover you. But I radioed ahead. Told them that you were coming and who you were. They'll let you down, but you'll have to be inspected."

"Inspected?"

"To make sure you're not carrying secret troops or anything that could be used against the settlement."

It seems fair enough, but then I think about Alpha back there in his cage. If anything could be dangerous to the settlement, it's him. But we're here, and we have nowhere else to go. So we're just going to have to talk to the people.

"So what's the name of this fancy new settlement of yours?" I ask.

"You know people," he says. "They like old names. Its name is Tamoanchan."

"Never heard of it," I say.

"It's Aztec," he says.

"What does it mean?" I ask.

I can hear the smile in his voice. "It means paradise."

✳  ✳  ✳

Things with the inspector don't go well.

I try to get in front of him, give him the news up front, that we're not trying to bring the thing onto the island, but he's not buying it. He calls for his backup and they come in armed to the eyeballs, and since none of us want to die just yet, we let them take us.

Ironically, they drag us off the ship and onto the ground, onto the island. There's pushing and shoving and then they wrap chains around us.

I protest, of course. Clay also mouths off, but they're having none of it. Two men grab me, one on each arm. A third drops a bag over my head that smells like old sweat, and they march us off.

After what feels like an interminable time being dragged across the ground (during which I wonder to myself why I ever left the sky after being back in it), they pull off the mask.

We're in a long hall—wooden by construction. They dump us on the ground, and the chains dig into my skin. I grit my teeth and get myself to my knees.

A woman stands in front of us, though not too close. Her face is anything but pleasant. Her blonde hair is cut short and she wears a red scarf around her neck. All her other clothing is dark—grays and blacks. The inspector said her name was Brana. Behind her are two more people—another woman and a man. They wear similar colors.

Anger comes off her in waves. "What were you thinking bringing that . . . thing onto my island?" Brana asks, though it sounds like more of a command.

"Please," Miranda says. "We're scientists. We're studying the Feral. He's a test subject."

"I don't care what it is," Brana says. "That thing is a source of contamination. What if it got loose? Rampaged throughout the city? We have people here who escaped the tragedy at Gastown. I don't want to see that happen here."

"We have him secured," Sergei says.

"Excuse me if I don't trust the word of someone I've never met before. I am responsible for the well-being of all the people here. You gained admission here because one of our own vouched for you. But that only goes so far."

"If you examine Alpha's cage, you'll see that it's secured," Miranda says. "We've minimized the chance of infection to virtually nothing. And he can't get out."

Brana looks directly at Miranda, being careful not to get too close. "Let me stress this for you. I. Don't. Care. I'm thinking the best thing to do is shoot your pet, then burn the ship and let it fall into the sea."

"No," Miranda says, trying to get to her feet. "You can't! He's too important!"

Brana shakes her head. "You people really are fucked in the head. You care more about that thing than you do about your ship."

"We're looking for a cure!" Miranda says, her neck muscles rigid. "What are you doing? Hiding away? Turning your back on the rest of the world?"

Tamoanchan's leader bends down so that her face is level with Miranda's. "I am helping to protect these people. Helping to give them a life away from Ferals. Away from raiders."

"So what are you going to do with us?" Clay asks.

"That's the problem," Brana says. "You know where Tamoanchan is now. We can't let you leave." The implication is left hanging.

"Can I talk to you alone?" I pipe up.

Brana frowns at me. "And why would I want to do that?"

"Because I'm the one Diego and Rosie vouched for. I'm the one that led these people here. And ultimately this is all down to me. I think we can hash this out just the two of us."

She narrows her eyes. "You're the one who took out the raider?"

"That was me," I say. "And if that bought me anything, I'd like to talk to you alone."

She scowls, but then she drags me up by my chains and pulls me into a small room at the back of the hall.

"Speak."

"I just think you should listen to what they have to say."

Her hands clench at her sides. "They brought . . . *you* brought a Feral to my island."

"Hey, believe me, I think they're crazy, too."

"And yet you're here. With them. On their ship. With that thing."

"Well, yeah. Doesn't mean it isn't crazy. Look, I'm out to survive. I know you are, too. Most of the people that are left, that haven't Faded, they're out to survive, too. Only I've seen a lot of people do a lot of horrible things in the name of survival. Hell, Gastown is what it is because of that. I was there. I saw what happened. Those raiders would come in here and clear you all out, spilling a lot of blood, in the name of survival."

Her eyes narrow. "What's your point?"

"My point is that Miranda and the others, they aren't just interested in survival. They're interested in stopping the Bug. In reversing it, if possible. And we need people like that. They might not succeed; they may even fail horribly, get infected by the Bug, but at least they're trying. And as long as people like Miranda are around, we have a chance. We have hope."

"That doesn't change the fact that you have a Feral onboard your ship. Or that I won't allow it into this city."

"I don't blame you," I say. "And nobody's expecting you to. But . . ."

"But what?"

I lean in. "A cure might be a ways off. But what if you could test for the Bug? How better to make sure to keep Tamoanchan free of infection than by being able to test for it?"

Her eyes widen. "Your friends can do that?"

"Not yet. But they're close. But they need that Feral to do it. And they need a place to study it. "

"Not in my city."

"No. Not in the city. But I noticed some other islands nearby. Small islands. Not worth your time. But give the boffins some space and maybe the ability to barter for materials. Let them build a lab there. Let them trade with the city for goods. With the assumption that if they come up with something, they share it."

"But the Feral . . ."

"Will be on an island. Contained. You bring supplies to them, if you need to. Drop them in by air. This way everyone gets what they want. But you get potentially more."

"I don't know," she says, but the look on her face says differently. I can see the idea working its way into her mind. Infection is still a threat here and the boffins could give her a way to protect against it. I think I might just have her.

"Give them a trial run," I say. "Control what gets in and out. Monitor the situation. Then we can go from there."

"You won't be able to leave," she says.

"*They* won't be able to leave. I'm not going with them."

"Oh?" She frowns. "Why not? I thought you believed in their cause."

"I do. But I believe in my own as well. I'm not a scientist. I'll just go stir-crazy cooped up with them." I want back in the air, I add silently.

She turns away from me, her arms linked behind her back. "What use is this place if it's just the long wait for the end?" I press. "These people are scientists. Smart people. I'm willing to bet they've accomplished more than anyone else has since the Bug hit. You have the means to contain them. And it's only one Feral. Put a guard there. You'll see. Isn't it worth the chance?"

She turns back to me, her face flat. "I'll consider it."

Then her people come and toss me into a cell. It's rough stone, hewn from the ground. I call out to Miranda and Sergei (not Clay), but no one responds.

I don't know how long I stew for. Maybe I was wrong. Maybe I misjudged Brana. Maybe she'll execute us all. And this was all my idea.

That's what you get for agreeing with Miranda, the voice says. But I know it's bullshit. This is all on me.

Even if it does work, I think, it means not seeing Miranda for a long while. That thought doesn't sit all that well with me, I find. But at least she'd get to do what she wants to do. We may have traveled together for a time, but our courses were always going to take us in very different directions.

After hours of me going back and forth in my mind, someone opens my cell. Brana steps inside. "Very well. I will put them down on a nearby island with some supplies and some barter. And two escorts. They will have access to some of our trade as long as they keep that thing under wraps and will be subject to inspection whenever we feel like it."

It's what I proposed, but it's a shit deal. Still, it's the best I see us getting. "Fine." I nod. "And I get passage into Tamoanchan."

She shrugs. "We have a three-day quarantine period. To make sure you're not infected. After that . . . I don't see why not."

"Good. Then we're agreed," I say.

They escort me back to the others, and I steel myself to break the news to Miranda.

# CHAPTER NINE

I walk down the streets of Tamoanchan and feel the need to look at myself in the mirror. I'm getting stares from some of the people on the street, and I wonder if it's from a red handprint on the side of my face. To say Miranda was upset when I told her I wasn't going with them would be an understatement. Of course I waited to tell her that part until the end of the quarantine period.

Of course she was only marginally more happy about the deal. I thought she was being a little ungrateful. And I told her.

"We're prisoners," she said.

"Listen, you have a place to stay. A place to do your experiments. That's what you wanted."

"And what's to stop them from changing their minds? Or from interfering? Or from deciding they'd rather not have us around?"

"Me," I said.

She snorted. Truth be told, it hurt my feelings a bit.

I feel naked without my father's revolver at my hip. But no weapons. Those are the rules.

Tamoanchan is no Gastown. At least not how Gastown used to be, but they seem to be doing something right. I can smell cooking food, and hunger sparks through me. I walk down the stairs along the city's streets. The buildings are built from cast-off materials, but unlike some of the other settlements, they use wooden frames. Which makes sense. There are no shortages of trees, at least. A carpenter here must eat very well. It makes me wonder if I'm in the wrong business.

Only, it's on the ground.

I think about gathering up supplies, but I don't have much on me. I only took part of the score from the farmhouse—enough to get me through the next few days. I left the rest for the boffins. And everything else I had was back on the *Cherub*. So now I have virtually nothing. Not even friends.

I go looking for a drink.

I figure I deserve one, what with losing my home, the next best thing I had to a home, and the closest thing I have to friends and family. I figure I've been dealt the short end of the stick and my one salvation is that I'm in what passes for civilization these days. And what better does civilization have to offer than a little hooch?

Tamoanchan is no different in that respect. Whether you're talking the Clean or the Sick, get enough people together and a bar will pop up. A tavern. A local watering hole. And while there aren't any wineries or breweries or distilleries anymore, there's still hooch.

I walk the streets of Tamoanchan and look for a drink. I listen for the sounds that would mark a bar—raucous laughter, cheers, the sound of cups clinking or clacking against one another.

I try not to think of Miranda.

I definitely don't want to think of Clay. Standing there, smug, superior, satisfied. That I was finally getting mine. That I had been brought down by my hubris and now he got to watch the last leg of the chair being kicked out from under me.

"I'm doing my best here," I'd said.

"And who asked you to?" Miranda pushed a strand of hair back from her face.

"Who asked?" I felt the heat rising up my neck and into my face. "Who asked? You goddamned asked. You brought me into this. To help you. To protect you. To cart your ass around. Only now the *Cherub*'s gone. And the Core is gone. And Gastown is on some kind of insane rampage across the sky. Pardon me if I thought that getting us all to safety was a priority. Pardon me for actually finding a place crazy enough to take not only you but your little pet."

I was yelling by the end and Miranda was silent. She just stared at me, her face blank.

Clay opened his mouth. I gave him a look that said I would stuff whatever words he was about to say back in his mouth along with my fist.

"And yet you're leaving," she'd said.

And there, I thought, is what's really bothering her.

"I have to," I said. "I can't stay cooped up here with you and that thing. Not now." Not after losing the *Cherub*, losing my wings, I was thinking. But I didn't say that.

She shook her head and turned away. "Go then." She waved her hand in the air. There was a small strip of cloth or linen wrapped around one of her fingers. I wondered what she did to it. "Go do whatever it is that you need to do. I'm sure we'll be here when you're finished." Then she turned back to stare me in the eyes again. "Only there may not be room for you then."

Despite my anger and my bluster, the words chilled me. Part of me wanted to apologize. Part of me wanted to explain and make things right. Instead I said, "I'll take my chances."

Then I left. As I walked out, I saw Clay put his arm around Miranda. Everything about that guy is like a persistent itch you just want to scratch at. Except in this case the scratching is me punching him in his smug face.

So, yes, alcohol.

I pass up one place that has some muddy-looking swill in stained plastic jugs on a series of tables made from wooden doors. Another place has the right atmosphere, but it's a brothel. I shake my head. Up until now I couldn't have imagined a brothel in the Sick. Fear of fluids is the law of the day. But here, where Ferals can't reach and access is carefully controlled . . . wow. The place seems well stocked with men and women, and I have to guess they do a brisk trade.

At last, though, I find what I'm looking for. A place with a plastic sign with the words "The Frothy Brew" painted on them. And I realize I'm in the right place. Because this place isn't slinging hooch. This place has beer.

\*   \*   \*

The first time I had beer—at least what could truly be called beer—was when my dad was still alive. We were somewhere over what used to be Oregon, or maybe Washington, and spotted a large house on the side of a mountain, the kind of place only the rich could afford back in the Clean.

It was likely, of course, that the place had already been cleaned out, but it wasn't very accessible from the ground, which meant it was likely to be free from Ferals, and it was shielded from view from above, for the most part, by a stand of redwoods.

Not to mention that Dad had a knack for finding good places to forage. So we brought the *Cherub* down behind the trees and descended to the ground.

Back then the ground made me even more jittery than it does now, but I had Dad with me, and his confidence—whether false or not—helped to calm me.

We entered the house through the upper windows and, as expected, it was stripped. Appliances and fixtures had been ripped from the walls—anything electronic or metal or glass carefully harvested for barter or use elsewhere. We found the hollow shells of a few computers, their guts long gone.

We descended. Two floors. All in the same condition. The house reeked of mold and urine, and we skirted a pile of dusty, leafy debris in one corner that might have been bones.

Then on the ground floor, Dad found the door to the basement. He was like that, always looking at the shapes of things, trying to figure out if there was something more than what was obvious. Turns out this door was hidden behind a knocked-over bookcase. Either the previous foragers had been in a hurry or had missed it.

I opened the door for Dad, while he kept his revolver ready. The bookcase might have been there for a reason, maybe Ferals had made a den down there. But nothing burst out at us, and we couldn't hear anything down below. No breathing. No snarls. Just a steady drip.

So we went down. Armed, of course. With a torch, of course.

What we found was a cellar. There was some furniture down there that we dragged up to the *Cherub*. Some metal pieces we later bartered. But the real prize, the true prize, was the alcohol.

Turns out the people had a nice collection of beer and wine. Much of the wine had been damaged in a partial collapse of the ceiling. And what was left was far too valuable to drink. But the beer, well, that was more accessible. Dad figured we had to check to see if it was any good. Figured it probably wasn't. So he popped the cap off and took a swig.

Something about the temperature down there, and probably the quality of the beer, kept it in pretty good condition. It wasn't as bubbly as it apparently was supposed to be and might have lost some of its flavor, he said. But he still drank the whole thing. Then he handed a bottle to me.

It may as well have dropped out of the past, through a hole in time. Something handed to me from the Clean. I eagerly popped it open and took a sip. Dark, earthy, nutty and with a nice alcohol kicker. It was all I could do to stop pouring it down my gullet. But I forced myself to take my time. To try to take it all in, remember everything about the taste, about the sensation, how the liquid felt in my mouth, how it finished on my tongue after I swallowed.

We packed up a box of beer and brought it up with us onto the *Cherub*, and it lasted us the better portion of a month. Some of it was the same dark beer as before. Other beer was lighter, more bitter. It was like a treasure chest of sensations. Drinking that last bottle was saying goodbye to something meaningful.

I've had drinks since that people claim are beer, but nothing like what we dragged up from that house.

For most of my life I'd learned that the ground held only death.

Bones and ruin scattered across a wasteland of the past. That day, I realized there was still some life in the ground yet.

✳    ✳    ✳

Things seem even better when I enter and find half of the wooden tables occupied. All of them with cups in front of them. A promising sign, I think, and sink into a chair in one corner. A couple of the people in the place look up at me, but there's nothing much to look at. I'm just another scavenger on the bones. Just like all the rest.

A woman comes over to me, short black hair tucked under a weathered bandanna. "What can I get you?" she says.

"What do you have?"

"Dark ale or light ale."

I think back to that first beer and know what it has to be. "Dark."

She returns with a cup of an ale so dark I can't see through it in the cup. I sniff at it and can smell something earthy and roasted. Then I take a sip. A flavor like the smell, something with a smoky, woody flavor at first, then a deepening almost chocolaty bitterness that finishes slightly sweet. It's remarkable. The bubbles leave my mouth feeling crisp.

I realize that my eyes are closed, so focused am I on the flavors.

As I toss back the mug again, taking care to try to disassemble the flavors in my mouth, I open my eyes and realize what's so different about Tamoanchan. People are walking around with their faces uncovered. I suppose it makes sense—entry is carefully controlled. Everyone here is confident they can't get the Bug. I find it almost dizzying. I scan the faces all around me, drinking them all in.

Then I see one staring at me. Frowning at me. Diego. He gets up and walks toward me. Maybe it's because I'm sitting down, but he looks even taller and broader than I remember. He takes the seat opposite me.

"What the fuck is wrong with you?" he says, his eyes hard.

"Look, Diego—"

"You didn't tell me you were bringing that thing with you."

I shrug. "I figured we'd keep you out of it. Clear it with the inspector first."

"And how did that go?" he says sarcastically.

I shrug again. "I'm here."

He shakes his head, his mouth tight in a frown. "I vouched for you. I said you were bueno. Clean. That stunt you pulled reflects back on me."

"Look, I'm sorry," I say. "Yes, you stuck your neck out. But it's sorted now."

"I don't know about that."

"Give it a little time," I say. "Once they see that the boffins are no threat, this will all die down."

Diego slams his fist on the table. More than a few heads turn to look at us. "Damn it! This is my life."

I look down at my beer, then finish it in one long draft. I think about how I would feel if our situations were reversed. I wouldn't much like it. "I'm sorry," I say. "Like I said—we were desperate. And believe me, I asked them to dump that thing more than once. But . . ."

He raises his eyebrows. "But?"

"Miranda's a crusader."

He purses his lips. "So why aren't you with her?"

"We had to part company," I say. "I'm just trying to figure out my next move. I need to get back into the sky."

"You just got here!"

"Yes, but I'm no good on the ground. I'm a zep. I belong in the sky with a ship around me."

He harrumphs and shakes his head.

I lean forward. "C'mon. You said there were opportunities for pilots around here. You said you needed me."

"That was when you had a ship," he says.

Ouch.

"That was also before you fucked me," he says. For a moment, I think he's going to hit me. Then he stands up. "Whatever you do from here on in, leave me out of it."

I sag back in my chair.

He turns before walking away completely. "You may want to get back into the air," he says. "But do you really think anyone's going to take a chance on you now? After what happened?" Then he leaves.

I feel like shit warmed over. That's it, Ben, the voice says. Keep making friends.

It's after my third beer, bought with the corn kernels from the farmhouse, that I realize I don't have a place to stay. And I didn't really plan on finding one. I was only hoping to be here long enough to find a ship to take me back out.

Of course Diego rightfully squashed that idea. Seems like Miranda's Feral has made me radioactive. And I can't imagine them trusting me to leave after that.

So I'm still grounded and I lost my one shot at getting back into the air.

So I buy a fourth beer and nurse it for as long as I can. Like most of these types of places, the people there stick around as long as they can manage. Dad used to tell me there were regular hours for bars back in the Clean. I can recall reading about that somewhere, too. In the Sick, though, if you have the barter, they'll serve you. Barter is just too damned important.

So it's a can of beans for a cup of the light ale and a long march toward the morning. At some point all the beer catches up with me and I have to dash outside for a piss. The Frothy Brew has its own outhouse, which I'm sure sees a lot of use. So I piss, this time without fear of a Feral biting off my cock, and then, as I walk back inside, I hear something I haven't heard in years.

I hear someone speaking Hebrew.

✳    ✳    ✳

Dad drilled me in Hebrew growing up. Mom probably, too, though I don't remember that. I learned it just as I learned English, and for a while I never questioned it. It was something my father was teaching me—that was enough.

It wasn't until I got a little older that I started asking him. What it meant. Where it was from. Why I needed to know it. It's not like we ever met anyone who spoke it.

He responded by giving me a copy of the Torah. Which was in English. But I was captivated. I'd never read anything like it. He explained its significance, started teaching me about Judaism. What it used to mean to people back in the Clean.

The story of Noah was probably my favorite. Followed by Moses. I was captivated by the image of God using water to cleanse the earth. I became convinced it would happen again. That God would wash away all the chaos and blood and tears of the Sick and we would sail through the air above it, safe on our own little ark, until the world was clean again.

Needless to say that never happened.

When I was older I wondered if maybe the Bug *was* the Flood. Not a literal washing away but a figurative one. Drowning humanity and leaving only mindless Ferals behind.

I didn't mention that theory to my father, though.

I remember once hitting a small town when I was a teenager. Foraging in small towns was often made more difficult by the overgrown vegetation that quickly took them over. It made them less desirable targets. Not to mention they were almost always infested with Ferals.

But both those things meant they usually still had valuables, and when you were desperate, they sometimes seemed like a good idea.

So we went down and used our machetes to hack through the plants to get into a stretch of stores to see what we could find. I remember there being some reasonably good salvage but not what it was. We also stumbled into a Feral nest.

They came for us. At us. All limbs and teeth. The strobing of our muzzle flashes lit up the dark interior. I could barely see a shape before it was on me, pulling the trigger of my pistol again and again. Reacting mostly on instinct.

My pistol went dry. Then my backup. And I began using the machete, the only other weapon I had, conscious of the blood flying everywhere, hoping none was hitting me or Dad.

Then . . . it was done. We stood there, the only moving objects, heaving, sweating. I turned to look at Dad and saw his expression—a mix of relief and fear, but fear unlike any I'd seen before. His eyes were wide, haunted, as if he were still seeing the attacking Ferals.

Then I looked where his gaze was and saw them. Tiny broken bodies. Young Ferals. Bleeding. Torn up by bullets or machetes or both. Some were maybe my age, but many were younger. I remember understanding then the ferocity of the attack. They were defending their offspring. I knew they were Ferals. I knew they wanted to kill us, but . . . I felt numb.

Then Dad grabbed me and turned me to face him, checking me for blood splatter, for wounds. The strange detachment still had hold of me as his gloved fingers examined me, as his flashlight shone in my face. Then, when he was satisfied that I was okay, he pulled me to him and held me for a time. My father wasn't a cold man, but that kind of thing wasn't common. I let him hold me until the numbness started to fade, then we grabbed our findings and prepared to leave.

As we were getting ready to climb the ladder to the *Cherub*, Dad stopped suddenly, his gaze on the building next to us. "Dad?" I asked. "We should go."

"Wait," he said. And I worried. Had he been infected? It wasn't like him to be so distracted. But he walked toward the building and hacked his way through to the door. As I followed him, I realized that I could read the words above the entrance, and that they were in Hebrew.

It was a synagogue. Long wooden benches filled it, with a raised podium on one side. "People used to pray here, didn't they?" I asked.

Dad nodded. "Ben, go back to the ship," he said.

"Dad?"

"I'll just be a moment. Take everything up to the *Cherub*."

"Okay," I said. Usually I did what he told me to without question. Only this time I didn't. This time I hid in the entrance to see what he would do.

He moved down the aisle until he was right in front of the raised podium. Then he fell to his knees.

I have no way of knowing for certain, but I'm sure my father was praying. The man who didn't believe in God was praying. And it unnerved me. I hurried out to the ladder and our stash and headed back to the *Cherub*.

I never asked Dad about that. Never felt comfortable bringing it up.

But right here on Tamoanchan, right now, hearing the Hebrew drifting on the night air, I wish I had.

I follow the sound, not too far from the Frothy Brew, to a simple wooden building with a Star of David hanging above the door.

Inside, there are rows of wooden benches and a scattering of people sitting on them. Up at the front of the room stands a man in traditional rabbi garb. He wears a wide-brimmed flat hat and hair curls around his ears almost merging into his long beard.

The words he's speaking are artifacts from another time. I can hear them, with my father's voice, his inflections, this kind of solemn weight they always carried. Like magic words from a story.

We were never really good at figuring out what day it was—either by date or by day—but every so often, we would observe the Sabbath, repeat the ritual words as our ancestors had done.

And then there was the Star of David.

My father had told me that his mother had given it to him when he was just a boy, an heirloom passed down through her family. It was made of gold, a worthless metal in the Sick but worth something once upon a time. I always thought it was special because our surname was Gold. Family names might also be worthless in the Sick, but Dad made sure ours wasn't.

He wore it all the time. Even when he bathed he had it next to his skin. I was always worried that he might lose it, but somehow he always kept it safe for all those years.

Ultimately, I was the one who took it from him.

I can still see those moments so clearly. See it gleaming around his neck, in that same moment that I saw the light of reason go out in his eyes. I didn't know that Dad had got the Bug. I don't know if he knew. But I realized, in that moment, what was happening.

I suppose I panicked. I don't even know what I was thinking. But I reached for the Star hanging around his neck and snapped the chain pulling it to me.

Then? Then I ran. I ran as far away as I could. It's a moment I relive again and again in my mind. A moment I'm still unsure of. For a long time I told myself there was nothing else to do. I couldn't shoot my father.

But there are times that I think I allowed him to live on like that. Like a thing. Allowed him to become what we'd always hated. Out there, with the ability to infect others. To hurt others. Killing him might well have been a kindness, to others as well as himself. But . . . that's not the way things happened.

But right now, with those words in the air, so much more musical than they ever were before, I can't help but feel him beside me, as if he were right there on the bench. Something loosens inside of me, some tension I didn't realize was there, and tears spill from my eyes.

I sit like that for a little while and when I open my eyes again, I realize the others have gone and the rabbi has stopped speaking. He's looking at me curiously.

"I'm sorry, Rabbi," I say. "I'll get out of your hair."

"No need for that," the rabbi says, shaking his head. "I haven't seen you here before."

"That's because I'm brand-new in town," I say.

"That's not an insignificant achievement," he says.

I smile a bit. "I'm well aware of that."

"I'm going to take it from your reaction that you're a Jew," he says.

I nod. "The last in a long line. My father, he taught me some of the prayers. I hadn't heard them in a long time."

"Well, I'm glad you came to sit with us, then," he says.

"Me, too."

"We have regular services every Shabbat," he says. "We would love to have you join us."

"I'm not sure I'm the praying kind," I say.

"Yet you're here."

"True," I say. "I just wanted . . . needed something from my past right now."

A half smile curls his lip. "Why does it have to be in the past?"

"I just mean it reminds me of my father." I look at my hands, clenched in my lap. "I've lost him and practically everything he gave me."

"Surely not everything."

"Almost," I say. "His airship, even his Star of David."

The rabbi frowns. "How do you lose an airship?"

"It was taken from me," I say, feeling fire spark in me.

"Oh, I see." He places a comforting hand on my shoulder. "I'm sorry. And what of the Star of David?"

I frown and look away. "I lost that in some trouble a while back and . . ." I don't tell him the rest. Don't tell him I kept the revolver and lost the Star.

He holds up a hand. "Please," he says. "Wait here. I have something I think can help." He shuffles off into a back room and comes back a few minutes later. He holds out his hand, and sitting in it is a coil of gold, upon which sits a Star of David. "Please," he says again.

I look at him, surprised. "You want me to take this?"

"To replace what you lost."

"Rabbi, I can't—" It's true it wouldn't be worth much as barter to your average person, but it definitely has value and significance.

"It is mine to do with as I like, and I would like for you to have it. Or do you wish to offend your new rabbi?"

I exhale, then reach forward and take the Star. "Thank you," I say.

"Just consider coming back again. That will make it worth it." .

I nod. "Okay, Rabbi. It's a deal."

"Your father would be proud of you," he says.

"How do you know that?"

"Because he obviously cared enough about our culture to teach it to you. That you're here, that you still care about these things, well, wouldn't it please him?"

I nod again, this time more slowly. "I suppose it would." Then I shake my head. "But what's the point, Rabbi? I don't have children; I'm not likely to."

"You still have some time left."

I stand up. "In this world? I don't know that I even want that. And so whatever's been passed on dies with me."

He flashes that half smile again. "Then I suppose it's a good thing you're not the last Jew in the world."

Then I smile. I suppose the future of the Jewish faith doesn't reside in me.

"Can I ask you a question, Rabbi?"

He says, "Of course. But let me guess. How can I still believe in God in this world? With all this going on around us?"

I wince. "I guess you get that a lot."

"Probably even more than you think."

"And what do you say?"

He sits down next to me. "People wonder how God can let all of this happen. The infection, the chaos, the death. They see it as a sign that He—or She, however you want to look at it—doesn't exist. That if He did, He would stop it."

"Wouldn't He?"

"And if He did? Then what? He fixes everything for us and then what do we do? Come to depend on God to make things right all the time? People said the same in ages past. Through all the persecutions, the expulsions, and the genocides. Why didn't He stop them? Maybe it's as simple as we were given this world and allowed to act with free will in it. And maybe, just maybe . . ."

"Yes?" I ask.

He smiles, and his teeth are surprisingly clean and even. "Maybe He's even rooting for us. Maybe He still has hope because he believes in us. Wouldn't that be interesting? Maybe He wants to see us do it on our own."

The rabbi's argument hasn't convinced me by any means, but it has given me a lot to think about. A different perspective. Here I am, expecting for someone to fix this or flush it away. Always someone else's problem. My own concern has always been survival.

"Do you have a place to stay here in Tamoanchan?" the rabbi asks.

"I'm afraid I don't," I answer. "I wasted too much time sitting in the bar."

"Then why don't you stay here for the night?"

"Really?" I just manage to stop shaking my head. "You'd do that?"

"I have a small room back here with space enough for you to sleep. I can't offer great comfort, but I have some soft pillows, a blanket."

"You don't even know me," I say.

"No. Not yet. But I'd like to. And you need to sleep."

Have I really become so calloused from the world that I'm on the verge of refusing this offer? But my fingers run over the edges of the Star in my hand and instead I say, "Thank you. That would be a big help."

I stand up. He stands with me and I shake his hand. "I don't even know your name," I say.

He smiles again. "It's Naftali. Naftali Cohen."

"Benjamin Gold," I say. "Thank you."

"Our people wandered for many years, looking for a home. Sometimes, though, it takes a little help."

The rabbi gets me set up in his extra room, but before I go to sleep I step outside for a moment and look up at the sky. At the stars.

It stills me for a moment. So many tiny little specks of bright fire lighting up the night's blackness. I remember being a kid and thinking that those were all the bits and pieces of the world that the Sick blew away, hanging over our heads as a reminder of what was. It was only later that I learned they were other stars, billions of kilometers away. I've often wondered if any of those stars have planets like ours and if any of them are as fucked-up as our dear old Earth is. I wouldn't take bets.

But it's beautiful, and peaceful, and with the smell of the ocean blowing in the air, I have a moment of calm. I hold up the Star the rabbi gave me. It's different from my father's old star—the planes are a little straighter, it's a little thinner, but it's also slightly bigger. I trace its lines with my finger. Then I take the chain and carefully drop it around my neck. The star falls against my breastbone, and something clicks into place inside of me. There, right then, one more thing is right with the world.

I look back up at the stars and some of my calm fades, as if stolen by the wind. Because staring up at the sky I know how badly I want to be up there. High above the ground, high above the sea, in another world. And closer to those stars than I am now. Closer to those reminders of how life used to be.

It's then that I make the decision. What I want to do. What I need to do. No more sitting around waiting. No more losing my grip on my future.

I'm going after the *Cherub*.

# CHAPTER TEN

I wake up the next morning feeling better, clearer, than I have in a while. I didn't even have many nightmares.

Rabbi Cohen isn't around when I get up, so I make my way out into Tamoanchan and start to look for Diego.

I don't know where he lives, or where he works, but I do know that he has a ship, the *Osprey*. So I ask around and head down to where they keep the airships. Diego is key to my plan, or at least the seed of a plan that is starting to take root in my mind.

Tamoanchan's way to keep the airships less visible is to keep them close to the ground. The area they've chosen is near a hill crowned with trees. It's a good idea. The trees provide extra cover and shadow, and with the sun in your eyes you might miss them all clustered on the ground. Of course many of these dirigibles would take a while to get up into the air if anyone was attacking, but they're hoping stealth will do the heavy lifting here. And it's a solid plan.

I scan the curves of the airships until I spot the green and silver colors of the *Osprey*.

I get stopped, though, before I get too close.

"Only authorized people can pass," a woman says. I notice she's missing the top half of her ear.

"I just want to talk to one of the captains."

"Then you'll have to talk to him back there," she says.

"It will only take a few minutes," I say.

She puts her hand on her sidearm and I back away, my hands up. "Sorry. Just . . . do you know Diego?"

She gives a quick nod. "Sure."

"Can you tell him I want to talk to him?"

"Tell him yourself," she says. "I think he went to the Council building."

"Council building?"

She sighs but gives me directions. I suss that Brana isn't the only leader here on Tamoanchan. Just the elected leader. They have a Council that helps make the major decisions.

I wind my way over to their headquarters, trying to think of a way to get inside, only it turns out I don't have to.

As I approach I see Diego having an animated discussion with a tall, slender blonde woman outside the building.

"You're lucky you're not grounded," she says, loud enough for me to hear.

With my scarf up, I get closer and duck around the corner.

"You would ground me?" Diego asks.

The other woman answers slowly. "You let a Feral get on the island."

"I had no idea it was even there."

"Well . . . it's just about killed your goodwill with the other Council members. Your judgment is suddenly in question."

"Vera . . ."

"It's not up to me," Vera says. "I wanted you to stand up for the fifth seat. I was pushing for it. But the resistance is just too much right now."

"So you're saying there's no chance for me to stand in the coming elections."

"Not unless you pull a miracle out of your ass." Then, "I'm sorry, Diego."

"Yeah," he says. "But not as much as me."

I poke my head around just in time to see Diego storm off. I quickly follow, giving him a decent lead but keeping a careful eye on where he's going.

In the end, he makes his way back to the Frothy Brew.

I slip in behind him and find him at the bar.

"Can I buy you a drink?" I ask.

He turns to me and I swear his eyes are about to spit fire. He holds up a finger. "You. No. Not now. Just . . . go away."

"I can't," I say. "I need to talk to you."

He turns away from me and back to the bar. "I don't give a fuck about what you need. Go away."

"Diego," I say. "Please."

He shakes his head and makes a face as if he just swallowed something bitter. "You have some fucking ego. Why would you think I want to talk to you? What could that possibly accomplish?"

"It could be beneficial. Helping me could help you."

"And how is that even fucking possible?"

I put my hands up as if to placate him. "Let me buy you a drink and I'll explain."

He growls. An actual chesty growl. But then he says, "Fine. A light ale." Then he stalks off to a table.

I get two light ales and go to join him.

I place his beer down in front of him before taking the seat opposite.

Diego takes a sip and then slams the mug down on the table. "Well?"

I inhale. "I need you to take me somewhere."

He barks a laugh. "Oh, of course. I should have known."

I sit back in my chair.

He leans forward. "I'm clearly an idiot. And a bad judge of character. I stuck my neck out for you and practically got it cut off. Now you want to, what, finish the job?"

"It's not like that." I take a swallow of the beer.

"So what is it like?" Diego asks. "Why do you need me?"

I meet his eyes and smile. "I'm going after my ship."

Diego stares back at me, incredulous.

"You're not going to say anything?" I ask.

"I don't know," Diego says. "I don't know what's crazier, the fact that you think you can get your ship back or that you expect me to help you with that."

"I only need a ride," I say. "And you can give it to me."

"It's a fucking ship," he says. "You can get another one. Eventually."

"The *Cherub* is not just a ship. She's part of my history. She's part of who I am. She's my home and she's a link to the past. My family. The world before."

Diego take a long draft of his ale. "Not my problem."

"It isn't. You're right. But you haven't asked me what's in it for you."

Diego looks at me like I'm brain-dead. Then he says, "Fine. I'll bite if it ends all this. What's in it for me?"

"I know you're in the shit with your people. I know that you're anxious to get back in their good graces. I can help you do that."

Diego shakes his head. "You must be out of your fucking mind if you think I'm going to get burned twice."

"Just listen to me."

Diego shakes his head again. "Where exactly is it you think you're going?"

"Gastown," I say.

Diego looks at me like I imagine I often look at Miranda.

"Gastown raiders took my ship," I say. "They either sold it, or they kept it. Either way, Gastown seems like the best place to start looking for it."

"They probably stripped it for parts by now," he says.

"Not the *Cherub*," I say, with maybe a bit too much force. "She's too good for that."

He rolls his eyes and I try not to be offended. He inhales deeply and spreads his hands out flat on the table. "So you really think you're going to go into the heart of enemy territory, among people who wouldn't think twice about wiping Tamoanchan out, with the location of this island."

It may be the beer, but I feel like I'm revved up here. Things clicking together. "That's just it," I say. "They are the enemy. And sooner or later they're going to try to wipe you out."

"You're not making your case very well."

"But that *is* the case. You should know about them. Know their capabilities. Their strengths. Their weaknesses. Learn all you can about them. How else will you know what they can throw at you?"

"They can't reach us if they don't know about us."

"But right now that's your only defense. And once that breaks down, then what? You're sitting targets. You're fucking plods, for Christ's sake."

"So you're saying what? I go with you? Poke around on Gastown?"

"That's exactly what I'm saying." I stand up. "Look, wait a second. Let me get you another beer."

He sighs. "Fine."

I grab another light ale and this time a dark ale for me, both for a can of beans. Then I return to Diego. "It makes perfect sense," I say. "Not only do you get to check out Gastown, but you get to keep an eye on me."

He gives me a skeptical look.

"You come with me, keep an eye on me, and if you think there's a danger of information getting out, you can deal with it." I leave this deliberately vague. I don't intend for it to be an issue, but in this case "dealing" with it could mean getting me out of there quickly or shooting me before I can say something.

He pulls back, frowns, but I can tell he's mulling it over. The sting of that Gastown attack is still fresh in his mind and maybe something else. Truth be told, I'm surprised I'm doing so well.

"You're in the shit with your people," I repeat. "Deep, from the sounds of it." I flash him one of my most charming smiles. "Maybe this can help dig you out."

He rubs at his beard. "I can't help but thinking that you're bad news." He slams back his beer.

I meet his eyes. "Look," I say. "I promise I'll make this up to you.

I'll help find a way to make up for what I did. Put things right. But I'm nothing without my ship. This way you get information on Gastown and another ship for the cause."

Diego drinks his beer. Then he stands up to leave.

"Just be aware that I'm going to do this with or without you," I say. "I'd rather do it with you. I'd rather you get something for your troubles."

He bends down until his face is level with mine. "You are my troubles," he says.

Then he leaves.

I, of course, continue to drink. This seems to be the best thing to do with my time. At least until I can think of a Plan B with regard to getting off of Tamoanchan. Diego was my best bet. He had the ability to come and go without scrutiny. He had reason to hate Gastown. And we had a prior relationship. Too bad I pissed all over that.

I'm so focused on trying to come up with an alternate plan that I almost don't notice when Diego returns to his seat a few hours later.

"You haven't moved," he says.

I shrug. "I don't have anywhere to be."

He laces his hands together on the table and looks at me across them. "That may not be true."

I tilt my head to indicate my cluelessness.

"I'll take you," he says. Then with a bump of his hands on the table. "I'll take you."

I stare at him with bleary eyes. I didn't think my pitch had worked. "You sure?"

He looks quickly away. Grits his teeth. "I don't really have a lot of choice."

I nod.

He points a large finger at me. "You buried me. In the shit, as you put it. I need to find a way to climb back out again. You're going to help me with that."

"Sounds good to me," I say. As long as it gets me closer to the *Cherub*.

"And Rosie's coming as well," he says.

I nod. I half-expected it. "What is she to you?" I ask.

"She's my sister."

"Ah. That makes sense." I guess they're not twins, which makes them rare. Not many people are having children in the Sick. Those who do tend not to have more than one. It's too difficult trying to protect little ones. Let alone little twos.

"When are we off?"

He stands up. "Soon enough," he says. "Morning. You have a place to stay?"

I nod.

"Then meet me down by the airfield tomorrow morning."

I stand up, feeling a little unsteady on my feet. I reach out my hand. "Thanks," I say.

He leaves my hand where it is. "Tomorrow morning," he says. Then he walks away.

I allow the smile once he's gone. I have a ride out of here. And I'm going after the *Cherub*.

I have preparations to make.

"What do you think?" Diego asks, turning to me as he pilots the *Osprey* across the sky. She's a fine-looking ship. Not the *Cherub*, of course. But nothing else is. The *Osprey*'s a cargo ship like the *Cherub*, but without the VTOL capabilities. But few enough ships have those.

"Good work," I say.

He keeps her differently than I would. He's cobbled together some comfortable seating, for one thing. And there are a few too many trinkets, from the look of it. Compartments, switches, doodads. I'm a minimalist when it comes to things like that. But there's nothing wrong with it.

"What's our play?" Rosie says. Her arms are crossed in front of her and she leans back on a console. This is the first time I've seen her unwrapped. She's lean, hard looking. Also lighter than Diego. Her dark hair is pulled back into a tight ponytail. There's something dangerous about her.

I shrug casually. "We go in as simple foragers. Looking for some business."

"So we're going to need to get some barter," she says.

I nod. "That's going to be the hard part."

"Oh, *that* is?" Diego says. "And here I thought trying to bluff our way through Gastown without getting ourselves killed was going to be hard."

I ignore him. We'll need to come in with enough barter to make it seem that we're ready to trade, but just enough so that it will look like we're desperate. "We need them to think we need them," I say.

"I know a place where we can go," Diego says. He moves to the controls, using a pull-down map to help plot his course.

I raise my eyebrows at him but don't press. It's not good etiquette. Thing is, secrets are not worth keeping in the Sick. Even if you do know of a likely place for spoils, you don't want to hold on to that. Every hour you waste, every minute, is a chance for someone else to find it, clean it out before you get to it. It's just bad business.

Really, I should just shut up and let Diego run the show. It's his ship, after all. But I'm not as polite as I used to be.

"Where are we heading?" I ask.

He looks at me, surprised, then back to his headings. "I got a tip."

I nod. "Okay. What kind of tip?"

"There's a stash. Nothing decent. Nothing too valuable, but enough that we can sail in with something."

"And where did you get the location of this stash?"

He stands up and squares off against me. "Do you think I'm an idiot?" he says. "I knew what we needed. I called in a favor."

I force myself to relax. I don't think he's an idiot, but I'm not used to relying on other people. I'm used to running the show. But of course he's thought ahead. I nod. "Good thinking. That will save us a lot of trouble."

"Don't I know it," he says.

"So." I look out the window of the gondola. "Is there a reason why this stash hasn't been looted yet?"

"You could say that," he says. Something twists in my stomach.

"Ferals."

He nods. "There's a nest right on top of it. My man swears that the salvage is intact. Mostly. Only it's crawling with those bastards."

"Great."

"We have weapons. And there are four of us. We can clear them out and grab a few pieces before moving on."

"Oh. Sure. You make it sound so easy," I say.

"There's nothing easy in the Sick," he says.

I'm forced to agree.

"Wait," I say. "Four?"

Diego looks down, then at Rosie.

"About that," she says.

I turn around.

Someone steps out of the back room of the gondola.

Miranda.

# CHAPTER ELEVEN

I walk toward her, grab her by the arm, and drag her back into the back room of the gondola. I can feel the heat rising in my face. But my momentary anger is drowned out by my shock.

"Miranda, what . . . what are you doing here?"

She tries to keep her face straight, but the hint of a smile flits across it. "Making sure you're okay."

"Miranda, you're supposed to be back at your lab."

"I left Sergei and Clay behind with Alpha. They'll have to do without me for a little while."

"How did you even get off that rock? How did you end up on the *Osprey?*"

Miranda sighs. "I begged them to let me stay in Tamoanchan. I spoke to Clay and Sergei, and we decided that someone—one of us, I mean—had to be free. We weren't expecting to be grounded. We need certain supplies. Things we don't have on the *Pasteur.* I figured Diego was my best bet, so I went to find him and he told me about your plan."

"They didn't have your supplies on Tamoanchan?"

Miranda cocks an eyebrow. "No. I checked. I even gave Brana a list. Someone had to fill in the gaps." She shrugs. "I have the most field experience."

It's true, I think. And for a moment I think of how annoyed Clay must have been and I want to smile, but then I'm back to Miranda. I drop my face into my hands. "Miranda, do you realize why I left you there?"

She walks forward. "Yes. Because you wanted me out of the way. Because you were trying to help. But I can't do what I need to do without these supplies. And . . ."

"And?"

"And maybe I wanted to help *you* this time."

"What are you going to do, Miranda?"

"Think, for one," she says. "And if you're dealing with Gastown, you're going to need some help. I remember what they did. I was there, too."

Images of dying Ferals with gaping chest wounds, spraying blood everywhere. Human faces contorted in fear.

I turn away. "I didn't want you involved in this."

"I know. You want to protect me. Keep me safe."

"That's my job, isn't it?"

"It's the job I hired you to do, yes," she says. "But it's also the job you quit."

I wince. I can feel a dull ache building behind my eyes. Maybe a side effect of all that beer. I rub the bridge of my nose.

"You put us down on Tamoanchan. I'm just trying to help make it work. And . . ."

I feel her presence like static, close to my body. "And?"

She stares back at me but doesn't say anything.

Before either of us can continue, Rosie appears in the doorway. "We've got ships out there," she says.

I spare Miranda a look that I'm hoping says "We'll continue this chat later" and then head back to take a look.

Rosie points out one of the windows. I look out and see several ships moving at an angle to us. It looks like they're moving away. "You worried?" I ask.

Rosie shrugs. "After last time we're a little bit jumpy."

"I completely understand."

"They're flying Gastown flags," Miranda says. She's holding a pair of binoculars.

"More of them?" I ask.

"They're up to something," Rosie says.

"I'm still surprised that they're flying Gastown colors," I say. "Pretty much everyone must know that Valhalla is running the show. Why the pretense?"

"Tell me more about this Valhalla," Diego says from the controls.

"You sure you can handle those ships?" I ask.

Diego fixes me with a look that shuts me up. "I'll keep our distance. Just . . . keep an eye on them. If they seem to take any interest in us, let me know."

"I will certainly do that," I say.

"Okay, then. Valhalla. It's out near what my dad called the Great Lakes. Colder country. Unlike Gastown, which hangs free, Valhalla is anchored to a building out there, one of the tallest in the country, I think."

"It's been around long?" Rosie asks.

"Pretty long. Before Gastown, certainly. Gastown was supposed to be the new, improved version. I bet that pissed off Valhalla something good." I pause for a moment. "Either of you know what Vikings are?"

Diego shakes his head, but Rosie nods. "I think so. Like barbarians or something, right?"

I nod. "Something like that. Valhalla is run by a bunch of freaks who follow those old ways. They're into conquering others, pillaging, taking what they want. They believe in violence. Their leader calls himself Odin, named after an old god. Valhalla is named after the hall where the warriors of the world would go or something like that."

"Rosie, you know about that stuff?" Diego asks. Rosie shakes her head. "She was the one who got all the learning," he continues. "I was too busy getting into trouble."

"I wasn't much for mythology," she says.

"I would stay away from anyone from Valhalla," I say. "They're crazy. You can see it in their eyes."

"Aren't we headed directly into a nest of them? After we get this salvage?"

"Well . . . yeah," I say. I shrug. "I guess you're out of luck, then."

"Hopefully not," Rosie says.

Miranda takes off her glasses and wipes them with the bottom of her shirt. "There's something that's been bothering me about Gastown," she says. "Sergei and I were talking about it."

"What?" I ask.

"Well, it's just that Valhalla's pattern, before Gastown, I mean, was always to sack a place and then leave. They would take what they wanted and then return to Valhalla. Like what they did to Apple Pi."

The mention of the Core makes my blood pressure rise.

"But they're holding Gastown," Miranda says.

I shrug. "For the helium, I'd guess. It's valuable."

"Sure," she says. "But they'd have to keep the operation moving along. It doesn't seem like something they'd be interested in."

"Maybe they have new leadership," I say. Which scares me even more. A bunch of violent, loco monsters I'm used to. Violent, loco monsters with a plan, well, that's another story.

I notice Miranda's look. It's like she has more to say. "What is it?" I ask.

"I just . . ." She puts her glasses back on. "It was hard to be sure from the wreckage of Apple Pi, but I think there were things missing. Not just destroyed. Taken."

"That's ridiculous," I say. "Why would they take anything?"

"Why indeed?" She stares at me. "What if they do have new leadership? What if their priorities have changed?"

I shake my head. "That doesn't make any sense."

Miranda opens her mouth, about to say something, but then Rosie cuts in. She's looking down from the window.

"We're here," she says.

✳    ✳    ✳

We hover over the Feral nest and I look down through Diego's scope at the buildings below. Several rectangular buildings form a hexagon surrounded by green fields and a crumbling fence. Like everything in the Sick, it is slowly being swallowed by vegetation, and plants mat its surface. "What was this place?" I ask.

"A school," Diego says.

"With that kind of privacy?"

He shrugs. "A special school. For smart people. Or rich people. They had those, you know."

"The people or the schools?" But I know what he's talking about. It's the kind of place Miranda might have gone in another life. The kind of legacy passed down through her family.

"Once the Bug got in there," he says. "Well . . ."

It would spread like wildfire. Kids, even now, are never the cleanest. And locked up in classrooms. Behind doors. Behind fences. Off on a hill. I wondered when the last of those kids had died out. Now their children's children roamed that hill. As Ferals.

"And no one has looted the place?" I ask.

"It's teeming," he says. "The guy I talked to pulled out after the first few rooms. But there's salvage to be had. Scientific equipment. Possibly some food that could keep."

Miranda walks over to us. "We're not going to have time to go roaming about the place, trying to find something. Our best bet is to pick a strategic target, the kind of place that will give us what we want, and go there."

I pull back the telescope and look at her in surprise.

"What?" she says. "I told you—I'm here for a reason."

"It's a good plan," I say. "Best to minimize our time on the ground. We go in, we get out."

Everyone nods back at me. "We should have brought more people," I say.

"Are you sure about that?" Miranda says. And she's right. More people would help, but I don't like to work like that. They could also get in the way. They could also get infected. Small was the way I liked it.

Used to be One was the way I liked it, but I guess I'm learning some new tricks after all.

I turn to Miranda. "Then where do we go?"

She looks down in the scope. "It's hard to tell—I don't know this place. But I used to raid schools with my folks growing up. Enough to give me a sense for the way they set these places up. I can't guarantee I'm right, but I'd go for that building." She points at one of the larger buildings, though not the largest. "I'd guess that's where they did chemistry based on the ductwork on top."

"I'm just going to pretend I know what you're talking about," I say.

Miranda smiles. "Why alter a winning formula?" she asks.

"I think we should stay high," I say. "We can use the ladder and bust in through the windows."

Diego takes a turn at the scope. "That could be tricky, though. Stabilizing the ladder for one thing. Staying clear of any Ferals that might be in there."

"I've done it before," I say. "My dad and I used to do it all the time. Safer off of the ground, give the Ferals limited access to you."

"Okay," Diego says.

"We'll leave Rosie here to man the *Osprey*. If necessary she can pull us clear. Diego, you and me will go down. One in, one covering. Sound good?"

"You left me out," Miranda says.

"I did," I say.

"Then let me correct that oversight. You need me, if only to identify the important salvage. You're going to need some decent equipment. Besides, I may be able to score some equipment that might fill out our lab back in Tamoanchan." She sets her jaw. "I'll go down second."

"Miranda . . ."

"You go in first, then me, and Diego can cover us."

It makes sense, so I don't argue. "Okay, let's go," I say.

I have a sinking sensation as I check my ammo and secure Miranda's clothing. She does the same for me. I don't want to go down there. On my own I'd never touch the place. But then I think about the *Cherub* and that's enough to keep me going.

When we're all secured, we walk to the airship's ladder.

Then we go down.

I always feel relief at airship ladders because they lead to the sky and provide exit from the ground. But they aren't the most secure of things. They're notoriously unsteady, no matter how much you try to weight them, and holding anything while navigating one is extremely hard. I once lost my Dad's revolver trying to fire while climbing one, and it almost cost me my life trying to get it back.

So I don't have the revolver out as I go down. Which makes me even more nervous. Damned if you do, damned if you don't.

This isn't going to be a stealth mission. At the height it was forced to hover to lower us, the *Osprey* is making quite a racket, and that will alert any Ferals around us. So the plan is to hit the top window, get myself as stable as possible, take out the revolver, and see what's inside.

I get to the bottom of the ladder. With Miranda and Diego above me it doesn't whip around as much as it might, but it still jerks left and right. I curl an arm around the ladder, tuck my boot under a rung, and pull out the revolver.

The windows at my level and below are all broken, which figures. A Feral never met some glass it didn't want to break. Especially windows. But the frames are still studded with shards, which makes it hard to peer in, especially backlit as I am. If I only had a flare. A while back I'd come upon someone bartering them and I'd traded him a good deal of my best stuff for a few. But they were all on the *Cherub*.

"Miranda," I call. I tuck the revolver back into its holster, and she hands me down the torch, already lit. I toss it through the window.

The light from the torch isn't great, but it shows a little of what lay inside the place. I don't see any movement, which is good. I do see rows of tables arranged neatly. Crap and refuse. Crumbling ceiling tiles.

I remove the revolver again and knock out most of the remaining glass from the window. Then, taking a deep breath, I climb through the window. Then I'm down into a crouch, the gun out, my ears strained to hear, my eyes constantly scanning.

Nothing. I pull back the hammer, half-cocking the gun. Then I wave to Miranda to let her know to come in.

She is mostly noiseless as she drops to the ground and, like I taught her, she stays low. I look out to see Diego taking up position, his rifle in his hands. Metal clips anchor him to the ladder, though that means he can't easily come in to support us if we need it.

I turn to Miranda and whisper. "Anything in here?"

She looks around, still staying low. "These are benches," she says. "For experiments. Chemistry, probably." She checks for storage beneath, pulls out drawers. I try not to pay too much attention. Then I can't check for Ferals.

She moves over to a set of cabinets against one wall, starts picking through them.

The smell in the place is bad Feral stench. Piss, shit, the usual. But not strong enough to indicate that it's often-used. I'm starting to think this might be okay after all. I doubt we'll score anything large, but we can pass up smaller things.

"Here," she says.

I resist looking over to where she's rifling through some cabinets. "What?" I say.

"Instruments. Microscopes. The optics could be useful. There are some old scalpels. I'll load up the tarp."

I nod and look back to the door. A noise creaks through the old structure. I can't tell if it's from the *Osprey* or from somewhere down below or just the wind. I tighten my grip on the revolver.

"Load up what you can," I say. "Then let's get the hell out of here." The hair on my arms prickles and my underarms slick with sweat. That voice in my head is telling me to get out of there.

"Almost there," Miranda says.

I breathe in. Breathe out. Keep myself calm. So many people learn the hard way what happens when you lose your head . . .

"Okay," Miranda says, after what seems like an eternity. "That should do it." She tugs on the line to let Diego know, and he'll signal to Rosie to pull the load up. I watch as it begins to slide across the floor and wince at the terrible scraping noise it sets up. But we'll be out soon.

I keep my eyes on the door.

I keep my eyes on the door.

I keep—

Something, glass or something like it, breaks, and for a moment I turn to see what it is.

Then the moment becomes a whirl of chaos and sensations. A heavy weight knocks me to the ground. I try to move, but I'm pinned. I look up into the bloodshot eyes of a Feral. My gun arm is pinned beneath me. I can smell his rancid breath, can feel the warmth coming off of him. Wild, tangled hair tickles my face.

My breath is fast and ragged.

Slaver drips from his open mouth. I want to scream, but even that is restrained, the Feral's heavy weight pushing the air from my lungs.

I try to signal to Miranda, try to see her, but I can't and I can't move my head and the Feral is on me and oh God he's going to Infect me and—

The world cracks in two. Or at least that's what it sounds like. What it *feels* like. Then the Feral's weight slides off of me.

I piece together what happened in the moments afterward. The Feral's head exploding, being swept away in a bloody pulp, as if flicked by the Hand of God.

I turn my head to see Miranda crouching low, the pistol still out, still aiming. She stands like that for a moment. I stare at her, both of us frozen. Then I remember where we are and I scramble out from under the Feral and get to my knees.

My movement breaks Miranda from her pose and she stumbles over to me.

"Am I—" I say. "Did it get me?"

Some of the glaze disappears from her eyes and she comes over, checking my face where it's not covered, paying special attention to my eyes, one of the most vulnerable places on the body. Running her fingers over my lips. Looking into my nostrils.

It's when she says, "You look clean" that I remember to breathe. I spare a brief glance at the Feral. It was a good shot. Blew everything out the side of the head. Away from me. No splatter toward me.

Miranda saved my life.

"C'mon," I say. "We need to get out of here." Already I can hear movement from the halls below. Scrabbling. Gibbers. Whether real or imagined they are enough to get me moving.

I push her ahead of me, keeping my eyes on the doorway, keeping my pistol out. Then she's on the ladder and climbing and I'm right below her, as usual. And something about this calms me, allows my hammering heart to slow.

# CHAPTER TWELVE

**D**iego brings the *Osprey* in to Gastown with his flags flying the sign for barter. All of us are conscious of the weapons they have mounted on the flying platform. Its evidence of the divide between Valhalla and the original Gastown. While the Gastowners were working on helium manufacturing, Valhalla was busy hunting down heavy weapons.

It's a sad admission that Valhalla ended up making the better choice.

Moments pass as we await their answer—either a colorful dance of flags or the staccato burst of gunfire. Miranda grips my arm, her fingers tightening with each minute. I don't think anyone is breathing right now. Time stretches, torturously.

The guns move to cover us. Then the flags move as well. They direct us to a mooring dock and, sweating, Diego follows their directions.

We are all armed. All prepared if they rush us when we open the doors. Diego's face is bundled up. Odds are no one who's seen him is on Gastown, but we can't be sure. One nice thing about the Sick is that it's easy to be hidden. No, it's ships that stick out, and that's the one thing I'm worried about. But we covered up the *Osprey*'s colors and her name and really it shouldn't be that recognizable.

I stand near the gondola door as Diego opens it, my hand very near my revolver. Funny thing is, as dangerous as this is, I'm a lot calmer than I would be on the ground. Psychopath blood is nothing compared to a Feral's.

Two rough-looking men push their way in, large, all swagger and scowls. "Barter?" one of them says.

Diego nods. I'm impressed that he looks so calm. I have to give it to him, the man seems to be a professional. "Got a recent score. Thought we'd come here and see if we could sell it."

"There's a tax."

"Of course," Diego says, nodding again. "What is it?"

"Fuel now. A cut of the barter later."

This surprises me. In a world where barter is hard to quantify, taking a percentage is often a difficult proposition. "How does that work?" I ask, unable to keep my silence.

He looks at me and frowns. "The person you barter with will work that in to their negotiations. Clear?"

I nod. I guess that makes a kind of sense, even if it is draconian.

Diego passes over the fuel. There are a few formalities and then we are out in Gastown.

Gastown bears some explanation these days, I suppose. It was the first city in the air, built from large platforms lashed together and held aloft by ballonets. As the city established itself, more people came to it, bringing their own ships, their own construction materials, and the city grew. It brought in more barter, and that brought in more raw materials. Ships are kept on the edges to help adjust its position and keep it in place, but it keeps swelling. Or at least it did.

It was, in many ways, a marvelous thing. As much as I had issues with the way the city in the sky was run, I appreciated it for what it was, a symbol of humanity fighting back against the decline of civilization. An attempt of reclaiming something we'd lost.

Of course it wasn't to last.

From the outside, Gastown looks much the same as it did. Aside from the addition of the ugly mounted guns and the brute constructions that house them. Inside, however, it's much different. It used to be—I don't know—almost cheery. At least as much as something in the Sick can be. It was almost irritating before. Now, the place is bleak, raw, stripped down to the essentials. This is no strike back for civilization. This is a sham. A place for greedy people to take all they can before sinking the ship.

We walk down alleys of reinforced planking, among "shops" that have seen better days. Armed people, rough people, sit in chairs or glare out from behind makeshift counters. Many of them are decked out in Valhalla's favored gear: animal skins, furs, bones, and teeth. They practically drip with weapons, from knives and swords to pistols and rifles. I think if they didn't have to worry about the Bug they would wear Feral skins. Maybe even human ones. All of this means that Gastown is much less hospitable these days—a shame, because that will keep the people away. And reduce the barter trade. But some will always come for the helium.

Miranda walks beside me. She's distracted. Bothered. She's no longer wearing her gun in its holster. We'd had a talk back on the *Osprey* that went about as well as most of our recent talks. It went something like this:

She stands in the back room of the *Osprey*, head bowed, shoulders hunched. "What's the matter?" I say.

She turns to me, a fingernail between her teeth. Her eyes are wide.

"Miranda," I say again.

"I killed him," she says.

"You saved my life." I place my hands on her arms. "And you did it perfectly. I am so proud of you."

"Proud?" Her face distorts in disgust. "I killed a person."

"You killed a Feral," I say. "Not a person. Not anymore."

"How can you say that so easily? How is it so easy to forget their humanity?"

"Not easy," I say. "It took me a long time to get to this point. Seeing my father Fade helped to convince me."

She stares up at me, her expression unreadable.

"Would you rather it had killed me?" I ask. "Or infected me?"

"Of course not," she snaps. Her eyes flash anger. "But I pulled the trigger. And I saw him die. Because of what I did."

"And you saved a life because of it. I don't get why this is so hard for you."

"Because I want to save his life, too. Because I see all these people that you think of as creatures, and I see the humanity in them. And I think I can give it back to them. I believe it. I have to."

"Why?"

"Because otherwise what point is there in going on?"

I don't know how to respond. It's like all her words are twisting around in my guts like writhing worms.

"I think you should take this back," she says, handing me the gun. "I don't want it anymore."

I shake my head. "No. I won't."

"Then I'll just leave it here." She places it down on one of the *Osprey*'s counters.

"Miranda, please. I know you're upset. I know that you want to distance yourself from this, but we're about to head into a very dangerous situation and I need to know you're armed."

"What for?" she says. "I don't want to use this again."

"Just . . . do it for me, okay?"

She looks up at me, then shakes her head and walks back to where Diego and Rosie are.

Now she's not wearing it, so I have to assume she left it on the *Osprey*.

"We should split up," I say. "Cover more ground that way."

"Good idea," Miranda says. "I'll go with Diego." Which is not what I had been expecting.

"Okay," Diego says. And before I can muster up some kind of protest, Miranda's grabbed Diego by the arm and they're moving off, leaving me standing next to Rosie.

I turn to her and shrug. "Meet back here in a few hours?"

"Uh-uh." She shakes her head to emphasize her point. "If they're going off together then that leaves me to watch your ass."

I sigh. You did get yourself into this mess, Ben, I think. "My ass is not my best feature," I say.

"I'm not likely to take much pleasure in it," she says.

"Fine," I say. "Let's go." I move off in the opposite direction of Miranda and Diego. Rosie shadows me.

"You know, we're going to be looking for different things," I say.

"I'm just here to watch you," she says. "Anything else is just extra."

"Well, I'm here to look for my ship," I say. "So maybe you can help while you're here. You remember what she looks like?"

"Freight ship, with a flattened envelope. VTOL capable. Red and tan." I nod.

"But they could have painted her." The thought makes me ill. The *Cherub*'s colors are just one of the things I love about her. On the other hand, repainting is a lot better than dismantling. "You paid close attention."

She flashes me a wicked smile. "Of course I did. I was looking for ways to blow her up." She pauses. "*If* it became necessary."

My jaw hangs open for the slightest moment. "I'm glad it wasn't."

We walk up and down the alleys and streets of Gastown amidst the yells of hawkers and the chittering of the patchmonkeys above us, amidst the smell of smoke and of exhaust and of humanity. I scan lashed-up airships and parts of airships, looking for the dirigible I know like my own heartbeat, my longest companion. But I don't see anything. And there are so many ships and so much ground to cover.

"Change of plans," I say. Then I head for the nearest bar.

As I mentioned earlier, the thing about gatherings of people is that there's always going to be a bar somewhere. A place for people to gather and forget the worries of the world for a while. And alcohol is one of the things we held on to after the Bug hit. Fermentation is one of the easiest, most natural processes in food production. And very, very tasty.

The place I find is called Fisherman's. I recognize it as a place that used to be called Sam's. But all that seems to have changed is the sign on the outside and the clientele.

I head to the bar, fetch two of the house liquors, then grab a table made out of an old wooden door, nicked and scratched. I place a cup down in front of Rosie. "What is it?" she asks.

I shrug. It's not clear but not quite brown. Places like this one have their own blend of hooch readily available. Usually it doesn't taste like much but it burns as it goes down and leaves some pleasant warmth behind, and really, that's all you can ask for.

We both slug ours back. It tunnels through me like a hot bullet. Rosie grimaces. "Jesus," she says. But she takes it. "Why are we here?" she asks. Just my luck, she's the inquisitive type.

"We talk to some people," I say. "See if anyone's seen anything. But first we have to make ourselves comfortable. Otherwise we'll just put people on edge."

She tips back the second half of her drink. She doesn't look too happy. But I'm here for the *Cherub* and that's what's motivating me. I become aware of a voice in my head. It's saying, "That's it, Ben. Just treat people as a means to an end. That's what you're good at."

Which of course makes me think of Miranda. Which makes me take another drink.

I scan the room, trying to take in the feel of it, the ebb and flow of human interaction. The mood is uneven. Some people sit at tables, not speaking to each other, eyes and faces dark and closed. Other tables are loud and raucous, drunk people laughing and slapping each other on the back and shoulders. Not a lot of women in the room.

The most active table, however, is a long one over on the left side of the room. My attention is drawn instantly to the figure at its center. She's tall and thin, with a shock of long brown hair rising up from a widow's peak. She otherwise seems nondescript, but it's clear from the way the others treat her, the deference in their posture, that she's someone important.

"You know who that is?" I ask Rosie.

She shakes her head. "Should I?"

"No," I say. "But she seems to be someone of importance. Could be a bigwig around here. Could know something about the *Cherub*." The engine in my brain kicks over and starts to hum. There, at least, is a start to my search. I drain the rest of my cup because every engine needs fuel.

I'm just slamming the cup down when the world turns and I'm flipped back in my chair. There's a moment of falling, disorientation, then I crash hard into the ground.

Instincts make me reach for my revolver. I grab it, pull it out.

A boot kicks it out of my hand and it slides, spinning across the floor.

Against my better judgment, I watch it for a moment, reaching for it. Another kick slams into my side, curls me around. Then a hand on the front of my shirt pulls me up.

I stare into a woman's face. Brilliant blue eyes. A jagged scar across one of them. Black hair spilling down shot through with gray.

"Claudia," I say. "Your scar is looking good."

She pulls me up more. "You're just saying that 'cause you're the one who sewed it up." She flashes me a humorless smile, then throws me back onto the ground.

I see Rosie standing up now, her weapon pointed at Claudia. "Put him down," she says. Her voice is low, steady. She's got balls, this one.

"It's okay," I say. "I know her."

"You're coming with me," Claudia says. She pulls me up roughly, then picks up my father's revolver, tucking it into her pants.

Rosie looks at me questioningly. I nod. Claudia pushes me out of the bar.

The first thought that crosses my mind after the pain stops sparking across my ribs is that Claudia looks damn good. Not many people can take a scar like that across the face and still carry it well. She looks a bit tighter, trimmer, too, and it suits her. She wears a long coat, a shotgun across her back. I like the look.

When the glamour fades, I start thinking of the past, and I try to remember when it was I last saw Claudia and how we parted. I can't remember giving her a reason to want to hurt me, but I can easily imagine it. It's not like things were ever conventional with her.

She pushes me ahead of her, and Rosie drags behind us. "Where are we going?" I say.

"Shut up," she says. And kicks me in the ass. People look at us as we pass but don't stop us or say anything. I notice Rosie still has a hand on her pistol.

"Who are you to him?" Claudia says at one point, to Rosie.

"No one," Rosie says in a way that slightly offends me. "Just a . . . business partner."

"Then maybe you'd better go elsewhere," Claudia says. "This is personal."

"I'm not leaving him," Rosie says.

Claudia narrows her eyes. "Why?" she asks. "You sweet on him?"

Rosie makes a disgusted noise. "Hardly."

"Hey," I say. "I'm right here."

"Relax," Rosie says. "Men don't do it for me."

"So then what?" Claudia asks.

"Let's just say I have a vested interest in him."

And there I am, trapped between two hard-asses who refuse to leave me alone.

Claudia guides us down several streets until we finally reach an airship. The *Valkyrie*. I remember her well. She's a damn fine ship, kept by a damn fine captain. I can't help a bit of the old hero worship from creeping in.

Claudia catches me looking at the ship. She smiles. "I can still keep a ship," she says.

Then she kicks me again. "Now get on."

✳   ✳   ✳

Rosie and I board the *Valkyrie* up the ramp after Claudia unlocks the door. She pushes us into the back cabin, which Claudia's done up nice for moments such as this. I sink into the old sofa feeling the same bite from the springs on the left side. Rosie takes a wooden chair that's seen better days.

"No," Claudia says. "Stand up." So I do, and then she throws her arms around me and claps me on the back, pulling me close, and I feel some kind of weight I've been carrying slip away from me a little. And I grab on to her.

"You're not mad," I say, despite myself.

"No more than usual," she says. "Though I think you're a damn fool."

"Then what was that all about?" Rosie says.

"I needed to get you on here and out of that bar," Claudia says. "Too many eyes and ears in there. But I didn't want people to know that we knew each other. At least not in a good way."

I shake my head. "Claudia, what the hell is going on?"

"Uh-uh," she says. "First, do you trust your friend?"

I look at Rosie, who's frowning at both of us. "You can talk freely in front of her," I say. "I owe her a bit of trust."

"Okay, then," Claudia says. "You first."

"I'm looking for the *Cherub*," I say.

"I thought that might be it," she says. "How in the hell did you lose that ship?"

So I tell her about Miranda and the Core and the attack by the raiders. She listens and doesn't interrupt. Then, "Scientists?" she says. "That's not like you." Then she looks at Rosie. "No offense."

Rosie shakes her head. "None taken. I'm not one of them."

"Let's just say they made a compelling argument," I said. "Not to mention the fact that they had clean water and soap."

"Heh," she says. She turns to Rosie. "Then who are you?"

"Just another forager," Rosie says. She gives me a hard look that says she doesn't want to mention Tamoanchan. I give a slight nod in return. "Ben helped me and my brother a while back. We wanted to return the favor."

Claudia raises her eyebrows. "That's some loyalty."

I give her a wounded look. "I've been known to inspire some from time to time." Then what she said sinks in. "Wait. How did you know I was looking for the *Cherub*?"

"Because I saw it here," she says. "And I knew you weren't on it. I thought you might be dead. Thought that would be the only reason you wouldn't have it around."

"I just got stupid," I say. "But I came back for her. Where is she?"

"You're not going to like the answer," she says.

"Claudia, tell me."

"Okay," she says.

"She's on the ground."

# CHAPTER THIRTEEN

"**T**he ground?" I say. "She crashed?"

"No," Claudia says. "Or at least I'm pretty sure she didn't. The Gastowners tasked her to transfer supplies for their helium runs. She moves back and forth between here and the plant."

"And where's that?" I ask.

She leans back against a cabinet and crosses her arms. "That, I wish I knew."

"Wait a second," I say. "How do you know all this? What are you doing here? It can't be for the ambiance or the company."

"You know me better than that," she says. "I can hang with a pretty rough crowd, but not these assholes. They give zeps a bad name."

"Then what?"

She slides into another chair. Drops her shotgun to the floor. "It's a bit complicated."

"We have time," I say, looking at Rosie. "Don't we?"

Rosie crosses her arms and leans back. "I think we do."

"It has to do with the helium," Claudia says.

"Go on."

"That's presumably why Valhalla attacked Gastown in the first place. Or at least why they stuck around. To get the helium. Smart barter seems to say that they wanted to control the helium and become the one place people can come for it. I mean, you know that both of us have put hydrogen in our babies, but people are still afraid of its flammability."

"And New Gastown wants to be the one place that has it."

"Right. But no one is sure where they're getting it from. Even the original people running Gastown were quiet about where it came from.

Has to be a natural gas operation. On the ground. But even then it was becoming scarce back before the Bug got up and running."

"So no one knows where they're getting it?"

Claudia shakes her head. "And it has to be a decent operation. Machines, extraction tools, things like that. They're still providing it, so they must have taken it intact when they took Gastown."

"But who's operating it? Not the Vikings, surely."

"I'm not sure," Claudia says. "They might have held on to the same crew from before. But I think there's something more going on."

"What kind of more?"

She shrugs. "The operation seems pretty complex. It seems beyond what I know of the Valhallans."

"So the *Cherub* is at the plant and the plant is on the ground," I say. "And possibly crawling with God knows how many Vikings."

"That just about covers it. It must be well hidden. No one has even seen their ships moving to it."

"Nobody has?"

"No one I've been able to find."

"Not even before *Valhalla* took it over?"

She shakes her head. "My guess is, back then they did it in the dark, blacked out, so as not to leave a big trail. These guys . . . I think they just go in big and with lots of guns. If you stumble onto the operation, they'll shoot you down."

"But I still don't get it," I say. "Why do you want to find it? You're looking to rip it off?"

"Not exactly," she says. "Let's just say I've been hired by some people to look into it."

"What kind of people?"

"People who were upset when the original Gastown was taken out."

I sit back and lace my fingers together. I smile. "We should work together."

"What?" Claudia says.

"What?" Rosie echoes.

"Think about it. You're looking for information. I'm looking for the *Cherub*. They're both down on the ground."

"Hang on," Rosie says. "I didn't sign up to go down to this helium operation."

"Then don't go," I say. "But my ship's down there."

"We need to let Diego know about this," Rosie says.

"Sure," I say. "But I'm going."

Claudia inclines her head. "It does make a kind of sense. Us working together."

"How are we even sure we can trust her?" Rosie asks.

I meet Rosie's eyes. "I trust Claudia with my life."

Rosie's eyes are hard. "I don't." She looks away. "And we know what happened when Diego trusted you."

I feel the heat rise into my face and I look away from her. Claudia raises her eyebrows, but I shake my head.

Claudia instead turns to face Rosie. "You're right. You have no reason to trust me. But maybe I can help you. You're clearly not here for the *Cherub*. What *are* you interested in?"

Rosie looks at me and then back to Claudia. "Information. On Gastown. Their defenses. Their weaponry. Things like that."

"Good," Claudia says. "I think I can give you at least some of what you want. I've been up here for the better part of a week, taking note of the defenses, the ships, the movements of their people. I can give you that information. A good faith gesture."

"That would help," Rosie says.

"Can you read?" Claudia asks.

Rosie nods.

"I can have it for you tomorrow."

Rosie closes her eyes for the briefest of moments. Then says, "Deal."

"Good," Claudia says.

"There are two more of us," I say. "Diego and Miranda. They might want to come, too."

"We'll need to figure out a way to get there first," Claudia says. "As you can probably guess, they carefully guard the location. Only a certain few up here even know it. Once or twice a week they send supplies down to the men and pull the helium back up here. But the ships are escorted by gunships. It's not like I can take the *Valkyrie* down and follow them."

"Then we'll just have to figure out another way," I say. "Can you share with us what you have so far?"

So Claudia does. She passes around her notes and a few photographs she took and was able to develop with an old-fashioned camera setup.

I flip through them. Detailed schedules of movements. Descriptions of ships. Supplies moved out. Supplies moved in. Diagrams. Schematics. Lists.

I pass some on to Rosie, hoping she'll see something in there. Some answer from all the data. I wish Miranda were here. She's really good at that sort of thing.

"Maybe we should take a few days with this. Bring in Diego and Miranda and see what we can find."

"You can," Claudia says. "But by my calculations the next supply run should be the day after tomorrow."

"Damn," I say.

"Yeah," Claudia says.

"And the longer we're here on Gastown, the more dangerous it gets," Rosie says.

"Then we just have to figure out a way to make this work for tomorrow," I say. I flip through photographs. Heavily armed gunships. People with boxes on handtrucks.

I feel my mind reaching for all the pieces, trying to make sense of them. Like a jigsaw puzzle. Only all the jigsaw puzzles I've seen have had pieces missing. And this plan can't afford that.

And then there it is. The answer. A photograph of people moving large drums.

I smile and hold up the photo. "This is it." Then I slap it down on the table.

"Explain," Claudia says.

"We can't take your ship," I say. "So why don't we use theirs?"

"What?" Rosie asks. She crosses her arms.

Claudia's eyes narrow. "We can't take out a whole crew. They're likely to have pilots and guards. I'm good, but I'm not that good."

I shake my head. "Agreed. A frontal assault would just get us killed. But what if we're disguised somehow. Like . . . cargo."

"That's ridiculous," Rosie says.

I point at the picture. "The drums. They bring these onto the ships, right? To bring down to the plant?"

"Yes," Claudia says.

"Look at their size. They're big enough to hold a person."

Claudia narrows her eyes. "You're saying that we load ourselves into these drums?"

"Yes! Then we let them load us on the supply ship and transport us down to the ground. No need for any ships. No need for an assault."

"And you think they won't find us?" Rosie says.

"Not if we take precautions. We pad the sides, minimize our noise. Make sure we have an easy exit."

"Okay," Claudia says. "Say that part works. How are we going to get into these drums? They're kept in a warehouse up here. Under guard."

"That's the part we have to work on," I say. "But if we get there early enough before the transfer, we might have a better shot. What do you think?"

"I think it's crazy," Claudia says. "But I think it might also work."

"You're both out of your minds," Rosie says.

"Maybe," I say. "But sometimes you have to be."

"We need to talk to Diego," Rosie says.

"Yeah," I say. "That's a good idea. Miranda, too."

"I have people to talk to as well," Claudia says. "I'll try to get more information. But then we have to be ready to move."

"Okay." I stand up. Rosie does the same. We make for the door.

Claudia mentioning that she still has people to talk to tickles my brain, though, and I stop and turn back to her. "Oh, by the way. Do you know that bigwig who was sitting at that big table back at the bar? Woman? Tall and thin? Big hair? Bigger entourage?"

"I don't know her name," Claudia says. "But I get the sense she's important. She's been here for a few days. I think I heard someone call her 'Professor.'"

"Professor?" I ask.

Claudia shrugs. "You know as much as I do. I just get the sense that Gastown, the new Gastown, that is, is reaching out to other folks. Making new alliances. That lot you saw was part of that."

I think back to the conversation with Miranda from earlier. "That scares me."

"All of this should scare you," Claudia says.

"Fair enough." I walk Rosie to the door and let her out first. Then I turn back to Claudia one more time. "It's good to see you."

"Likewise." She grabs my face and kisses me hard. It brings back old times. I can't help smiling.

"You still use the bow?" I ask.

"Of course," she says. "Only people up here don't respect a weapon like that. So I thought it better to keep it tucked away."

I picture her suddenly, the bow stretched back in her hands, the arrow flying true and clear when she releases. It's such a perfect picture, I think about it often. I realize I want to see it again.

"I'll check in tomorrow then," I say.

"Tomorrow," she says.

Then I walk off of the *Valkyrie* despite wanting to stay all night.

✳   ✳   ✳

Not long afterward, we're sitting with Diego and Miranda in an entirely different Gastown bar, and Diego's saying . . . something. Frankly, I'm not paying attention because I'm too preoccupied with the fact that Miranda won't meet my eyes and for some reason that has me all tangled up inside.

I notice that Diego's looking at me expectantly. "I'm sorry. Say that again?"

"I'm saying, I know you want your ship back, but what point is there getting caught up in your friend's helium thing?"

"Really?" I say. "You don't see? Gastown has all but declared war on any other settlement in this region. Including . . ." I look around, recognizing that this is hardly a private conversation. "Including your home. And this is a way to get intelligence about their most valuable resource. Maybe we could even figure out a way to sabotage it."

"You trust this woman? Claudia, was it?"

"Yes," I say. "I've known her a long time. She's trustworthy. She's had my back lots of times."

Miranda is still not looking at me, and it's like this annoying insect buzz in my mind that I'm finding it hard to work past.

"So now what?"

"We meet up tomorrow, coordinate, and then move out."

"All of us?" Diego says.

"I thought we should stick together."

Diego tilts his head to one side, then rubs his beard. "See, I thought maybe I could get more done up here. I've already met a few people. Made some progress. Staying up here makes more sense to me."

I bite back my response. I realize that retrieving the *Cherub* is what's driving me, and that has no meaning for him. "Okay," I say at last. "Then maybe I'll take Miranda, and you and Rosie can do what you need to do here."

"No," Miranda says, still not meeting my eyes. "I'll stick with Diego."

It stings more than I want it to. Rather than feeling the urge to punch Diego as I would expect, I just feel beat-up. "Fine," I say softly. "I guess I'm on my own."

"Not quite," Rosie says. Great, I think. She's decided to stay on my ass and she's not going to budge.

I nod. "Okay." I take a slug of my drink. "If you change your mind, be ready to meet us at Fisherman's the day after tomorrow."

Diego nods. Miranda doesn't respond. And then my skin is itching and I want to get away from that table as quickly as possible. So I throw back my drink and then stand up. "I'm going to do some preparing," I say to Rosie. "Meet me at Claudia's an hour before we go. You remember how to get there?"

She nods.

"Good. Then have a good time, all." I walk out of the bar trying to look calm, cool, but I'm not sure I'm pulling it off. But then I don't care.

Gastown passes in a blur—people and shapes and smells I don't identify because of the buzz that's in my head.

Then I'm back at the *Valkyrie* and even though I know Claudia said we shouldn't be seen together, I find myself at her ramp and I rap on it to get her attention.

She comes to the door and looks down at me. "What's wrong?" she says.

I shrug. "I just needed to see a friendly face."

She laughs and points to her scar. "You call this friendly?"

Without mirth or humor, I nod.

She wraps an arm around me and pulls me inside.

✳    ✳    ✳

Those early days are imprinted so strongly on my brain. I can remember everything about them. The sound of my father's voice, and Claudia's answering back in the midst of Feral howls. The smell of the ground, of the Ferals, that scent of Claudia's that she still has—metal and oil and sweet vanilla. The taste of Claudia's grog. The feeling of hands and bruises and cuts from our adventures and patching each other up. And . . . other sensations.

We hooked up with her back when my dad was still around. Did a job together. She didn't have the *Valkyrie* at the time. And we all made a good team. She was older, yes, but nicely in between me and my dad and served, in a way, as a bridge between us.

I sometimes wonder if Dad was hoping for something to happen with her. There certainly was as much of a difference in age between them as there was between her and me. But I guess Claudia had other ideas.

I think about that night often.

We had gotten word of a stash. Some ritzy mountain home we were going to check out. Those were always potentially good scores. Back in the Clean, the rich were the ones who could barricade themselves away from everyone else. They were likely to have better salvage. They were likely to have stockaded goods.

So we took the *Cherub* in. Of course we were worried about Ferals. No matter how defensible a place looked, you always had to expect the Ferals had found it. And even if they hadn't, what if the Bug had?

Once we lowered the ship in and next to a stand of trees, we descended the ladder. Dad never liked to take the *Cherub* down to where Ferals might be able to reach her. It's something I carried on after he died.

Dad had his revolver out. I had a worn .45 that I had scrounged up somewhere. It wasn't a great weapon, but I remember being so proud of it. Because it was mine and I took care of it as well as I could.

Claudia had her bow. I remember being skeptical of it at first. I was young, impressed by guns and ammo. Not that I'm not now. But a bow seemed, well, it seemed ridiculous.

Yet the first time I saw her use it, I was a believer. I watched her pull back the string and loose arrow after arrow in fluid, graceful movement. And I watched Feral after Feral fall before her. What made it even better was that it was easy for her to collect ammo. She wouldn't collect the shafts from used arrows—they were covered in Feral blood and, therefore, the Bug—but she could cut and carve new shafts from trees, and arrowheads, while not easy to make, could be fashioned from cast-off metal or flint or any number of materials. Not quite the same as bullets.

Dad brought the *Cherub* down to the house. It was a sprawling, massive structure, composed of asymmetrical elements. Lots of glass, though that could always prove a problem. Most of it looked intact, though. Behind the house was a large pool that Dad said had been used for swimming. Swampy water filled it, nature reclaiming the structure.

We lowered the ladder and Claudia was first down on the ground as usual. She kept her bow up, an arrow fitted to the string, scanning for any Ferals. I came down after her, my .45 in my hand. Dad brought up the rear with his revolver.

We moved one at a time, covering each other's movements. We'd worked like this so many times it had become routine. Still, I felt as anxious as a cat between two Ferals, the way I always did when it was my turn to cover. I was good at spotting Ferals—I knew that—but it was something that if you fucked it up, you weren't likely to get a second chance.

Everything looked good by the time Claudia got to the house. We'd discussed how to get inside but in the end had opted to smash through one of the windows. It would create some noise, possibly attract any Ferals inside, but it was the quickest way and no one liked to be fumbling at the lock while potentially under attack.

Claudia pulled a long rod from her belt and swung it at the window. I moved my eyes back to scan the surrounding area and waited for the sound of the glass cracking.

It didn't come.

I couldn't stop myself from turning back to look at her.

"Fuck," she said. "It's reinforced."

Which made sense of the fact that they were unbroken. Something like that would hold up to the wind and to Ferals. But it also meant that Ferals were unlikely to be inside. Unless, of course, some fool had left a door or window open.

"We'll move around to a door," Dad said. "Keep your eyes open."

We followed the outside wall and soon came to a small set of stairs leading up to a door. The wood of the steps had rotted through, but again, this meant that Ferals were unlikely to have penetrated the building.

"Cover us," Dad said to Claudia. Then he hoisted me up to the door. It was locked, of course, and I couldn't see a way to get inside. "Should I shoot it?" I said.

Dad didn't answer at first. Firing my gun now would alert anyone in the area. But we were up on a hill and the trees would cover us. It wouldn't necessarily give away our position.

"Okay," Dad said at last. So I shot the lock and with a few hits from the butt of my pistol was able to get the door open. I pulled myself inside, flattened down to the floor, the pistol still out, alert for any movement.

I didn't see any, nor did I notice the smell that characterized a Feral dwelling. Still, that didn't mean anything. Willing my hearing to its best ability, I reached down my hand for the next person.

Dad boosted up Claudia next, and with me pulling and him pushing, she was soon up by me and able to cover me from the inside. Then Dad came up last.

"Smells good," he said. Claudia didn't seem convinced.

Dad shut the door behind us. It was one of the things we had often disagreed on. I was of the opinion that it helped to have the door handily open in case, for example, the house was filled with Ferals and we had to go running to get away from them. In this case, we couldn't just go through the windows to escape.

Dad, on the other hand, felt that leaving it open was an invitation to any Ferals that happened to wander by, and he didn't want a Feral sneaking up on him while he was exploring.

Dad always won this argument.

We moved through the house. It looked like someone had been in it, had cleared some of the things away, but not everything. There was bound to be some decent salvage inside. I resisted the urge to start tearing everything apart and stuff it into my pockets. That was another thing Dad had taught me. And yet another variation in salvage philosophy.

There are some who would say that in a strange place like that where you're not sure if you're walking into a Feral den, the best thing to do is to grab what you can as quickly as possible and then get out as quickly as you can. Those people would likely tell you that any salvage, no matter how good, is no use to you if you're dead.

I can understand that line of reasoning. I like living, prefer to keep that going as long as I can.

But Dad liked to play a longer game. Sure, we could have cleared off with the first things we saw. Taken some books, some small electronic equipment. That might have got us by for another few months. But a bigger score meant more security, and Dad always trusted his instincts in situations like that. And he felt that there was something more important there.

We stuck together, moving throughout the rooms of the house. Dad never let us separate, not that we were likely to. It always was better to have someone cover you.

We moved through what was once the house's galley to a few sitting rooms and then to one large room that was filled with some old-fashioned games. I recognized a few of them from other houses, but whatever the rules were, or how they were played, were beyond me. Dad didn't even know. And the odds of finding a full set of anything, after all, was highly unlikely.

So far I had noted what could have been a decent haul. There were books. And small electronics and what must have been art pieces that could be used for raw materials—steel and glass, stone and fabrics. But Dad kept us going.

We went up to the bedroom, which had a huge bed, now covered in dust but piled high with blankets and pillows. Claudia looked at me and raised her eyebrows. I rolled my eyes at her, but I couldn't help smiling.

"I don't think there's anyone here," she said. "Maybe they left and this place was just too tightened up for anyone else to get in."

"Maybe," Dad said. "But something doesn't seem quite right."

I tried to figure out what he meant. I felt it, too, but I couldn't put my finger on it.

"Here," Dad said, interrupting my thoughts. He stood before a wall in the room.

"What?" I said.

"There's something here," he said.

I walked over and examined the wall where he was looking. He was right. It wasn't natural. You could tell where the ends met. Things weren't completely flush. The angles were all wrong. "What is it?" I asked.

"Some kind of hidden room," Claudia said.

I looked at Dad and smiled. The hidden score. Concealed objects tended to be valuable.

"How do we get it open?" I said.

We looked around for some kind of hinge mechanism, a place where the door would move from, but it wasn't obvious. I prodded at the wall, tried to find some kind of opening device or a switch or panel. It reminded me of some of the books I'd read as a kid, mysterious temples with secret doors.

Eventually we found the seam of the door and tried to jam things into it to lever it open. With the three of us pushing on it, we were able to open up the gap a tiny bit, but something prevented the door from moving. Either there had been swelling over the years or an earthquake shifted things or maybe it just malfunctioned.

Then Dad had an idea.

He made me open one of the bedroom windows which I did easily enough. Then he pointed up to the *Cherub*. "If we can't crack it, she certainly can."

"But if you take her up, anyone around will see," I said.

"I think it's worth the risk," he said.

Claudia nodded. "Yep."

All three of us went outside, covering Dad until he was onboard the *Cherub*. Then Claudia and I returned to the house. Dad lowered the winch from the *Cherub*'s gondola, and we snaked it into the open bedroom window and hooked it to the edge of the door, ratcheting it into place. With a shake from me, Dad started winding the winch in.

The line went taut, and nothing budged, then with a desperate, wrenching squeal, the metal pulled back from the wall and scraped against the floor. Dad was able to tell that it moved and shut down the winch.

The excitement of the moment died down when I realized that we didn't know what, or who, was in the room. Claudia and I exchanged a glance; she had her bow up and ready and I had my gun up and out. We moved around to the entrance, ready to cover each other.

The stink that rolled out from the room almost had me firing my gun because I'd only smelled the like near Feral dens. But my brain soon sussed out the difference. This was not the smell of filth and shit and rot. This was the smell of death. Even Claudia raised her scarf to her face and turned away.

I moved forward. I didn't know what else to do. And I was still motivated by what might be in there.

Dust, or what I thought was dust, swirled in the entrance. Dim lighting cast shadows throughout the room. It was some kind of safe room. Lockers and storage units and cots lined all the walls. But that wasn't what drew my attention.

In the center of the room, near the door, was a figure. Dead. Partially decomposed and contorted. I gave it a wide berth and beckoned Claudia to come in with me, partially because we needed to go through the room as quickly as possible, especially with the *Cherub* still above us, but also partially because the sight of this body disturbed me.

The score we were hoping for, frankly, wasn't. It was evident that at one point the storage units had been filled with food and water. There was still some water left, but not enough to be truly valuable. Besides, water was never that much of a desperate thing. There was some clothing, blankets, and the like. But nothing we could use.

There were also bones. Bones that weren't quite dry. Piled up in several of the storage units. I won't go into the details or the smell. Not all of them were adult bones.

Claudia and I were able to piece together what must have happened. This apparently well-to-do family knew the Bug was coming and they hid themselves away with what they thought was plenty of food and water and supplies. Only it wasn't enough. Or maybe the door just got stuck before they could come out to resupply. But the food was all gone. And people started to die and . . . well, those remaining ate the others until there was only one left.

I'll be honest—it made me gag. Cannibalism wasn't uncommon among Ferals when food supplies were low. It was one of the things that made them animals. Monsters. Other. But here was a family of human beings, seemingly uninfected, who had ended up acting just as monstrously.

I turned away, stumbled out of the room to get something resembling fresh air. Claudia came out after me. Putting one arm around me, pulling me close. For the first time I saw that she was shaken, too. We held onto each other for some time.

As we separated, I looked into her eyes and saw . . . something I'd never seen before. Something bright. Something intense. Something desperately alive. And it sparked with something inside of me.

We separated and started gathering up what meager salvage we could, attaching it to the winch to be pulled up to the *Cherub*. Then we did what we could to get out of that house and back up to the sky.

Later that night, Dad collapsed into drunken sleep. He had been counting on a score, and all we ended up with was what we might find in any number of other places. I hovered at the edge of Claudia's room, the supply area we had converted into her quarters. She looked up at me. Not smiling, really, but with something bright and hungry in her eyes.

I walked in. She stood up and turned to me.

The space between us disappeared and suddenly my mouth was on hers and hers on mine. We were hungry, desperate animals clawing at one another, pulling, grasping. Needing to find comfort in skin and in touch.

Sex is . . . rare in the Sick. The fear of infection touches everyone. Fluids. That's where the Bug lives. And you can never really tell if someone's hiding it. At least not normally.

But I had been with Claudia for weeks now. Had spent most of my time with her, knew the last time she had encountered Ferals. Had been with her at the time. And even if I hadn't, there was something about her that made me think it was impossible. That she was too smart and savvy for that.

So . . . we tore at each other, stripping off the carefully layered clothes we assembled to brave the outside world. But that was far away. Kilometers. And we were safe in the air, removed from Ferals, removed from death and the fallout of the Bug. And we were alive.

We fell to her sleeping mat, naked, our skin hot. Something surged through me, a feeling so strong and powerful that I thought it might bear me away. I don't remember distinct details, just impressions—the sensation of skin on skin, her mouth on mine, tongues intertwining in our mouths. Her teeth on me and mine on hers. Nails digging into backs. Legs snaking around legs. And hunger. Mad, desperate hunger to be close to someone. Inside of someone. To be lost in something so instinctual and natural and yet mostly forbidden.

There's another reason sex is rare in the Sick. And that's because it often leads to babies. And who wants to bring a baby up in this kind of world? People do it. I've seen kids, of course. But I know I wouldn't want to inflict this world on some innocent soul. And I sometimes realize this is probably the end of the human race. At least the uninfected human race. So other things happen, I'd done them, but never sex. I had never had sex before.

So I was understandably surprised when she grabbed my cock and guided it inside of her. My whole body blazed with pleasure. And even before I knew what I was doing, I was moving, thrusting, rocking my pelvis against hers, both of us gasping.

Tingling fingers stretched over my chest and up my neck. A powerful tightening built around my waist. Thought, perception, rationality fell away from me.

It built and built and I almost couldn't take it anymore. A noise I didn't recognize as coming from me escaped my mouth. I tensed.

Then she pushed me back, and the sudden movement and contact initiated my orgasm. I fell back out of her, shuddering, against the floor. I lay there, panting, tired, still coming down from the sensation of sex.

"I'm sorry," she panted. "I . . . I just couldn't."

"It's okay," I said between breaths. "I understand."

I moved over to her, put my arms around her, and pulled her close. And we lay like that, together, close, until sleep took us both into its arms.

# CHAPTER FOURTEEN

'm roused from sleep by a persistent knocking sound that alerts me to the fact that there's an equally persistent pounding in my head. A moment later I realize it's Miranda before my brain actually processes that it recognizes her knock.

I'm only half-dressed, my shirt off, my pants still on. I look back to see one of Claudia's muscled legs peeking out from underneath a sheet. More skin than I've seen in a long time.

Again, the knocking. I fumble for my shirt and quickly shrug it on, rushing to the door. Last night is a blur in my mind. I pull open the door.

Miranda stares up at me from the boarding ramp, a look of . . . what? Annoyance? Obligation? Something's in her eyes and I don't know what. Her eyes flick over me and then she reddens, looking away.

"Is everything okay?" I ask.

"Yes," she says quickly. "I mean." She looks down at her feet. "Ben, I need your help."

It makes a change from the last time I saw her. She's coming to me for assistance. "What's up?"

She looks around, at the docks behind her. "Can I . . . um, wouldn't it be better if I came inside?"

It's my turn to redden as I think of Claudia still lying in her bed, that one leg emerging from beneath her covers. "Right," I say. "Just . . . give me a moment."

I shut the door—not all the way, but most of it—and I go back to the bed. I gently prod Claudia. "Claud, we've got company."

She sits up suddenly, her hair tousled. "Who is it?" she asks. I can see the tension in her posture. She's ready to move, to act.

"It's just Miranda," I say. "But she wants to come in."

"Then let her in," Claudia says.

I grimace. "Maybe you should put on some more clothes then."

Claudia gives me a look of disapproval and then she sighs. "Okay. I'll make myself presentable. Go let her in."

I move back to the door, open it, wave Miranda in. She looks as uncomfortable as I feel, so I try to focus on the matter at hand. "Is it something with Diego? Are he and Rosie okay?"

"They're fine," she says. "Everyone's okay."

"So what do you need my help with?"

Miranda leans against one of the counters in the *Valkyrie*. Crosses her arms. "After you left last night, things got interesting."

"Go on . . ."

"I noticed that some of the people there didn't look like the usual Valhalla thugs. They didn't wear the same gear, they didn't look used to combat. They weren't seasoned in the same way."

"Visitors?"

"Maybe." She shrugs. "I got curious so I moved closer to some of them and overheard them talking about, well, about experiments."

"Experiments?"

"These were scientists, Ben. Like me. Working with Valhalla."

I think back to our conversation about the Core. Why they hit it. The thought makes me sick to my stomach.

"Could you tell what they were working on?"

She shakes her head. "Only a little. I decided to find out more about what they were talking about."

The thought makes me so anxious I have to remind myself Miranda's okay. It's not that I don't trust her to handle herself. I do. It's just that Miranda's not the best person when it comes to artifice. Lying, bluffing, they're not her thing.

"Go on," I say.

Miranda shrugs. "I figured the best approach was a direct one. I bought one of them a drink. I told him, well, the truth. Mostly. Told them who I was, where I grew up. What I studied. All I left out was what I've been doing the last few years, working on the cure, Apple Pi. I knew enough about some small scientist settlements that we talked to when setting up Apple Pi to fake who I'd been working with."

I nod. "You baited your hook well."

"I thought so. It seemed to work. This man, Templeton, seemed to like me, so I stayed for a few more drinks."

Big mistake, I think. Miranda could drink most people under the table.

"Templeton seems impressed by my background, and so he basically tries to recruit me. He says he's part of this cadre who have hooked up with Valhalla. He starts showing off by talking about some of their research. Ben . . . they're researching the Bug."

I wait for the bombshell.

"He said they want to remake the world."

"I don't understand," I say. "That sounds like what you're doing."

She shakes her head. Then slams the console. I jump. "Not that way," she says. "They're . . . social engineering. They're planning to set up a new society. Stratified. With them on the top and everyone else below them. Using the virus as just another tool."

I go cold. Miranda and her boffins want to cure the Bug. These people want to use it. Like a weapon. It brings me back to Ferals on hooks. Even if this cadre didn't come up with that idea, it's more of the same.

"Miranda," I say. "That's—"

"Yes," she says.

"So what do you need my help for?" I ask.

"I need to get a look at what they're working on. I have to find out what kind of research they're doing. I set up another date with Templeton. For tonight."

"I still don't get it."

"My plan is to get him drunk and convince him to show me some of the research. They apparently have a few facilities up here. I need you and Diego as backup."

I try to absorb all of this through the pounding in my head. "Miranda," I say. "We're getting ready to go down to the ground tomorrow. To this helium plant. I don't know if this is the right time to start poking our noses into new places."

"Ben, we need to know about this." A pause. "I need to know."

I shake my head. "What if this puts the whole city on alert?"

"That's why I need you." She says it like she didn't want to come to me with this. "You can help us get in, keep it quiet. Then tomorrow you go down to the plant, get your ship, and get out of here."

"It's a dumb idea," Claudia says, choosing this moment to emerge from the back of the gondola. She's fully dressed, thankfully.

"Miranda," I say. "This is Claudia. Claudia, Miranda."

Each of them takes a moment to size the other up, then they say hello. Politely but coldly.

"I'm sorry, Claudia, but you don't have to be involved in this."

"Ben," Claudia says. "We're about to head down to a hidden location, using a crazy scheme you cooked up, surrounded by a city full of homicidal maniacs. Do you really think now's the time for something like this?"

Miranda steps forward. "Ben, you told Diego to come here, to find out what he can to help . . . his people. This could help them. Knowing what they could be up against. Knowing what these people are planning."

I shake my head. I don't want anything to do with this. I'm only here for my ship, I tell myself.

Then Miranda takes the killing shot.

"Ben, you owe me."

And there's no way I can protest that. I owe her for getting me back up in the air. And more importantly, I owe her for saving my life.

"Okay," I say softly.

"What?" Claudia says.

"Okay," I repeat.

✳   ✳   ✳

After a quick planning session on the *Osprey* with Diego and Rosie in attendance (Claudia refused to involve herself, calling us all fools), I'm back at Fisherman's with some of their rotgut in hand. I can't decide how I feel about anything. On the one hand I'm glad Miranda is talking to me again. On the other, I'm annoyed she pulled me into this mess.

But if it involves watching her back . . .

Diego comes in after me, takes a seat by me. He smiles, to help keep up the cover, but I can tell it's forced.

"Were you in favor of this little operation?" I ask him, smiling.

"You were the one who said we needed to find out what was going on here. What Valhalla was up to." His smile fades. "So yes, I was."

I take a sip of my drink in response. It drowns the bitter taste in my mouth with the harsh tang of alcohol.

Diego pulls out a wad of playing cards and puts them down on the table. We're here waiting for Miranda, but we need to look like we belong. It seems as good a way as any to pass the time.

Most of the people I've played cards with use homemade ones, written on scraps of paper or cardboard or whatever. These are actual cards from back in the Clean. There's even a little bit of shine to them. They must be one of Diego's prize possessions.

"Nice set," I say.

He gives me a flat stare but then deals out the cards. Poker, a game I know well. Dad used to always say that people like to hold on to the comforts of the past, and cards seem to be one of those comforts. We certainly played quite a bit in quiet times on the *Cherub*. I imagine a lot of other people did as well.

I like to think I'm good at poker, skilled at the bluff and reading my opponent. Diego is clearly better. He takes the first three hands and most of the rest. I tell myself that it's because I'm distracted with everything that's going on, but that might well be bullshit.

We play for a while, nursing our drinks as much as we can. We don't really have anything to play for, but Diego keeps score on a ratty old piece of paper. I wince a little as I see all the marks on his side of the paper.

Then I catch sight of Miranda entering the bar. I nod my head toward her so Diego can see. Her wavy hair, usually piled up in a tousled bun now hangs free, curling down around her face and neck. I haven't seen it like that in ages. It looks good on her. I think she might also be wearing some kind of makeup, something shiny on her lips and cheeks. I find myself sitting up straighter in my chair.

She's still mostly covered. A scarf draped around her neck and shoulders, a sweater, the worn, fingerless gloves, but I spot artful gaps in her clothing. Bared skin at the chest and neck. Bands at her wrists. She put a lot of thought into this, I think. But then again, that's Miranda.

She walks up to a man standing at the bar, with a few men around him. I size him up as best I can. He's tall, medium build, with curly hair and bright-blue eyes. He looks like a boffin, yes, but there's something different there, in the stance and the gaze. A kind of domineering swagger. The boffins I know approach the world with a sense of curiosity and discovery. This one approaches it like it's his, to peel open and expose. Or that's what I get from him anyway.

When he sees Miranda, he calls to her and excuses himself from his companions, moving to meet her. He calls for a drink, puts it into her hand.

I focus back on the game. No need for me to catch the blow-by-blow of Miranda flirting with her mark. He'll go for it, I'm sure. Not many wouldn't. And he seems to appreciate women.

I'm so focused on my cards that Diego is the first to spot Miranda leaving with Templeton. Their arms are linked and he's gesturing in the air like he's describing something grand. He holds a small plastic bottle of liquid, and his movements are exaggerated. Miranda seems to hang on his every word.

After they exit, I collect my cards and count to ten. Slowly. Then, with a nod to Diego, I stand up and walk toward the exit. He follows.

There's no great complexity to this plan. We just follow Miranda to the lab and then see if we can get inside.

Diego and I make small talk, discussing our haul from the last job, what we might barter with it. I make up that I'm looking for some new parts for my radio. He says he needs a new pair of boots, or to at least find someone who can repair the ones he's wearing.

Miranda and Templeton continue to thread through Gastown.

We put on a good show. We stop from time to time, look at a shop or stall, check out an airship. Bend down and pretend to pick something up. But Miranda's always in sight.

Rosie's back at Fisherman's. Her job is to keep an eye on Templeton's buddies, make sure they don't follow him. She's there to keep our way clear.

Occasionally the night air brings across Miranda's laugh or an exclamation from Templeton. They seem to be having a grand old time.

Eventually, they arrive at a building, large for Gastown. Unlike most of the other buildings that are assembled from corrugated metal and old car parts and mismatched wooden panels, this one looks well-constructed with some kind of light metal walls and a flat roof.

I flash Diego my open palm and we get out of the line of sight against a nearby structure that looks abandoned. Templeton leads Miranda up to a door guarded by two men. He opens the door and lets Miranda look inside.

At this point I'm guessing Miranda doesn't have to act interested.

Templeton moves to close the door, but Miranda looks up at him, and I can tell she's pleading, begging him for a few moments inside.

For a moment there's stiffness in his body language, but as he looks at her, it fades and he pulls her against him. Then Miranda leans into him, nestling her head against his chest.

Something hot and bitter moves through me.

Templeton fishes for something in his pocket, a key I realize a moment later as he fits it to a big metal padlock, and then he's pulling Miranda through the door, closing it behind him.

"That's our cue," I say.

Diego walks out of the shelter of the building and straight toward the lab. I wait a count of two, then follow.

The two guards are tracking Diego, one stepping forward to intercept him when I step into sight with my weapon out and shoot him carefully in the neck.

As the other guard turns toward me, Diego leaps forward and grabs him, spinning him toward me. I shoot him in the neck, too.

Neither shot makes a sound. That had been Miranda's idea. When we were planning this crazy scheme and I asked how we were going to keep things quiet, she pulled out this strange-looking gun and laid it on the table.

It took me a moment to place it. "A new tranq gun?"

She nodded. "We worked a couple of them up for use on Alpha. I took it with me when I left the *Pasteur*."

It had been a good idea. No noise. No fuss. Put them down fast.

"Wait here," I tell Diego. Then I enter the lab.

Miranda is standing inside with a single light on. I don't see Templeton at first. Then I see a crumpled form at her feet.

"You did that?" I ask.

She shrugs. "He had a lot to drink. I think he slipped and fell."

Her eyes aren't on him, though. Or on me. They're on what's in the lab. Frankly it looks a lot like some of the boffin's setups. Steel tables, cobbled-together computers, beakers, microscopes. Science gear. All over the place.

"Take a look around," I say. "I'll get Diego." Which I do, and the two of us drag the bodies inside.

"Do what you need to do fast, Miranda," I say. But she's already bent over a computer screen, a sheaf of papers in her hand.

I toss Diego the fur cloak one of the guards was wearing. I swap my leather jacket for the other guard's fringed coat. "You watch these guys," I say. "If I need you, I'll knock three times on the door."

He nods back at me.

Then it's back outside, into the cold dark. You don't see the stars on Gastown. All the balloons they use to float the place block out the firmament, as my dad would say.

I feel the tension ride my body, leaving me feeling tight. Any moment now one of Templeton's buddies could walk up and check in. Or there could be a guard change. I'm glad I brought along my revolver in addition to the tranq gun.

Miranda seems to be taking ages, but then again she always seems to take a long time. This is the way we operate. I look for threats, she looks for science. She feeds on curiosity; I choke on paranoia.

Just another day on the job . . .

A shape appears off on a nearby platform. I knock three times on the door, making sure my revolver is accessible.

Diego emerges from the lab and takes up position on the other side of the door.

The shape approaches, then turns off down a different walkway.

I exhale and feel my heartbeat slow.

"I'll go get Miranda," I say, and walk into the lab.

Miranda is bent over a different table, her hair once again tucked up behind her head save for one wavy strand that threads down her face and around her glasses. As tense as I am right now, as strongly as I want to yell at her to get out. Now. So we don't get captured and killed. In spite of all that, I can't help but be captivated by her, standing here, now, doing what she does best. Think. Process. Calculate. Solve.

So, instead of yelling, I say, gently, "Miranda. Do you have what you need?"

She looks up at me, and it almost seems to take her a moment to recognize me. She nods quickly. "I think so." She tucks a few rolled-up papers inside her coat and stuffs something else in her pocket.

She walks toward me, then points down at the bodies. "What do we do about them?"

"Leave them," I say. "Nothing else to do."

"And when they wake up?"

"The alarm goes up. But hopefully by that time we'll be off of Gastown."

I hold the door open for her and we exit. As I replace the metal padlock, hoping it buys us some time, I ask Miranda, "Was it worth it?"

When she meets my eyes, I see something in them that I almost don't recognize, it's so unusual. Fear.

"I think it was," she says.

We walk off into the night.

# CHAPTER FIFTEEN

I wait at the rendezvous, and Diego and Miranda are nowhere to be found. Rosie, however, is there. "Where are they?" I ask.

She shrugs. "I thought they'd be here."

"They were supposed to lay low."

She glares at me. "Miranda said she had something to do and Diego went with her. To keep her out of trouble."

I get that familiar sinking feeling in my stomach, that worrying-about-Miranda thing.

"We don't have a lot of time," Claudia says.

"Damn." I shouldn't have spent the night on the *Valkyrie* again, I think. I should have stayed with Miranda. But I didn't. Her coldness returned after we left the lab and I couldn't bear it. So I went back to Claudia.

Claudia is now looking at me. I know that look. No mirth. Her face is a stone wall. "Ben," she says.

I know what she's going to say: we don't have time to wait around. If we miss this window, we miss everything. So I wave her off.

"What if something happened to them?" I ask out loud.

"What if something didn't and we miss our chance to get down to that plant?" Claudia says. "Not to mention this place is going to be on alert any minute now. The longer we wait, the more likely it is that we all get picked up."

It's hard to know exactly what is the most likely scenario. It's quite normal for Miranda to get something lodged in her brain and to focus on it to the exception of all else.

"I'm going with or without you," Claudia says.

She wants to see the plant. I don't really give a shit about that, but the *Cherub* . . .

Rosie meets my eyes. "Diego can take care of himself," she says. "Can Miranda?"

"Yes."

"Then let's go," Claudia says.

Maybe it's for the best, I think. Miranda only muddies things up for me.

"Then let's go," I say. Rosie doesn't protest. She must have a lot of faith in her brother. I wonder if it's time I start to put some in him as well.

We move to another section of Gastown, shadowed by large ships. "Do you see them?" Claudia asks, gesturing at their bulk.

"You mean the heavily armed gunships?" I say. "Yes, how could I miss them?" They're heavy-framed ships with weapons bristling off of them, probably bolted onto the skeleton. Ugly, but effective.

"They're ready for the run," Claudia says. "Gastown air control will suspend all incoming and outgoing flights for at least a couple of hours. During that time the transport ship will bring the supplies down to the plant and then return with the helium."

I move forward, my hands reaching for a railing, gripping it tight.

Rosie gives me the hard stare. Around us Gastown is slowly shaking to life, but her eyes are locked on me. "Are you really going to do this?"

"Yes," I say. "I came here for my ship. I'm not leaving without her. You don't have to come with me if you don't want to. If you think this is bullshit, stay. Go find Diego and Miranda."

She scowls but doesn't say anything.

"This is it," I say to them. "We go now or never." I think I'm convincing myself more than either of them. I look at Claudia. "You good with the plan?"

She shrugs. "I don't love it," she says. "But I like it."

"Everyone have their gear?" I ask.

Nods all around. Each of us is carrying some extra padding from the *Valkyrie*. We're likely to be knocked around a bit inside the drums, so some blankets and other cast-offs will help. They'll also help us to seem less hollow if anyone ends up thumping the containers around a bit.

Then there are the weapons. I take the revolver, of course, but also a long-bladed knife that Claudia gave me. I typically don't use blades or anything with that short a reach, but we're not going up against Ferals here and stealth is the magic word.

Rosie carries a worn automatic with a white grip.

Claudia insists on taking the bow. "It will fit," she says. "I measured it."

I want to grumble at her, but I can't. Again, the bow is quiet where a shotgun would be noisy.

So we tuck away our weapons, sling blankets around us, and trek over to where Claudia leads us. It's a structure constructed from what looks like some kind of beaten metal. But the edges are all secured with barbed wire. "That's where the drums are," Claudia says.

"Okay," I say. "We get in and load a couple of empties in place of the full and then we'll be transported with the others."

"As easy as that?" she says.

"Well," I say, "It might be a little harder than that."

Claudia flashes me a concerned look.

"Oh, come on. You love this."

Whether or not she does, I do. I'm not the cloak-and-dagger type, but this is the most excitement I've felt in a while. And Miranda is no longer lurking in the forefront of my mind.

"Ready?" I ask.

Claudia looks at Rosie. "Ready?"

"Ready," she says. Claudia repeats it back to me.

"Follow my lead," I say.

We've been watching the building for a little while. We've only seen one person inside.

I walk up to the door of the building and knock on it. Loudly, firmly. No stealth in that.

A man, harried-looking and perspiring, opens the door and glares at me. "What the fuck do you want?"

"I got a delivery," I say.

"What?"

"A delivery. Cloth. Linen. Textiles."

"Tex-what?"

"Textiles," I say loudly and slowly.

"Look, I don't—" he begins.

I grab his arm firmly and pull out a worn, folded piece of cardboard, trying to make it look like I'm gently escorting the man inside. Once he clears the door, I shove him all the way in. Rosie and Claudia quickly follow.

I kick the guy's leg out from under him and push him to the ground. His head bounces hard against the floor. He snarls, so I do it again and he goes out.

"What are we going to do with him?" Rosie asks.

"We can't leave him here," Claudia says. "He might wake up while we're down there. Raise an alarm. It would be best to kill him."

I wonder who this man is. He doesn't look like one of the Vikings. He could just be someone trying to get by. "I don't feel comfortable killing him. Especially while he's unconscious."

"Then what do you want to do?" Claudia asks.

I rack my brains trying to think of something. "Why don't we put him in one of these?"

"What? In the drums?"

"We can gag him," I say.

"Oh, this gets better and better all the time," Rosie says.

"There's not much else we can do about it," I say.

"Yes, there is," Claudia says. She bends down to the man and grips his nose and mouth firmly. Soon he starts to buck, but she keeps her grip firm. Then he goes limp.

"Claudia," I say.

"What? You think he's innocent? No one in this operation is. This way he can't fuck us."

"You didn't have to kill him."

She stares at me, frowning. "You want your ship back or not? Ben, you need to pick a side."

I stare back at her, my jaw set.

"If he was a Feral you wouldn't have thought twice."

"But he wasn't."

"Argue later," Rosie says. "We need to get rid of him."

"Look for a place to stash the body," Claudia says.

The building is mostly just a big storage space, but we find a small cavity in the floor that holds some boxes and a few smaller canisters. We're able to wedge the body down into it. We cover it carefully with a wooden cube that seems to exist as seating.

Claudia rustles up a crowbar and we start prying off the lids of the drums.

I can't help but think of the dead man. I couldn't do what Claudia had done. Yes, if he'd been a Feral I would have done it without compunction. Done it again and again and again. Hell, I have. But not a man. Not like that.

It makes me think of Miranda. She feels that way about the Ferals, too. That they're all people who can be saved. Humans. Just because I disagree doesn't mean I don't understand.

Still, the one attacking me wasn't unconscious. It leaves a bitter taste in my mouth.

"So," Claudia says. "Into the barrels?"

I nod.

Each of us picks a drum and lines the inside with the blankets and other padding. "How are we going to seal them up behind us?" Rosie asks.

"Well, we don't want to seal them too tightly," I say. "Or else how will we get out? Just pull it on and I'll give it a few taps." We try playing with the lids for a bit and I find a way that we can get them to stay on and still get them off again. Claudia hands out some cardboard, torn into thin strips, which gives us enough room that the lids don't seal completely.

"What about breathing?" Rosie asks.

"We poke holes in them," I say. "But keep them small and not noticeable. There's supposed to be liquid in these drums."

Eventually we all climb in. I make sure Rosie and Claudia are secure before I help seal the lids. Then I get into my own.

From here it's all waiting. Our drums stand on a pallet with wheels. We moved some of the full drums off to one side of the room. When they come for these, they'll wheel us onto the transport ship.

It's all waiting from here.

And that's something that I don't do very well.

The inside of the drum smells of chemicals, something like oil but sharper, an odor that tickles my nostrils. I try to shift into a comfortable position, but it's hard. My legs are bent up under me, and my arms don't have much room to move. I try to stretch and relax my muscles when I can, but I know that when I get out of this thing I'm going to be sore and stiff and hurt.

I try not to think about it. Instead I think about the *Cherub* and seeing her again, but my body keeps trumping my brain and bringing me back to where I am and how goddamned uncomfortable it is.

My breath sounds loud in the enclosed space and I hope it's not audible from outside. It sounds like all of Gastown can hear me.

I hate waiting.

Of course it could be worse.

Much worse.

It has been. In the past. One time in particular.

It was back when my dad was alive. At some point after Claudia had left us, off to do her own thing, tired of tagging along after a father and son duo, despite the activities she and I had got up to when my dad wasn't around.

The *Cherub* needed repairs, and Dad was working on those, but he sent me down to the ground to look for some food. I said we never separated, and that was true for scores, but he figured the *Cherub* was nearby and there was no sign of Ferals in the area.

I was supposed to stay near the ship, see what I could scrape up, if anything. More often than not, there was nothing. Maybe some berries. Maybe mushrooms. But this, like most of the stops, yielded nothing. I didn't think Dad would mind if I roamed for just a bit. Everything seemed clear.

So I did. I walked down the slope of the hill I'd climbed down to. There were some bushes farther down the slope and I figured they might have something edible on them.

I was moving quickly—no sign of danger, but then again I was on the ground—and then I slipped and fell and tumbled into a hole.

I fell through earth and roots and rocks, getting scraped and banged up by the descent, and all I could think of was holding tight to my gun. A man without a gun was an easy target, and Dad had always taught me to hold tight to mine.

Then I hit bottom and the wind blew out of me and it took a moment for me to orient myself.

The smell hit me first. The unmistakable scent of Ferals.

I fought against the rising panic inside of me. Stifled my breathing so it wouldn't give me away. It still sounded loud in my ears. Then I heard the rasping and gibbering of Feral voices. Close. Not on top of me, but very close. And there were several. How many, I couldn't tell. But more than I could take on by myself in the dark with who knew what flying around in the air. And the fall had ripped some of my coverings loose.

The thought made the panic surge again. I could be lying in Feral piss. Feral shit. All contagious. All swimming with the fucking Bug.

I started to move, slowly, tentatively. Still on my belly. Trying to figure out what was around me. Each scrape against the ground made me sure the Ferals would find me. That they would hear with their sharpened hearing. Or smell me with their sharpened smell. In a way, the grime and muck of the hole would help me in that regard.

I managed to crawl my way to a pile of dead leaves and twigs and other cast-offs that must have fallen in the same hole I had. As much as I could, I burrowed my way into it. Then I lay there, and waited.

I didn't know what else to do. If I went out with my gun blazing, the Ferals would have me in no time. I couldn't see. And they had the advantage.

Of course I didn't exactly know what I was waiting for. It's not like Dad was going to know where I went. And even if he did, what could he do without landing himself in the same predicament.

I waited and I listened. Sometimes the noises would get fainter, farther away, and yet they would sometimes return. They ran the gamut of Feral sounds—howling, yelping, barking, snuffling. Little sighs that repeated over and over.

But I waited, and I hoped, and maybe even prayed a little, that I would figure out a way out of the mess.

I don't know how much time passed. It could have been an hour. Or hours. I had no way of knowing. I just lay as still as I could, breathing as softly as I could, waiting and hoping and sweating with my fear. At one point I found myself trembling, and it was all I could do to make myself stop. All of my will was bent to keeping myself still. Otherwise I knew my teeth would chatter and that would give my position away.

Then, after some time, I heard shrieks. In the distance, then growing fainter. And then . . . silence.

I decided it was the only chance I had to make my move. I scrabbled free of the deadfall and tried to make my way out of the hole I had fallen in. But the sides gave me no purchase. I couldn't find a way to haul my weight back up it.

So I moved forward. I reached the stone of a cave wall and then kept following it, still doing my best to minimize my noise, breathing through my mouth as much as possible, my free hand on my gun, ready to bring it up and start taking out any Ferals that might come at me.

Yet none did.

Eventually I saw light and then, beyond, an opening to the outside.

I ran for it. It might not have been the smartest thing, but I couldn't help myself. I ran for the blessed light, my gun still ready in my hand, and I ran out into the light and it was the most glorious thing I could imagine.

Dead Ferals littered the ground outside the cave entrance. Nothing moved. Still, I kept my gun up and gave them a wide berth.

A shrill whistle got my attention and I looked up the hill to see my father with a rifle in his hand, looking down at me. I learned later that he had come looking for me, had seen the hole and had followed the hill down to the cave entrance. When he saw Ferals there he had started shooting from a place of cover. The nest had emptied to go after him, but he had taken them all out. It wasn't a big nest, but he'd still taken down five or six of them from his position.

I wanted to hug him when I saw him. I wanted to thank him. But the look he gave me stopped me cold. There was, of course, the ammo that had been wasted taking out the Ferals. For no good reason at all. No salvage. No food.

But even worse, I had been down in the dark in a Feral nest and he could see the places where my coverings had torn away.

He checked me over, his face serious. Amazingly, there were no cuts, no lacerations from the fall. My clothing was all that was torn, though I was badly bruised.

"You kept your mouth covered?" he said.

"Of course."

He checked my face anyway.

Then, after he was satisfied, he nodded and we headed back to the *Cherub*, both of us with guns out, scanning for any stragglers.

He didn't yell at me. He didn't have to. I knew he was angry, disappointed, and it hurt. It would've been easier if he had yelled. If he had hit me. All he did was shake his head and give me silence.

Even worse, he kept his distance for the next day or two. And I knew why. Though there were no apparent signs of infection, there was still a chance the Bug had won out. That the persistent fucker had worked its way inside of me and started the process that would turn me into one of Them.

Thankfully, I was clean. But the silence continued for at least another day beyond that.

Eventually, because it was driving me crazy, I went to him. "I'm sorry," I said yet again. "It won't happen again."

He gave me a stone face. "See that it doesn't" was all he said.

That was my Dad.

I think about him and that moment as I am forced to wait inside the drum. I think of him and realize how much I still miss him. How much I would take his stone-faced silence over losing him. How I would gladly suffer his displeasure and disappointment if it meant that he were still around. But wishes die in the Sick. They choke and drown on infected blood.

Then, after some time, I feel the drum moving and I know we're off to the transport ship.

My futile wishes go with me.

✳    ✳    ✳

There's no sense of movement as the airship we'd been loaded on takes us down to the facility. Down to the ground. I'm fairly certain they've loaded us into some cargo hold somewhere and that it would be okay if we all got out to stretch ourselves, but that's sloppy thinking. So I stay crumpled up like a piece of old paper and focus on breathing.

The smell inside the drum makes me wish it wasn't all I had to focus on.

Then, after an indeterminate amount of time, I feel actual movement, close by. The jerk of the drum as the cart is pushed off the airship. There's a moment of panic as I feel gravity pull at me and I realize we're going down a ramp. A moment of fear as I wonder what will happen if all the drums tumble to the ground. But then we're on level ground again and I exhale my held breath.

We move and then we stop, then we move again and stop again. Each time, I hope this new stop will lead to me being able to exit and stretch my legs. Each time, I can feel the disappointment as physical pain, as we move.

Then we stop for a long time.

I shove down the hope. Tamp it down.

Then there is a tapping at the top of my drum. I almost don't hear it at first I'm so focused inward. Then I recognize the pattern that Claudia drilled into us back on Gastown and I push at the top of the drum. With a creaking hollow bang, the lid comes off and Claudia is looking down at me, a lopsided smile on her face.

"Thank fucking God," I say. "My back feels like it's about to break."

"Don't be such a baby," Claudia says, pulling me up. It's no exaggeration. I feel creaky and bent beyond tolerance. Pains twang through most of my muscles and as I stretch them out, several start spasming, almost dropping me on the ground.

I grit my teeth and try to limber up as best as I can.

Claudia pulls Rosie out, though she seems to be handling herself better than me, massaging her limbs but not even grimacing in pain. I tell myself she's younger, more flexible. I'm pretty sure Miranda's complained a number of times about my rigidity.

After a few minutes of massaging and stretching, the worst of the pain seems to have subsided. That is, the fire has faded to a smoldering, steady burn. It will do.

It helps that the knowledge of where we are is actually sinking in. I'm so much closer to the *Cherub*. That is, if Claudia is right.

"Now what?" Rosie asks.

"Now we go get my ship," I say.

"Uh-uh," Claudia says. "You and Rosie get your ship. I have other plans."

I frown. "What? Where are you going?"

"I have other business." She smiles, and it's like an old leather coat, worn but comfortable. "This is what I was hired to do—investigate all of this. Now I'm here. Thank you for that."

I grab her arm gently. "You can do that with us. C'mon. It'll be like old times.

Her smiled deepens, then fades. "I can't waste this opportunity. And I can move more quietly on my own. Go. Get your ship. I know your father must be squirming in his grave."

"Claudia—"

"No. Go. Take Rosie. Do what you have to do. I'll do the same." She turns away from me, then looks over her shoulder, the smile now back on her face. "Besides," she says. "I'm not splitting the pay with you."

I shake my head, then shrug. I tell myself that Claudia's a grown woman. She's been handling herself this long. It's her choice.

"Okay," I say to Rosie. "It's just the two of us."

"Oh, joy," she says dryly.

"Try not to make too much noise," Claudia says, then she heads off down a corridor to the right.

I look at Rosie and she shrugs back at me. "I guess that means we have the one on the left."

We move. "If you see anything," I say, "signal, and try to stay hidden. If we have to . . ." I trail off. "If we have to kill anyone, put them down quickly and silently. No hesitation. If they find us here, if the alarm is sounded, we're dead. Any problems?"

She shakes her head. "I know the deal," she says. "Nothing I haven't done before."

I raise an eyebrow. "Good," I say. "Let's go."

With Rosie following me, I move down the left passage.

# CHAPTER SIXTEEN

**W**e move as lightly as we can through the corridors of the factory. The walls are largely bare—painted stone and concrete—but here and there pipes jut out from the walls or pace them like racing birds. The whole place hums and thrums with movement and power. It's a strange experience. For most of my life, power, energy, has always been so temporary. I wonder how they run it.

"I don't like this place," Rosie says. "It makes me nervous."

I want to shush her, but I nod instead. The place is eerie. We go through three twists of the corridor with no encounters and then come to an area that has three doors. One ahead and one on either side.

"Now what?" Rosie asks.

Good question, I think. Each of the doors has a window in it, and we're luckily not close enough for anyone to see us through them. "Stay down," I whisper. "I'll check it out."

I crouch low and move toward the doors. Then, being as stealthy as I can, I raise my head to peer in each door. The door to our right is occupied. I see boxes, switches, and three men milling about. All with long protective coats. I lower my head quickly and turn to the room on the left. It doesn't go anywhere but appears to be empty. There are tables and machinery, but no apparent exit.

As I look into the door ahead of us, I see that it is another corridor, or rather a continuation of the one we're in. It seems to be what we're looking for, save for the four people walking toward the door.

Walking toward us.

Crouching down below their sight level, I turn and grab Rosie and drag her into the empty room.

Correction. The room I thought was empty.

As the door shuts behind me, I see that a man stands in the room, just behind the door where I couldn't see him.

He looks up in alarm. Rosie has her weapon out, but I grab for the man and hold him tight, my hand over his mouth, my knife pressing against his side. "Don't make any noise," I hiss into his ear. I know what I told Rosie, but we can't risk a sound with people in the corridor outside. I pull him back with Rosie behind the door where we can't be seen.

"Cover the door," I tell Rosie. We're screwed if they decide to come into this room. I can't take four people with my knife.

I crane my head and wait for the dark shapes of the approaching men to come into view.

They come toward the room . . . then continue on.

I exhale loudly. Rosie nods at me. I look around for something we can use to tie up the man, think about cramming him into a closet and leaving him there. Then I reconsider.

Idiot, the voice in my head says. You need to start thinking more like Miranda. Because we're blind here in this plant and this man likely has a better idea of where things are. Right now, information is extremely valuable. If this guy can get me to the *Cherub* faster . . .

"I'm going to remove my hand from your mouth," I say into the man's ear. "But not the one with the knife at your side. You make any sound other than a whisper and I will gut you so quickly that you'll have time to see your entrails spill onto the floor before you die. Do you understand?"

He nods.

Taking a breath, I move my hand away. I hold the knife steady.

He only breathes. Then he says, "Please. I'm no one. I just work here."

"That's good," I say. "Because all we need are directions."

He's sweating and I can't stifle the urge to move my head back away from him. Away from his fluids. "We need to get to the airships moorage," I say. "You're going to tell us how to get there."

"Why?"

"Because if you don't, we're going to have to find someone else who will and we can't leave any witnesses behind."

"No," he says. "Why do you want to go to the airships?"

I look at Rosie, who shrugs back at me. "Because I'm going to get my ship back and take her out of here."

"I'll show you," the man says.

"Good," I say, feeling satisfied.

"But you have to take me with you."

I'm about to refuse, but again I reconsider. Directions aren't going to be much good down here. It's a sound idea.

"Okay. You come with. You show us the way."

"No," he says. "You have to take me out of here. Out of the plant."

"What?"

"Please. When they took this place over, they didn't allow any of us to leave. They said they needed us to run the place. But it's like a prison now. We're watched and guarded all of the time. We don't have any freedom. Please."

I stare at my boots. They're scraped up pretty badly. "Just take us to the ships and we'll see what we can do."

That's apparently enough for the man. "I can take you a back way," he says. "Over near the service tunnels. They're not very traveled. Of course we'll still have to pass through an open area, but that should be the easiest route."

It sounds like a good plan, but I know I can't trust this guy. Still, it seems worth a shot. "Let's go," I say.

"What's your name?" Rosie asks him, and I roll my eyes. We don't have time to make friends here, and he's just a means to an end. But he answers. "Atticus."

"Get moving, Atticus," I say, waving the knife at him. "And remember, you try anything and you get cut."

He swallows and then moves to a metal panel that I now see is a door. He pulls on it, using all of his weight, and with a clang it opens. Beyond I can see more pipes lining the walls and ceiling. "It's in here," Atticus says.

"You first," I say.

I follow close behind him, and Rosie trails me. She slams the metal door back into place, and it sounds so loud in the tunnel that I worry the whole complement that mans the place will come to investigate. But I take a deep breath and tell myself to calm down. The tunnel smells like dust and stone and plastic. "What do all of these do?" I ask Atticus.

"They're all for the helium production," he says. "Some of them are power, but most of them aren't."

"And you help maintain this place?"

"Yes," he says. "I worked here when Gastown first started. It was . . ." He stops and turns to look back at me. "Nothing like that had been attempted before."

"Since the Clean," I say. "I know."

"They were good to us. They needed us. I mean, it must've been hard enough to gather up the people needed to run this place. Some of the people had been working here since the Bug hit, trading helium for goods, but it wasn't in full production. Gastown changed that. But then . . ."

He doesn't have to say it. I was there when Valhalla raiders decided they wanted Gastown, and its helium, for themselves, as I've mentioned. I try not to think about it much.

"So they force you all to stay here?"

"Some try to run," Atticus says. "Those who do are usually tracked down and made an example of. Shot on sight or just . . . disappeared. I mean we're scientists. Mechanics. We can't match them. They're thugs. Well, most of them are. But if you can take me with you . . ."

"I said we'll see." I wipe some sweat from my forehead and switch the knife to my other hand. "What do you mean, most of them?"

"Most of the men who came here are just guards, here to keep us in line. But there are some other people here as well. Scientists, I think. They're different. They know what they're talking about. I think they're the ones really calling the shots."

The sinking sensation returns. Of course it would make sense that Miranda's cadre be part of the running of the plant. "Why don't you all just work together against them?" I ask.

"When they first came down here, we did," Atticus says. "We said we wouldn't work, none of us, and they wouldn't get their helium. So they took one of the techs and they killed him. Shot him in the head. Then they said they would continue to do that until we went back to work. They would pick at random, too. So there was no telling who they'd choose. They said if we weren't working anyway, it wouldn't matter if we all were dead. So . . ."

"So a few of you gave in and then the rest of you had no choice."

He bobs his head in the affirmative. "What could we do?"

I have a few thoughts, but he's right—they're scientists. While they've been working, trying to rebuild the world, others have had other priorities. They're no match for men who have been surviving, and killing to do so, for most of their lives.

Which is not to write them off. Miranda could hold her own, as recent events proved. But these people were probably outclassed in the violence department. And I couldn't look down on that. I had gambled on those smarter than myself to help bring about a better world.

We move on.

✳  ✳  ✳

After some further crawling, we arrive at another door similar to the one we came through. "This is the tricky part," Atticus says.

I feel my stomach sink. "What do you mean?"

"This door opens onto a larger room. They keep some . . . specialized machinery in there. There might be people inside."

"What kind of specialized machinery?" Rosie asks before I can.

"Um . . . that's the other thing," Atticus says. "We have to be careful."

"What the fuck is going on, Atticus?" I ask.

He turns to look at me and licks his cracked lips. "They keep explosives in there."

"What?"

"A lot of them."

"Why?"

"They say some of them are for construction but . . . I think they're a safeguard," Atticus says. "There's even supposed to be something really big in there. I haven't actually seen it up close. I didn't want to. But I talked to some of the others about it. They figure that if anyone were to try to take this place, they would set it off and take the plant with it."

"That's insane," Rosie says.

"They are," I respond. "Okay, we avoid anything that looks like a bomb. Atticus, you go first. See if anyone is there, make up some excuse if you need to. But be aware that if you try to rabbit, I will make sure I slit your throat. Even if there's an army on the other side, I will kill you with my dying breath."

"I want to get out of here, I promise," Atticus says, and I hear the fear in his voice. "You get me out of here and I'll take you to your ship."

"You take me to my ship."

Atticus's hand curls into a fist, and for a second I think he's going to take a swing at me. Then he squeezes his eyes closed and says, "Okay. I'll do it. Just . . . please consider."

Atticus opens the door to the next room and, on a whim, before I can think twice about it, I crawl out after him. He looks back at me, startled, but I nod and keep my face straight as he turns back to the room.

Rosie stays in the access corridor.

I scan the room and see only two people. One is thin and balding, and by his dress seems like he might be working there. The other one is from Gastown. I can tell by the furs he's wearing and the two-foot-long machete at his hip. Only one guard. I relax some of the tension out of my shoulders.

Both approach us, but only one of them has his fingers near the handle of his weapon. "What are you doing here?" the thin man says.

Atticus scratches his head. "We need to get to the shipyard. I thought I'd take a shortcut."

The Gastown man's eyes are narrowed, discerning.

"This area needs to be kept clear," Thin Man says. His eyes wander over to me, then down to my knife, and then back to Atticus. I think he takes me for a Gastown punk.

"Sorry," Atticus says.

I shake my head. "I told you," I say.

"Okay, okay," Atticus says. "Since we're here, can we just cross over to the access corridor? I'm needed in the shipyard and I'm already running late."

"Okay," Thin Man says. "Just be quick about it."

We both nod and move toward the far end of the cavern. I try to catch a look at the equipment. There are large stacks of machinery for unknown purposes. Cranes, scaffolding, and carts as well. And then I catch sight of the large box near the center of the room and the writing on its side.

I'd never seen one before, but Dad talked about them when I was younger. And you'd sometimes hear mention of them in tales from when the Bug first hit. A Firestorm bomb. A tool the government never got the opportunity to employ the way they wanted to.

When the Bug started to spread, they needed a way to contain it. The Firestorm was their answer. A nuke wouldn't make sense—the radiation would be impossible to contain and the blasted area would be contaminated. A Firestorm used a combination of high-yield explosives and incendiaries to basically scour the area. They had apparently planned on using them in infected areas, burning any Ferals (and innocents) to a crisp, sterilizing the land.

Seeing one, here, makes me stop and start to tremble.

The Gastown thug sees me falter, realizes something is up, and I see him in my peripheral vision coming toward me. I whirl around, the knife in my hand and slashing through the air. It slices him in the throat, catching and tearing it open in a spray of red that I actually don't cringe from.

He goes down, gurgling, the machete in his hand clattering to the floor, and the other man cries out at the violence. Atticus grabs him from behind and pushes him toward me.

"What's that for?" I hold the knife out to the man, blood still fresh on the blade, and point at the box in the center of the room. The massive fucking bomb.

"Don't, please," Thin Man says.

"Tell me," I insist.

"It's a Firestorm bomb," he says.

Atticus exhales loudly.

"I know that. What's it here for?"

Thin Man looks at his feet. "It's insurance for Gastown," he says. "If someone attacks and tries to take it . . ."

"They'll make sure no one else has access to it."

Thin Man nods.

"Where did they get it from?" I ask.

"A raid, I don't know. I think one of the Brains knew where it was. We didn't exactly have a conversation about it."

"Brains?"

"Yeah. The smart ones. The Brains. The others are just the Muscle."

"And you're in charge of this bomb?" I ask.

Thin Man shrugs. "I know my explosives. That's why they brought me in. I know how they work."

I shake my head. This man is the flip side to what Miranda and her friends are doing. He's a man of Science, keeping the tradition alive, but not to help anyone, not to improve anything. For himself. For a position, for power, for survival—for something. But only for himself.

Like you, Ben, the voice in my head says.

I pull back my arm and hit him in the face as hard as I can. Then I do it again. And again. Atticus is still holding him up so he doesn't fall. When I'm done expelling my rage, his head sags on his chest, blood leaking from his mouth and lips. I quickly wipe my gloves on his shirt. "Lay him down somewhere over there," I say. "See if you can tie him down somehow."

Atticus goes off to take care of it and I go back to grab Rosie.

Her eyebrows raise as she steps out into the room. "Did it all go okay?"

"Mostly." I point to the bomb. "That right there is a Firestorm. The big boom."

Her eyes widen. "That thing is massive." She shakes her head. "They can't really think—"

"They don't think," I say. "They just hunger and they take. They're no better than the Ferals."

Atticus returns. "He's tied up. I found some cables." I stare hard at him. "You don't trust me?" he asks.

"Would you in my position?"

"Look, I'm in this now. With you. Do you think I can still stay here even if I wanted to?"

"You didn't kill anyone. And this was all under duress." I think for a moment, then look at Rosie. "Check to make sure he's secure."

She runs off to the man.

Atticus hangs his head.

"Nothing personal," I say. "We just can't afford surprises."

Rosie returns a few moments later and gives me a nod. "He looks secure. Pretty beat-up, too."

"He looked at me funny," I say.

She gives me a hard look but then smirks. "Now can we go and get your ship?"

I look around the room. In addition to the Firestorm there are boxes and crates of all kinds. There's probably dynamite, C-4, explosives of every variety. They must've raided a military facility.

"What?" Rosie asks.

"I'm wondering if we should figure out a way to set all this off."

She looks at me like I'm crazy. It's not that different from how she usually looks at me. "You want to blow this place?"

I shrug. "Valhalla controls the helium now. We blow this place and they don't have that anymore. They lose something big."

Rosie nods her head at Atticus. "There are innocent people here."

"You heard him," I say. "They're prisoners. Some of them might even get out as a result."

"What about Claudia?" she asks.

And she's right. I have no idea where Claudia is. How this would affect her plans. But it's still hard to walk away.

"These people almost killed you and your brother," I say, meeting her eyes.

"Yes," she says. "They did. And I want to hurt them, too, but this isn't the way. There are too many unknowns."

I close my eyes and grit my teeth. Inhale. Exhale. You're not here to save the world, Ben. You're here for your ship.

When I open my eyes, I nod. "I'm still taking a few of the smaller explosives, though," I say. I grab some of the C-4 and a few detonators. You never know when this stuff will come in handy. Then I turn to my companions.

"Let's go," I say.

My ship awaits.

# CHAPTER SEVENTEEN

We continue on down the next stretch of access corridor. I try to put the Firestorm out of my mind, but I can't. It's bad enough that Valhalla has become more aggressive. That they've enlisted scientists in their cause. But to have that kind of firepower. . . . With that they could take out a whole city. Not just Gastown. Tamoanchan. All those people at risk. Diego. Rosie. Rabbi Cohen. Sergei. Miranda.

Someone needs to stop them.

But not you, Ben. Right?

Fucking voice.

"How far ahead is it now?" I ask Atticus.

"After the end of this passage we have to cross another corridor." He mops at his neck with a handkerchief. "After that I think it's just one last service tunnel and then that should lead us directly to the moorage."

"You think?"

"I don't come this way very much. I'm not really sure what they do over here."

"But you still know where we're going?"

Atticus nods.

"Good," I say. "I'm anxious to get the *Cherub* and get out of here."

"Me, too," Rosie says.

We reach the end of the access corridor and stop at the metal door. Just like in foraging, this is the tricky part. Is there anything—or anyone, in this case—on the other side? If so, which direction? Are they armed? How many are there?

I place my hand flat against the metal surface, inhale, then open it.

As Atticus said, it opens onto a corridor running perpendicular to ours. It's wider than the previous corridors. It goes down some distance to our left, but to our right it leads to a set of double doors, heavy dark steel with bars across them.

The corridor seems empty, so I step into it, my revolver out but down by my side so it won't seem obvious to anyone who might happen by. Then I hold the door open for Rosie and Atticus to come out.

Atticus steps out and wipes his neck again with his handkerchief. "We have to move down to the left," he says. But his eyes stray to the heavy metal doors.

"What's over there?" I ask.

"I don't know." He shakes his head. "They don't usually lock things up so well around here."

I wonder what's beyond the doors, but I push the thought aside. I'm here to get the *Cherub* and get out.

But Rosie moves toward the door. "What are you doing?" I hiss. "We need to keep moving before someone finds us."

Rosie shakes her head. "It looks like there's something important behind here."

"Then it's likely to be guarded," I say.

She turns to face me. "You were the one who said we could get intelligence down here. I think it's worth a look."

I look to Atticus, but I can tell he's interested too. "Give me a hand with these," Rosie says, and together she and Atticus begin sliding aside the bars.

"Goddamnit," I say. But I move closer to them, ready to shoot if anything comes out of the door.

Rosie pulls open the door and a smell comes out. Death. Rotting meat. Shit. I raise the revolver and push past them into the room.

It's a large room, the largest I've seen in this place, and I come to a railing that looks down over the rest of the room, which is something like two floors down. In the center of the room is a pit, dug out of the floor, and in the middle of the pit, pacing, is the largest Feral I've ever seen.

This one's female, long greasy hair trailing down its back, no clothes to speak of. Grime or dirt or worse darkening its skin. But as it moves I can see the muscles bunch and ripple. Its shoulders, arms, legs, everything are huge. It's terrifying.

Also in the pit, pushed to one side, are the remains of something that was once human. I don't know if it was a Feral or not. I can't even tell whether it was male or female from what's left of it.

I tense up. From where I am, there's no real chance of infection. I'm a floor up from the pit, and the floor goes down a ways. The Feral couldn't climb up. Any fluids it could sling would fall far short of reaching me, but I can't seem to help myself.

"What are they doing keeping a Feral in here?" I say to Atticus, who along with Rosie has joined me.

"I . . . don't know," Atticus says.

I raise my revolver and try to figure out if I can hit the thing from here. Whatever it's being used for can't be good. Before I can fire, though, I hear a sound from below us and I pull Atticus and Rosie down. But while the metal walkway is not see-through from the bottom, it is from the side.

"Move!" someone barks.

"No," another voice, quavering, answers.

Then three people come into view. The one in front is a man, face uncovered, balding with a fringe of copper hair. Pushing him ahead is a Valhalla thug with an animal-skin coat and a rifle. Behind both of them is a woman with a black cap.

Fuck, I think, and pull Rosie and Atticus back. But the metal walkway starts clanging under our movement and so I stop.

The man below is still chanting "no" over and over again as he is pushed forward.

"Wilson," I hear Atticus say. One of his coworkers, perhaps?

When Wilson nears the edge of the pit he starts to scream. A high keening sound that reverberates through the room.

"You shouldn't have run," the woman in the back cap says, loud enough that the sound carries to where we are.

Then the thug pushes Wilson down into the pit.

Wilson's screams are joined by a lower-pitched howling as the Feral within the pit recognizes fresh prey. Then the screaming intensifies, joined by grunts and wet, tearing sounds.

I grip the edge of the railing tight. I've heard sounds like that before, but it never gets easier. I want to rise up and shoot both figures in the pit, but that will give us away and there's not much I can do for Wilson anyway. So I force myself to be still.

Atticus is not nearly as successful in his self-control. I look up to see him standing, screaming, his face red, the tendons in his neck like rigid cable.

The two below turn to him as one and begin firing before I can do anything.

The moment becomes chaos and disjointed thoughts. Almost immediately Atticus falls back to the floor of the walkway. His throat is spurting blood and one of his cheeks is gone.

The bullets are still flying.

I grab for Rosie, and together we scrabble as fast as we can, as low to the ground as possible, toward the door. Hoping the sound of the bullets will cover our own sound. Hoping they didn't see us.

The air of the corridor is a welcome change from the stink of the room with the pit. Rosie and I get to our feet and run down the corridor.

"Where do we go?" Rosie says.

"Look for another access tunnel," I say.

Any moment now, the thug and the woman in the black cap could burst out of the room behind us. There are doors in this corridor, but we have no time to stop and investigate them. Though we may need to take cover in one.

Fuck, I think. Fuck fuck fuck. I can't banish the image of Atticus's eyes as he fell back to the walkway.

"Here!" Rosie points to another metal door in the corridor side. This one has been painted white. As we both work at it to pull it open, I look at the doors opposite me. These have small glass windows cut into them reinforced with metal links. Through the windows I see cages. At least a row of them. And in the cages, naked figures. I go cold because I'm sure these are Ferals. They look cleaner, better-groomed, but something about them, something in their posture, screams at me that they're no longer human.

Then Rosie pulls me into the access corridor, pushing me in front of her. She pulls the door closed with a loud clang and we move, knowing we have to keep going, knowing they could be right behind us. "What are they doing?" I gasp.

"I don't know," Rosie says. I can hear the horror in her voice.

Ferals. They're playing with Ferals.

They need to be stopped, I think.

We run away as fast as we can.

"Diego said you were brother and sister," I say, wanting to distract myself. Wanting to push through the numb shroud that seems to have enveloped me.

"Half," she says. "We had the same father."

"Wow," I say.

"What?"

"He convinced not just one woman but two to have his children."

She smiles for a moment, though there's not much joy in it. "That was my father. He had a way of making the people around him feel safe. I guess our mothers believed it enough to chance having us."

"Who's older?" I ask.

"Diego. Dad met his mother first. He was a zep, too. The story goes that he swooped in, took her up into the sky. It must have seemed a lot safer that way."

"What happened?" I ask.

"She got infected," Rosie says. "No one seems to know how. Probably while they were bartering. Dad . . . he had to put her down."

"Oh," I say. "I'm sorry."

"Dad took care of Diego after that, but it was hard by himself, so I think he looked for someone to help him out and then he met my mother. Of course Dad being the romantic, he fell in love with her."

"Are they still around?" I ask.

"No," she says. "Mom died when I was a kid, she caught something—not the Bug, but just a normal human disease. She got real weak. We tried to give her antibiotics, but they didn't help. After that, we kept on with Dad, but then his mind started to go. He would forget where he was, what he was doing. He'd forget about getting food. That's when Diego started taking control. We kept Dad with us for a while, but that proved to be a mistake. One day while we were out looking for food, he left without us."

"How did you survive?" I ask.

"Diego," she says. "He found a place for us to take shelter, guarded it from Ferals. At least we'd found some food. We stayed there for a few days, then started making our way back west."

"On foot?"

She nodded. "That was when Diego started teaching me how to handle a gun, and a knife. How to kill and skin animals. How to cook them. It helped that we were young. We could climb trees and squeeze into small spaces."

"How old were you?"

She shrugs. "I don't know. Maybe ten years old? Eventually we found a settlement, did some work there. We took work on a freight airship helping to find salvage. Worked that way for a while. That's how we got the *Osprey*."

"You stole it?" I ask.

"No. We bought it. The previous owner wanted to upgrade, so he sold it to us."

They earned their ship.

I stop for a moment. Rosie looks at me questioningly.

"Why are you here?"

"You brought me here," she says.

"No," I say. "You had your chance to stay up on Gastown. You chose to come down here with me. Why?"

She looks down at her boots. Then back at me. "I wanted to keep an eye on you."

"You didn't trust me?"

"Do you think that I would after you fucked Diego?"

"I didn't mean to do that."

Rosie shakes her head. "I don't care. He's my brother. I have his back. And you fucked him good and proper. He was on his way to being a Council member. That was all he ever wanted. He used to dream about being part of a real settlement, helping to take care of other people. And your Feral sabotaged all of that."

"If I had known—"

"What?" Rosie says. "You would have done things differently? Don't shit a shitter, Ben. You do what you need to do to get by, same as plenty of others."

The words sting.

"I didn't know what would happen to Diego."

"But you really didn't care. I've watched you. I know how you feel about your ship. How you feel about Miranda. You would sell me and Diego out in a second if it would help you save either one of them."

"That's not true," I say. But I instantly wonder.

"Whatever."

"So you're here to watch me?"

"Yes." Her hands are on her hips. "Diego somehow still thinks you have some value. Despite being burned by you he still signed up again. He's a good man, but he's too trusting. So it's up to me to watch you. Make sure you don't fuck him again. Make sure that you do what you say you're going to do. And if not, if you're about to fuck us, fuck Tamoanchan, then it's up to me to put a bullet in your head."

Her eyes are hard. Unyielding. I'm the first one to look away.

"I understand," I say.

She shrugs. "I don't need you to. But if it makes you feel better."

As I continue on, she says, "There is one other thing."

I turn back to her. "Oh?"

"Whether or not you believe what you told Diego, about Gastown one day coming for Tamoanchan, I do. It's only a matter of time. And the more we know, the better off we'll be. So I came to Gastown. And I came here. And if I can find a place to hit them, to make them weak, I will."

I believe her.

We move on through the corridor.

*　　*　　*

We reach the end of the passage and I spare a look back for Rosie. Despite what she told me earlier, she seems ready and gives me a nod, her hand curled around her automatic.

I open the door and see the airfield. Above us, zeppelins, blimps, dirigibles of all sizes float, moored to the ground by tethering cables. And there, like the sweetest sight I've ever seen, is the *Cherub*. All I can see are her tail fins and her rear, but I know her better than almost anything in this world and something inside me that I didn't even know was crawling stands up at the thought of flying her once again.

Of course we have to get to the ship first.

I turn to Rosie. "I'm going to try to get to the ship. Stay here." I think of telling her to keep an eye on me, but it seems redundant.

Rosie shakes her head, her face tight. "I should go with you."

"No. I'd feel more comfortable with you covering me from here. If we're both out in the open and they catch us, we'll go down quickly. If you hang back here, well, I'm hoping that will be a lot harder."

She scowls but doesn't argue.

"If it goes wrong. If they take me down." I look at the *Cherub*. "Find a way to get back to Tamoanchan. Steal one of these ships. And tell Miranda and Diego I'm sorry."

There's a lot more I would want to tell Miranda, but . . . there's not time for that now. Sorry will do. I'm feeling now that I have a lot to be remorseful for.

"And if they do get me," I say. "Make sure you get them back."

She shakes her head. "Don't get all sentimental on me. Just go," she says. "I'll watch your back." She pulls her pistol out of its holster and holds it down by her side."

"Fair enough," I say.

She looks me hard in the face. "You really love that ship, don't you?"

"Yes," I say. Because what else can I say. "The ship is all I have. You have your brother. You have Tamoanchan. I have the *Cherub*. She's the only thing that's ever made me feel safe. The only thing that's ever made me feel good about myself."

I say those things, and most of them are true. But I realize as I'm saying them that it's not entirely true. Miranda makes me feel good about myself. But she's back on Gastown.

Rosie nods. "Go get her."

To my surprise, I only see one guard on the airfield. Then again, what do they need to guard against? The plant is well hidden, the location protected. All they're really worried about, I suppose, is some boffin getting antsy and trying to make a break for it. But they're already broken, and so one man with a rifle seems to be all that they need. And if he fires, I'm sure others will start running.

Knowing Claudia, she would take the stealthy approach. Approach the guard from a distance. Maybe just shoot an arrow through his throat and walk past him as the body was still twitching.

I walk up to the man calmly. Confidently. The fact that I can see the *Cherub* gives me some of that confidence. The rest I fake.

"What are you doing here?" the guard says. He's unshaven, fair-skinned, wearing a wool cap down low on his head. He unslings the rifle that's strapped to his back. His eyes narrow.

"I got a report that one of the scientists saw something in the utility tunnels."

"What kind of something?" he says.

"He thinks it's a Feral."

The guard's eyes widen, and I can see his expression shift as a number of questions flit through his mind. But the one thing that must be at the forefront is the possibility of a Feral being there.

"Look, just help me check it out," I say. "It's probably just a rat or something, but, well, you know protocol."

He looks at me questioningly. "Look," I say. "I'm working inside with Kressel. You know, the skinny bomb guy? And he stopped working when he heard it and I just want to at least show that it's fine. That we're airtight."

The man relaxes a slight bit. "Did you tell Boggs?"

I sigh. "You, too? Look, come with me and we'll tell Boggs together."

He looks back at the field. "But . . ."

"Two minutes. In the access corridor. This way I can say you were there."

He starts moving with me back to the compound, and then I grab him around the throat to take him down.

Only he's holding his rifle in a strange way, up high near his neck, and it blocks my arm. He elbows me in the chest and spins away.

"Fuck," I gasp as he starts to raise the rifle. I bat it to one side, but he recovers quickly, chopping at my face. He catches my neck instead and I can't help reaching up to grab it.

Then I see a blur racing toward us and I recognize it as Rosie.

I kick at the man's legs, but he skirts back away from me.

But a few steps closer to Rosie.

He raises the rifle.

Rosie tackles him with all the force of her momentum, and the two of them go flying to the ground. The rifle spins away on the ground.

It seems that they're both on their feet in an instant. The man clearly knows how to fight, even without a weapon.

But so, apparently, does Rosie.

The guard aims a kick at her head, but she blocks and kicks him in the groin. Hard, from the look on the man's face. Then they're attacking each other so quickly I can't track their movements. Throwing arms and legs, fists and feet, against each other.

I scurry to the rifle and grab it, getting to my feet.

It's not a time for gunshots, though.

I move closer. Wait for Rosie to aim a vicious kick at the man's mid-section. He pulls back. And I slam the butt of the rifle hard into the back of his head.

He crumples to the ground. I smack him again with the rifle butt, then I give him another kick just to make sure he's down.

"Thanks," I say, massaging my neck.

Rosie smiles. "Wouldn't want to lose my ride out of here."

Together we drag the guard back to the access tunnel and drop him inside to keep him out of the way.

Then I run off toward the *Cherub*.

# CHAPTER EIGHTEEN

They keep the *Cherub* in the air, opting to use the ladder rather than bring it to the ground. I climb that ladder up to my airship, and it's like coming home. Each rung on the thing is familiar to me. I wonder how many times my fingers have curled around them, how many times my boots have pressed against them.

I push through the hatch and up into the gondola. The smell of it fills my nostrils. A lived-in smell that probably wouldn't appeal to many other people, but it's like the smell of your father. Even down to the undercurrent of sweat.

I'm smiling, enjoying being back home, when I realize I'm not alone. Music is playing on the phonograph. My music. And I catch a whiff of something smoking. People have found a lot to smoke in the Sick, but cannabis is the most common. This, though, smells like tobacco smoke. I find that smell even worse.

Someone else is in my fucking ship. Like that story, Goldilocks. Sleeping in my fucking bed.

My joy turns to anger. I pull the knife from my belt.

He's standing at my console. Moving slightly to the music. Smoke curls around his head.

He doesn't hear me with all the noise.

I think about sneaking up behind him, knifing him in the kidney, or cutting his throat. And I want to do this. I want to punish this man who's had the nerve to invade my home. He might even be the one who stole it. But . . .

But I hear Miranda's voice in my head. She's telling me to think. And I do. Instead, I stride up to him, grab his arm with one hand, his head with the other, and swing him down, as hard as I can, into the console's edge, far enough away from the instrumentation.

He's off-balance, from his dancing or what he's smoking or both, and he goes down. Hard.

I feel the impact move back into me as he crashes against a bank of the *Cherub*'s controls. Then, just to be sure, I do it again.

He collapses to the ground.

The *Cherub* is mine again.

I give her a once-over, checking the controls, checking the rooms. Checking my things.

The controls are all in order. Everything else is a fucking mess. A lot of my gear is missing. The food, the water, all my supplies are gone. My sleeping mat looks used—I'll probably have to burn it. But like I said before, the Sick has taught me that possessions are temporary. The *Cherub* is okay, though, and that's all I care about.

I find some rope in my utility closet. At least my collection of junk is still there. I bind the man up tightly and stuff some rags into his mouth.

Now that I'm there, I don't want to leave. I want to fly away. And as soon as Rosie climbs aboard I will.

Where is she?

I look down at the airfield but don't see her. What the hell happened?

With a sinking feeling in my stomach, I return to Goldilocks and take his red scarf and red gloves. I trade mine for his, then descend down the ladder back down to the airfield.

She seems to have disappeared.

I stand there for a moment with my hand on the handle of the revolver, scanning for some sign of her. Should I go back to look?

Then she appears from the direction of the access tunnel and trots over to me. "What happened?" I ask.

"I thought I heard something," she says. "I wanted to check out the tunnel."

"Clear?"

"Except for the guy we dumped in it."

"Okay, let's go then."

I push her in front of me and she climbs up the ladder. I stay down, the revolver out, making sure I keep her covered. All of me wants to get back into the *Cherub* now that I'm here, but we're still in the open and someone has to keep an eye out. I see her boots near the gondola door and then she's in. I'm about to follow her, my hand on a rung, when I hear the gunshot.

Before I know what's happening, I'm hitting the ground, and my face rasps against the asphalt. Pain sears through my chest and I shudder on the ground. I can't move. I can't think. It takes a moment for things to make sense.

Gunshot.

I've been shot before. Several times, in fact. But this time it keeps me down. I try to roll over and push myself up, but my body refuses to obey.

And I know the shooter is coming toward me.

And I know he's going to finish the job.

And I know the *Cherub* is hanging just over me. So close. But far enough away. I still can't move.

That changes as the shooter rolls me over with his boot. I can see the *Cherub* for a minute above me, and then I'm staring up at his face. Or rather her face, I correct. The woman wears a black military cap and has a large pistol aimed at me. She wants me to see her shooting me. A smile crosses her face.

I look at the *Cherub*. If I'm going to die, I want to die looking at her.

But I can't help thinking about Miranda. I never . . .

A gunshot echoes across the space, but it sounds so much smaller than I'm expecting. So much farther.

The woman and her gun disappear. I look back to the *Cherub* and see Rosie on the rope ladder firing down at the woman.

But Black Cap isn't hit and she fires back up at the *Cherub*. At Rosie. Sending her scrambling for cover.

I tell myself to grab the revolver. Shoot her now. But my hand doesn't work.

Black Cap is good. She snaps off a barrage of shots and then smoothly draws a second weapon, bringing it to bear.

A shot catches Rosie, and I hear her scream and fall back.

Grab your gun, I yell at myself. Shoot her.

Black Cap smiles again and looks at me, and I know this time the bullet's coming.

I swear I see her arm tensing.

Then something long and sharp punches through her throat. It takes me a moment to place the shape with it covered in blood.

An arrow.

A second thuds into her shoulder. A third punches right through her midsection.

Claudia.

Then she's there, running, her hair streaming, the bow in her hand.

"Get up," she says, throwing her free arm around me and helping me to my feet.

"Can you climb?" she asks.

"I don't think so," I say. My arm still doesn't want to obey and I definitely need both of those for the ladder.

"Damn it." I know that tone, I think. It's the one she uses when she's really worried. When was the last time I heard that? She slaps my face gently. "Ben. Stay with me. I'm going up to the *Cherub*. I'm going to bring her down. We'll get you on that way."

"Good idea," I mumble.

She pulls my revolver from its holster and places it in the hand that I can actually feel. "If anyone else appears, try to shoot them."

Then she's scrambling up the ladder, the bow now strapped to her back.

The airfield starts spinning around me and I think it might be a good idea to lower myself to the ground.

It feels like half of my body has been switched off. Everything's off-kilter. Out of balance.

Any moment now, I think, an alarm is going to go off. Or the guard is going to be found.

I feel as good as done.

I hear the *Cherub*'s engines above me and I look up to see her descending. Claudia bringing my baby to me.

She touches down and I begin crawling toward her, dragging my body over the ground. It's the first time I see the blood. On my arm and then on the ground. Rosie lowers the cargo bay door and comes to get me, helping me up to my feet. She's bloody, too. The movement sends pain screaming through my body. I grunt and black out for a few seconds. But I fight my way back.

"C'mon," Rosie says. "Those gunshots probably roused someone. We need to get out of here before the whole place is on alert."

We move toward the ramp and I'm almost crushed beneath the pain. The world spins around me. I try to focus on Rosie, my arm around her shoulder, my weight leaning against her. Did I come so far, find my way to the *Cherub* only to die in her cargo bay? I can feel myself withering with every step.

I close my eyes, and my fingers find the hard shape of the Star of David underneath my shirt. I think about saying something to God but then see that for the bullshit it is. I stopped believing in God a long time ago. I think of my father, though, and all he did for me. All he did to the *Cherub*. His ship.

My ship, I think, as I grip the Star. My foot hits the ramp and I make my way into the cargo bay. The *Cherub* is mine again.

The *Cherub*'s scent is all around me, the machine smell of the bay. Rosie practically drags me inside and closes the ramp behind us.

She lowers me to the ground. She bends over me, checking the gunshot. I can't even tell where it hurts. The pain is everywhere. Her face swims in my vision. My eyes roll and come to rest on my old inflatable yellow raft. The one I found and decided to keep for emergencies. Somehow that being there makes me feel better.

She moves me some more. I think she might be talking, but the words are all slippery and I can't hold on to them. But then we're in the gondola and Claudia's there.

"How is he?"

Words with shapes but no meaning.

"I'm worried about him losing too much blood."

Blood, I think. It's all about blood. Alpha's blood. My blood.

"Don't give me Alpha's blood," I say.

"What was that?"

"He's delirious. Help me find the medical supplies."

I've had enough of blood, I think. Fill me up with fuel and let me fly.

Then something bites me. A moment later I gasp and the loose weave of reality shrinks and tightens around me. I'm on the *Cherub*. Claudia is standing over me with a syringe. I recognize it as my Juice, zep parlance for a potent mix of painkillers and stimulants. I sit up, coming back to myself.

"What happened?" I ask.

"You got shot," Claudia says. "I saved you. And then I gave you some Juice."

I turn to Rosie. "You got shot, too."

"I'm okay," she says, but blood stains the sleeve of her jacket. "It just tagged me. Went right by me."

"Good," I say.

"Yours, however, is still in there," Rosie says. "Bitch got you in the chest."

"It'll keep," I say. "Help me up."

"You shouldn't move," Claudia says.

"I need to fly."

"I can fly the *Cherub*," Claudia says.

I give her a hard look. "No."

She steps back from the console.

"Now help me up."

They both help me to the console. I see that the man on my ship, my Goldilocks, is still unconscious. Claudia and Rosie push me against the console much gentler than I did for him.

Claudia's already retracted the anchor. Only one of my arms is working, but I know the *Cherub* well enough to work her even like this. Still, I give the others some instructions. The engines warm up. My girl's full of power; her solar panels have soaked up the sun while she's been resting.

I don't even feel my wound as much and I run my hands over the *Cherub*'s controls like an old lover. I try to ignore the bloodstains my hands leave. I can hear her engines and I know that Sergei's fuel is still inside of her. And that gives me even a little more strength.

Then I push her, looking for nothing from her but speed. And I pull away from the airfield and up into the air.

Back to the air. Back to freedom. Something, like the awe of God, washes over me.

"Look for any pursuit," I say to Rosie.

But it's not pursuit I need to be worried about. Because as we break through the cloud cover, I see it. The Gastown gunship.

Coming straight for us.

For a moment I think about making a break for it, trying to outrun the gunship, but that would certainly draw their attention and I'm not sure I can make it in the condition I'm in.

Instead I shuffle over to the Gastown man on the floor and drag him up with my good arm. Pain streaks across my chest, but the Juice is already kicking in and I feel it like the pain is reaching me from underwater.

I push him to the console and make sure he can see the gunship in front of us. "See that? That thing's going to splatter us all over the sky unless you talk them out of it. If you don't, we're all going down. So, you have a choice. Talk to them, get us through, and I promise on my ship, on the one important thing that's left to me, that I will drop you somewhere, unharmed. But if I yank this rag from your mouth and you fuck me, I will cut your throat, just enough that you can watch us get shredded to pieces. Do you understand?"

The man's eyes are wide and he doesn't look happy, but he nods.

"Is this a good idea?" Rosie asks.

"If he doesn't do it, he's as dead as we are. They're not going to take prisoners. And I'm not letting them take this ship."

I pull the rag from the man's mouth and he spits and coughs. "What frequency?" I ask.

He tries to speak, but the words don't come out. Then he swallows and rasps, "Seventy-two point five." I dial the radio to the number.

I hold the knife close to his throat. "You're on," I say.

He moves to the radio. "Reaver, this is Hernandez. I'm returning to Gastown to pick up some supplies," he says.

"Passcode?" a voice crackles over the radio.

"Leviathan," Hernandez says.

"Proceed," comes the reply. And I exhale the breath I've been holding. I look at Hernandez.

"Copy," he says. Then I flip off the radio and let my body relax. I put the knife on the console.

"Where are you going to put me?" he says.

"Don't worry," I say. "I'll honor my word. Just keep your mouth shut and you'll be safely on your way soon."

Rosie raises her eyebrows at me, but I shrug and return to the controls.

"That Juice isn't going to last long," Claudia says.

"Long enough to get us back to Gastown."

"Are you sure it's wise to go back there?" she says.

"Diego and Miranda are there." A streak of pain shoots through me. "And so is the *Valkyrie*."

Rosie looks pointedly at Hernandez. I just used names in front of him.

"It's okay," I say. "We're getting them and then getting out."

"Good," Rosie says.

I push the *Cherub* as fast as she'll go back to Gastown. I send Rosie to see what she can find still left in the cargo bay, and Claudia helps out with the controls. Which is a gift because I'm working with only one arm.

"You're pushing yourself too much," Claudia says.

"I'm fine."

"Let me look at the wound again," she says.

She lifts my jacket away and pulls me into the light.

It's then that Hernandez makes his move. Claudia pushes me out of the way as he comes at us with the knife I left on the console.

I fall to the ground but scramble back up to my feet to see her grappling with him. But he's bigger and he's stronger and the knife is moving closer to her.

And for a moment, I think of Miranda and what happened back at the school.

Then my hand is pulling out the revolver. I lift it and pull the trigger.

The sound fills the space and I realize it's the first time I've fired a weapon in the *Cherub*.

The bullet punches a hole through his chest and out the gondola's window, spraying blood against now spidered glass. Hernandez slumps to the ground.

"I wasn't lying," I say. "I would have let you go."

Then his eyes go blank and he slides down to the floor.

Claudia is breathing hard. "Thanks," she says.

"Likewise."

She helps me up, back to the controls, with Hernandez's body still at my feet, and we push for Gastown.

I'm already feeling the wound getting to me, the Juice wearing off, as Gastown comes into view. The multicolored balloons up in the rigging seem to blend together as I bring the *Cherub* in.

"So that's it?" Claudia asks. "Grab Miranda and Diego and go?"

"That's the plan."

"Why don't you come with me?" Claudia says. "They can all go back to wherever they're going and we can go . . . elsewhere. I could really use your help with this latest job."

I'm touched. And it's a good offer. Working with Claudia again, falling back into that old lifestyle, would be so easy. And so comfortable. And she seems to be doing good work.

I place my good hand on her face. "That sounds really great. It does. But . . ."

"But you're not going to." She pulls away from me.

"I can't," I say. "I know you're working against Gastown in your own way, but . . . I need to stick with the boffins."

"Need to?"

"Yes," I say. "I've been fighting it, I know. But they are the one bit of hope I've discovered left on this earth and I need that. It's not enough to just survive anymore. Not with Gastown. Not with everything going on. I need more."

She gives me a sad smile.

"I'm sick of all the death," I say. "I'm sick of not being able to save anyone. Claudia, I want to be able to save someone."

She grabs my hand and squeezes. "Then let's go get your friends."

✳    ✳    ✳

All three of us are tense as we pull in toward Gastown. To them this is now a Gastown ship—the *Cherub* is even now flying her colors—and they'll be wondering what I'm doing back.

I flip on the radio, still at the channel Hernandez had left it on, and I repeat the same passcode that he had given the gunship. If it doesn't work, the considerable guns on Gastown, and its attendant gunships, will almost immediately begin to fire on us, so my hands are near the controls, ready to push off, hoping I can outrun them.

But bluffs are based on confidence. So I push the *Cherub* in on a slow but steady course.

The line crackles to life, and they direct me to one of the docking platforms. Again, I exhale, and Rosie looks at me and smiles. "So far, so good," she says.

I bring the *Cherub* into the appropriate docking platform and I am well aware that my condition is forcing her to wobble far more than she usually would. But then I bring her in smoothly and we're back at Gastown.

The body of the man is still on the deck, and Rosie and Claudia both help me drag him to the storage room and cram him into a utility box. But not before I strip him of a few of his outer items of clothing. I take his hat, his mask, his scarf, and his jacket.

I try not to worry about the hole in the back of the jacket. The one caused by my bullet blowing through Hernandez's back. It's not uncommon to have torn, beat-up clothing, I tell myself. But will that escape people's notice?

I turn to Rosie, who looks more with it than I must do. "How do I look?" I say.

"Like shit."

I put the mask and cap on. "Now?"

She shrugs. "Can you move without showing off your wound?"

"I'll do my best," I say. She's scraped together some bottled water and a half-bottle of hooch to help rinse off her jacket. Neither of us will stand up to scrutiny, but hopefully we won't have to. Claudia's hair is bound up and a scarf wrapped around most of her head. Rosie is similarly covered.

We all makes sure our weapons are accessible.

Together we move down to the exit.

Gastown guards greet us as the door opens. "Hernandez," one says. "We weren't expecting you to get back so soon."

"Need to replace the forward glass in the gondola," I say in my best imitation of Hernandez's voice. The mask helps muffle the sound. They will have seen the glass missing.

"What happened?" the other guard says. He has greasy hair sticking out from under a cowboy hat.

"Let's just say I was a little too vigorous." I mime jerking off with my good hand and they laugh. "We'll catch up with you later. Gotta get this taken care of, then get back."

Then I walk, with Rosie, out into Gastown.

I exhale as soon as we turn down one of the alleys, out of sight of the guards.

"I can't believe that actually worked," I say.

Rosie shakes her head. "Me neither. Let's get to the *Osprey* and get the others."

"You'd better hurry," Claudia says. "Pretty soon what happened on the ground is going to get back to the folks up here, and Ben, you're going to want to be gone with the *Cherub* by then."

"You go out with Diego," I tell Rosie. "I'll take Miranda out."

Claudia stops me. "Are you going to be okay? That bullet is still inside of you."

"It will keep until we get out of here."

She shakes her head.

"Besides," I say. "Rosie has my back."

Rosie doesn't respond.

"Then I'm going to head back to the *Valkyrie* for a moment. I was able to recover some documents from the plant. I want to make sure they're secured." She kisses my cheek. "I'll try to catch you before you leave."

I nod.

Then, staying close to Rosie for support, we head off to the *Osprey*.

The ship's where we left it, thankfully. But when we knock on the gondola door, no one answers. We try again and again, but nothing. I try not to be aware of our time ticking away.

"Goddamnit!" I slam the door in frustration, then look around to see if I attracted any attention. "Where are they?"

Rosie removes a key from a pocket and uses it to open the door. I should've thought of that. I barrel past her, looking in the *Osprey*'s gondola, trying to find any sign of Miranda or Diego.

"They're not here," Rosie says.

"Then where are they?"

"They could be anywhere in the city," Rosie says. "We need to find them." What she doesn't say is that they might not be okay. That things could have gone terribly wrong.

"We need to find them," I say, "but I don't know how long I can keep this up." Already I feel the Juice wearing off. The pain is coming back, as well as the weakness. My legs are shaking. And I'm starting to feel nauseated. Not to mention I think I'm bleeding through the bandages Claudia put on me.

"Then what do you want to do?" Rosie asks.

"The *Valkyrie*'s not far from here," I say. "Maybe Claudia can help us look. She might have more Juice, too."

Rosie doesn't look too happy with this, but she knows that three pairs of eyes are better than two. And that I'm not going to last very long.

The dock where the *Valkyrie* is moored seems to be clear of guards or watchers, so I walk over to the door to her gondola and knock on it.

All this movement is shaking me more than I want to admit. Amidst the churning nausea in my belly as the Juice ebbs, I feel something, like hard, jagged ice scouring my insides.

Claudia opens the door and flashes me a surprised look.

"Miranda and Diego," I begin, then my legs go soft and I'm pitching back, falling. Rosie moves forward, catching me, and together with Claudia pulls me into the gondola.

They escort me to a chair and put me down. Claudia grabs a plastic bottle full of water and hands it to me. I drink some of it, careful not to take too much, knowing it's probably some of her good supply.

"You need some rest and some medical attention," she says. "Only I don't know that it's a good time for that."

"Miranda and Diego aren't in the *Osprey*," I say. "We need to look for them."

Claudia frowns. "We don't have much time."

"Which is why we need your help. And maybe some more Juice."

Her frown deepens. "I have some, but you shouldn't have too much in such a short time. Too much of that stuff will kill you, too."

"Claudia—"

"No," she says. "My ship, my call. You're only going to slow us down anyway. And we can't afford to be slow right now. You stay here. Rosie and I will do a quick search and then bring your friends back here. Then you can all get out. Okay?"

"Claudia . . ."

"Just say yes. Or try to stop me." She flashes Rosie a smug look and then they move toward the door.

As another trembling fit hits me, I realize they're right. "Just . . . hurry," I say.

Claudia nods, then they leave.

I swear I'm only going to close my eyes for a second. Just one second to rest them, to get the fatigue to relax its grip on me. But I feel like it's longer than that.

What eventually rouses me is Claudia gently shaking me. I grunt and wince as the pain returns, even stronger than before.

"What is it?" I say as soon as I can focus on her face. There's something wrong. I can tell.

"Is it Miranda?" I ask. I can hear the panic in my voice. "Where is she? What happened to her?" I start getting out of the chair.

Claudia pushes me back down and lifts the bottle back to my mouth. "Not Miranda," she says. She flashes a worried look at Rosie. "Diego."

"What?"

"I checked with one of my contacts. He was able to confirm that Diego got hauled off by the city's thugs."

"What about Miranda?"

Claudia shakes her head. "I don't know. My contact didn't know anything about her. She could've escaped."

"Or she could've been taken, too. With Diego."

"We have to get him back," Rosie says.

"It'll have to be fast," Claudia says. "These boys aren't the gentle types."

I nod. "You'll have to sew me up as best as you can."

"You can't go with us, Ben. Don't be crazy."

"I need to go with you."

"Ben—"

"If he's being held somewhere, we'll need someone to be ready to get him out of there. On a ship. One person is not going to be able go in after him alone."

"He's right," Rosie says. "We need him."

"Not if he's just going to pass out on us."

"Then cut me open and sew me up," I say.

Claudia sighs, then shakes her head. "I suppose it's time I return the favor."

"Yeah, I guess I have this coming."

Claudia starts removing my shirt and pulling back the soaked bandages. "At least Rosie had the good sense to let the bullet pass through. You have to do everything the hard way, don't you?"

I try to shrug, but the pain stops me. I grit my teeth. "It's a gift."

I move over to the counter on one side of the gondola that is secured to the wall and I lay myself down on top of it. It's not the first time it's been used for medical reasons. Or others. Claudia disappears and returns with a bottle. I recognize it as some seriously strong rotgut that I picked up a while back, back before the raiders took over Gastown. It's the color of rusty water. She holds it out to me and I flip off the cap and take a long swig. It's harsh, and it goes down my throat like whirling blades. But as the acid taste fades, a torrent of warmth follows it and I can feel the alcohol swim out into my muscles. I take another swig, then another, and then I lie down.

"Try to make it quick," I say.

"I'll do my best," Claudia says.

I roll over onto my stomach, and Claudia hands me a wooden stick, which I slot into my mouth. We both know the drill. I did the same for her back when she first got her scar. It seems like another lifetime ago.

As the knife pierces my skin, cutting through to where the bullet is lodged, I focus on that memory and call it to me.

It was back when Claudia was running with us—after the night we'd had sex, but before she'd got the *Valkyrie*. That's a different story—an epic story—but not the one that's flooding through my pain-filled mind.

Dad was at the controls of the *Cherub* while Claudia and I were on the ground, preparing to forage. Our target was a fancy apartment building in Seattle. Dad had read about it in an old magazine, of all places. The article had mentioned how this was one of a slew of new buildings that used biometric locks on all the doors, even those on the stairs and elevators. "Biometric locks mean that Ferals can't operate them," he'd said.

"But then how do we get in?" I asked.

"Through the windows. We can smash through those. We just check out the apartments, see if there's anything there."

"But what if the security has failed after all this time?" Claudia asked. She was always pointing out flaws in Dad's plans. It was something he hated, but it was valuable. I used to get a big kick out of it.

"It may well have," Dad said. "But I know the ways these things work. I've seen enough security systems in my time. If they're off, they stay closed."

So it had seemed worth a look. We brought the *Cherub* in, and while the lower windows seemed to be completely smashed in, and thus off-limits, the upper windows seemed mostly intact.

So Claudia and I went down on the ladder and smashed our way into one of the rooms, a living room, from the looks of it. We got in without any problem, but as we were brushing glass off our coats, we heard a loud engine, and gunfire.

Looking out the window, we saw another ship—a rigid—firing on the *Cherub*. Dad began to pull away.

We had a plan for this, of course. If the *Cherub* took fire, Dad would pull away, get to safety, and then come back for us when he was able. Our job was to find a safe place to hole up and forage for what we could. Seeing as we were in the building, it seemed like that wouldn't be difficult. I was even excited by the idea of the two of us having some time alone together, with Dad not being around.

It's not that I didn't care about Dad's situation—of course I did—but I knew he could outrun that other ship. He'd done it before. And as I've always said, the *Cherub* is fast. He knew the tricks, how to take advantage of the terrain. I was sure he'd be fine.

Of course, safety first. We started exploring the apartment. Everything inside was covered with a thick layer of dust, muting the colors of the furniture and the artwork that hung on the walls. It was largely untouched, and already I saw some valuable salvage—a computer, for one. Other electronics. Plenty of books. We walked into the kitchen. Loads of pots and pans. Again, valuable for their metal content. It was, in any terms, a score, and it was just the first of many apartments.

Claudia looked at me and smiled. I smiled back. Then she kissed me. I kissed her back. We escalated in that way.

I know what you're thinking—it was unprofessional. And it was. But we were quick about it. And we got on with our business. And I didn't feel badly about that at all.

We gathered together everything we wanted to take, moved it by the window, and then Claudia said, "Should we try for another?"

I shrugged. "Why not? We have to wait for Dad anyway. Might as well make the most of our time." There were, of course, other ways to spend our time. Reading, talking, fucking our brains out again, but we were high on the score and it was singing in our blood.

"What about the doors?" I said.

"The locks won't work on the inside," she said. "We can prop this one and then see if we can get in anywhere else. If not, we come back here."

"What if there are Ferals in the other apartments?" I said.

She shook her head. "Anyone trapped in here when the Sick came down would have died off long ago. We should be fine." And it made sense. So, like she said, we opened the front door and propped it open with a sturdy chair. Claudia ventured out into the dusty hallway and I followed closely behind.

We tried the next apartment door and it wouldn't open. It appeared as if Dad had been correct. But Claudia wanted to try a few more, so we tried the next one, and the next one. It seemed that Dad's hunch was right and we felt secure enough, so we were making noise and laughing.

Claudia was just walking up to the next door when we heard a snarl, and a shape flew out of the doorway and into her. I saw an arm flash out, and Claudia was falling back.

Even back then I had been programmed on how to respond to Ferals, so I jerked out my pistol and fired across the corridor. Once, twice, three bullets, four, until it dropped to the ground.

I ran to Claudia.

She was reeling, leaning back against the wall of the corridor. And when I saw her, I almost backed away. The Feral's long nails had torn her face from her cheek to her forehead. Blood gushed everywhere and I wasn't even sure if her eye was still okay. I reached for her.

"It got me," she gasped. "It got me."

I wanted to hold her, to go back for water, to do what I could, but my upbringing overrode all of that. So I turned to the open door where the Feral had appeared from. And I saw why the door had been open. Someone had wedged it. When the Sick came down, when people were trying to escape, someone must've not wanted their doors to be locked and they wedged something wooden underneath it, and it had stayed that way all these years.

I pushed into the door, which smelled of Feral, and I took the place room by room, my body on fire, my veins pulsing with my racing heart, adrenaline sparking through my body. It was a similar apartment to the one we'd seen, but it was wrecked. Glass was broken. All the belongings had been shredded or mishandled. Ferals had been here. But it seemed like none of them remained.

I rushed back for the front door, kicked free the wooden block that held it open. Then I grabbed Claudia, still in shock, and pulled her back to our original apartment. Then I closed that door behind her and got her onto the bed in the bedroom.

The blanket was thick with dust, but I pulled that off and put her down on the sheets beneath. Already blood was soaking into the white. "Water," I said. I pulled free my bottle of water and, holding her down, splashed it over her face.

She gasped, but in that moment I could see that her eye appeared okay. A moment later, the blood had welled up from her cuts.

"Is it bad?" she said. She was gasping and kind of whimpering, but no more than that.

"It's bad, but your eye's okay, thank God."

"You'll need thread," she said.

"Oh shit."

"See if you can find some."

"Oh shit."

The miracle of that day was that I found some. And a needle. So I threaded it and stood over her. And paused.

A Feral had cut her. I had been so concerned about how she was that I hadn't stopped to realize. A Feral had cut her. Its nails had torn into her. It wasn't, strictly speaking, a fluid exchange. But how could we know? It was only the one strike. It didn't even get close to her. But still. A Feral.

Yet it was Claudia. A friend and the closest thing I had ever come to that notion of Love I'd read so much about in the old books. The thought of leaving her to this, of not doing something, made me frantic. I felt tears forming in my eyes.

Claudia looked up at me with her good eye, seemed to realize the same thing. "You can't touch me," she said.

"Shut up."

"No, you can't touch my blood."

"You shut the fuck up," I said.

And then it came to me. "I'll use my gloves."

She stared at me, blood still pouring down her face.

And so I did. It didn't give me the best control, but I used the gloves and the needle and thread, and with a hairbrush handle between her teeth and about a half bottle of vodka inside her (and some for the cut), I sewed up her torn face.

She passed out somewhere between her cheekbone and her eyebrow, and after I finished I stood over her, holding a towel in place over her face. I stood (or later sat) like that for hours.

My pistol never left my other hand.

It wasn't until the next morning that Dad came back with the *Cherub*. He had to lower her almost level with us before I could get Claudia aboard. I explained to Dad what had happened. What I'd done. I expected him to be mad. If there was one thing he'd always said, it was to get as far away from Bugged-up fluids as you can. Even if you weren't sure. Even if you were covered. It was too persistent. It was too easy for the Bug to win. I was sure he was going to rip into me. Or maybe give me the silent treatment again.

Instead, he looked at Claudia, then back at me, and nodded like he understood.

For the next two days we kept a vigil by Claudia's side, switching off to take over the controls. We looked for any sign of the Bug. If she was sleeping and began to stir, I would hold the gun up to her head and question her until she said my name or began using words.

In the end, as you can already tell, she survived. She didn't have the Bug. What she did have was a nasty scar, the result of bulky gloves and a shaky hand.

I always felt bad about that. About feeling caught between the two strongest impulses I had ever felt—of my will to live facing off against my will to love. Seeing her again, even after all this time, brings all of that back.

But with the pain I'm in, I feel like this is payback. Somewhere between the knife entering and the bullet leaving, I pass out.

✳   ✳   ✳

When I come to, my chest and shoulder are throbbing, but I appear to be patched up. "How is it?" I ask.

I hear Claudia's voice behind me. "I'd say I did a damn better job on you than you did on me," she says.

"Well, you watched me," I say. "You had a good example."

She helps me up to a sitting position. "Hand me my shirt."

"You need to rest," she says.

"I can't," I say. "They have Diego and they may have Miranda, and I'm not letting either of them sit in there for a moment longer than necessary." I look to Rosie for support. "You want to go in now, don't you?"

She grits her teeth and nods.

"I suppose you're set on this?" Claudia says.

"Yes. So you better get me that Juice."

Claudia sighs and shakes her head, but she rummages in a nearby chest and mixes me up a shot. She isn't gentle when she plunges it into my arm.

Once again it's only an instant before it starts to take effect and I feel a surge of wild energy and everything becomes hyper-sharp and clear. The pain from my chest and shoulder starts slipping away, unable to get a grip.

"Do you know where they took Diego?" I ask.

"There's really only one place where they keep people," Claudia says. "They converted one of the larger warehouses to serve as a prison." She looks down, then away. "Everyone else they dump down the murder hole."

"The what?"

"There's a section of the platform they cut a hole in. People they want to make an example of, they, well, throw in."

"Oh my God," Rosie says.

I try to imagine plummeting to my death from up this high. It's not a pleasant thought. "There's no chance that . . ."

"No," Claudia says. "I don't think so. They seemed to want to question Diego. He was caught poking around. They'll want to question him first." The implication is left unsaid. Once they're through with the questioning . . .

"How many guards would you say watch this prison?"

"Probably four or more," Claudia says.

"Okay," I say, thinking. "Two of us will have to deal with the guards and get inside. The third will prepare our exit. Bring a ship around to ferry Diego off."

I look at Rosie. "You'll be the exit."

"What?"

"Claudia and I will go in and get Diego out. You bring the *Osprey* in and take him out at the closest ramp."

"If I get clearance to leave, though, they won't let me cross over the city to get to you. The guns will take me out."

"Then we'll just have to create some kind of diversion. Draw their attention elsewhere while you come around the city's periphery. We get Diego aboard and then you take him straight back to Tamoanchan."

"I'd rather go in with you," Rosie says. "Claudia can bring in the *Valkyrie*."

I shake my head. "Sorry, Rosie, but Claudia is the best shot I've ever seen with a bow and arrow, and we're going to need that to take out the guards without alerting every thug in this place."

Rosie's glare looks like it's going to burn through my skull.

"We need you to get Diego out. It has to be you. You take him and you sail off into the sunset and you leave us to clean up. It has to be that way."

Rosie grits her teeth but nods.

"Good." Then we get down to planning. Timing. Strategies. As much as you can with this sort of thing. A lot of the time it comes down to watching for a bit before you act.

So that's what we do. Claudia and I, I mean. Rosie heads off to get the *Osprey* ready and set up the distraction. I jury-rig one of Claudia's spare radios to work off a battery, which we'll take with us. When we send Rosie the signal, she'll bring the *Osprey* in and take Diego away.

The night is cold as we exit the *Valkyrie* and I'm glad for the wrappings I'm wearing. Claudia is wearing a hooded cloak that all but hides the shape of the bow slung across her back. It's something of a thrill knowing she's carrying it. I picture it in action, the perfection of it. I should have learned how to fire one, I think. And not for the first time. Me, I have the revolver and my knife. But once again this kind of operation calls for stealth and that's not my usual way of doing things. But Diego's life is at stake. And maybe Miranda's too.

My last piece of prep is overly dramatic and definitely the result of reading too many books. But, before we leave, I take out the Star of David the rabbi gave me. And, jury-rigging up a pin, I fix it to the front of my shirt, like the stories of the old lawmen of the West. My very own sheriff's star. I wonder what Miranda would think of it.

Thinking of Miranda sets my stomach twisting even worse than my wounds do. Every so often a wave of nausea hits me and I'm not sure if it's coming from one or the other. But there's no time for that, so like everything else, I push it down and press onward. There will be time to rest and reflect later. Or else there won't be.

We move through the Gastown streets. Time of day doesn't seem to matter here. People are out, still operating their stalls or just hanging out in the streets or alleys, warming themselves before fires in large metal barrels. Fire, at least, is easy to make in the Sick. There's plenty of fuel to be found if you don't mind chopping wood.

My palms start getting itchy as we move to the other side of the city.

They're also shaking. But it doesn't take too steady a hand to kill a man. I should know.

Claudia is quiet, but I know this is how she is. She uses this time to focus. She used to do the same back when we were foraging together. Dad and I would chatter on, but Claudia was silent as stone. And just as hard. I realize what we're about to get ourselves into, and there's no one else I'd rather have with me right now. At least not for this kind of thing.

We stroll past the street the warehouse is on where Diego's being held. The first time we're quiet, heads down. But we look. I see two guards. Near the entrance. Nothing on top of it. I wonder if that's because of structural integrity or because the chattering of the damn patchmonkeys is too loud.

We make our way around the warehouse, walking a block or two away, then come back, playing amorous drunks. Claudia runs ahead of me, I pursue. This time we make noise. And watch again. Still just the two guards. But they're vigilant. They look up as we pass by. Their hands are steady on their guns. Semiautomatics. Ready to cut us down in a spray of bullets.

Wonderful.

We duck down the first alley we pass.

"So, just the two of them?" I say.

Claudia nods. "I couldn't see any others." She shrugs. "I thought there would be more."

"They probably have more inside."

She nods again. "No way of telling until we get in there."

"So what's the plan?" I say. "Stab and strip?"

"Can you think of anything better?"

I can't. So that's what it is.

And this is where we split up.

As I walk away, I look back to see her pulling down the bow, stringing it with her sure fingers. I can't help it. It makes me hard.

I check to make sure my knife pulls freely from its sheath. I check to make sure my hands are working well enough.

Then the fun begins.

The guards are still looking vigilant as I sway my way over to them. I make sure not to be too loud, but if I'm doing my job, they'll think I'm drunk. The worrying thing is that it's not that hard to do. My wound is wearing down my calm and my cool. But I'm committed right now. Have to see it through.

One of the guards moves forward, one hand securely on the gun grip, the other stretched out to me in a warning gesture. He is wearing an animal pelt like a short, dirty cloak. "Walk away," he says in a firm voice.

"Huh?" I say, staying in character.

He raises the weapon and shows me its profile. "Find somewhere else to be."

"But isn't this Tom's place?" I say. I raise my hands like I'm just harmless. Like I'm just looking for my friend, Tom. The other guard is firmly gripping his weapon now.

He's still gripping it when Claudia's arrow takes him in the head. My guard turns at the sudden crunching sound, and I draw the knife and plunge it up through his chin, grabbing his body with my other hand and lowering it, softly, to the ground.

Then we're in the trenches. And it's only a matter of time before someone finds us. Or before one of the people inside feels that they need a piss and walks out. So I drop the guard (which is a relief since he feels pretty heavy on my bad arm) and I begin stripping his clothing. Not all of it. But the coverings that matter. The ones people use as identifiers. And I put them on.

The fur smells, but there's nothing doing for that. I strip off a dull metal necklace, some wrist bracelets. And make sure to wrap the semiautomatic around my chest. I hope they'll be enough to disguise me.

Claudia jogs up a moment later and begins doing the same with the other man. He has a full face mask with only the eyes cut out. It's good and bad. It covers her face, but it leaves her eyes free. And that could be a problem. That kind of get-up draws attention to the eyes. And Claudia's are bright blue. And her scar is visible. But there's nothing else to do.

Then there are only the bodies to deal with. We each grab ours and drag them to a nearby alley and shove them in the shadows as best we can.

Then, assuming our best swagger, and wearing the guards' semiautomatics, we move to the door.

Claudia and I have this all worked out. She stands outside while I open the door and go in.

A man looks up from where he's sitting at a table. "What are you doing here?" he says. I catch a glimpse of gray hair and a grizzled, curly beard.

I walk up to him without stopping and say, "There's a bit of a problem." His eyes are on me. So he doesn't see the door open and Claudia step to the opening.

I spin the man around and Claudia puts an arrow through the back of his neck. I see it erupt from his throat. See the spray of blood, hear the choking rasp he makes as he falls to the ground.

There's no one else in the room. Just a door in a makeshift wall, and I move to that.

"I got the door covered," Claudia says.

I nod. There's no time to stop. No time to think. The room stinks of death and we only have minutes to make sure everything goes right.

I open the door, and the smell in the next room is worse. It smells of blood, too, but stale blood. And sweat. Of shit and urine. And it's enough like a Feral nest that it's all I can do to stop myself from jerking out my revolver.

There are two people in the room, but only one of them is moving.

He's standing, and as he turns to me, his eyes wide in surprise, I notice that he's carrying a knife, too.

It would be so easy to shoot him, I think in that second. But that's not an option. And the knife is in my hand and we dance.

He comes at me, his knife out, and slashes at me, and it's then I realize my mistake. The semiautomatic is still slung around my body and it slows me down. I duck away, but the knife slices across my chest, cutting through my jacket and shirt and carving a line of fire through my skin.

I swing at him, but the man pulls back. He's strangely bared, I notice. No real coverings, just a short-sleeved shirt splattered with blood and wet with sweat. Less to cut through, I think.

He reverses his knife in a back-hand grip. He's used to this kind of weapon. He holds it like you might hold your hand. As part of your body. And I'm much better with guns.

His stance is easy, light. He practically glides across the ground, like a snake. I feel like a lumbering cow.

He comes at me again, and I raise the semiautomatic just in time to catch the knife then thrust up with my knee, aiming for his groin, but I only catch his thigh.

His next attack cuts the gun from my shoulder and it clatters to the floor.

He comes at me again.

I follow the gun.

Somehow it gets caught in my feet and I go down and he's on top of me, the knife driving down, and I throw up my hands to stop it. Still, a good inch of the tip digs into my side.

I throw my legs at him and push him to the side.

My arm whips out and my knife slides against the ground and into something soft.

Something happens to my mind in that moment. I'm tired, I hurt, and all my nerves are raw and close to the surface. But that moment of victory sparks some kind of bloodlust in me. I feel my lips curl back from my teeth in some kind of sick smile.

I roll over onto him and bring the knife back. A kind of wild fury fills me and I bring it down.

Then he head-butts my wound, and the world blanks out in pain. He twists my wrist, and the knife falls away from me. Then he throws me to the side and I fall off of him.

There's this voice in my head that starts screaming at me to get up and I do, somehow finding my feet through the pain and disorientation.

And I go for my gun. The only thing I know to reach for. The only thing I know to kill my enemies.

He comes up, back in his light stance, the knife still there, an extension of him. I can fire at him. I have the range. I have the thunder. But I know it'll give us away and I know the figure slumped in the chair is Diego. Only I can't focus on him right now. My eyes are on my opponent.

He raises his chin. Daring me to fire at him. Instead, I drop my guard. He moves in. I drop my shoulder and pivot, bringing the revolver around, my finger on the trigger guard, my grip firm. He cuts me, somewhere near my bullet wound, and the pain threatens to blank me out again, but I am now a machine. An engine. And there's no stopping the movement. My hand comes around and the pistol slams into the side of his head.

We both go down.

I'm aware of only two things—my hand and, by extension, the pistol and his head. And I bring the two together. As hard as I can. Once. Twice. Again. Again.

I think of Diego. And Miranda. Mostly Miranda.

I am a machine. The pieces move of their own accord. Back and forth. Back and forth.

A voice breaks me from the cycle. "Ben."

Then again. "Ben."

I look up at Claudia. Then look down to see the ruin that is the knife fighter's face.

"I think he's dead," Claudia says.

I nod. Regain myself. Then I climb unsteadily to my feet, wincing as every fiber in my body screams at me.

We both turn to look at Diego. He's slumped in a chair, his arms and legs bound behind him. There are cuts all over his body. Burns. Blood. They've tortured him.

His face is as much a ruin as that of the man I just killed. He's almost unidentifiable below the bruises and dried, crusted blood. His head slumps down over his chest. He's out. Which, from the looks of what has happened to him, must be a mercy.

I walk over to him. Claudia starts untying his bonds. He doesn't stir. I slap him lightly on the face, afraid that if I hit him any harder he might start bleeding all over me.

"Diego," I say. "It's okay. We're here."

He still doesn't stir. Claudia hands me a water bottle and I splash some on his face. Some more gentle shaking causes his eyelids to flutter.

"Diego," I repeat. "It's me. Ben. We came to get you."

He looks up at me through his swollen eyes. I'm not sure he's seeing me. "Ben?" he says.

"Yes. We came to get you out."

"Ben . . ."

"It's okay," I say. "Rosie's okay. She's going to take you back home."

"No," he says.

"It's okay," I say again. "You're safe now."

"They . . . they tortured me," he says through swollen lips, his voice a croak.

"I know," I say. "But that's all over now."

"No. You don't realize. I told them."

"Told them what?" I say.

He chokes and shakes his head and we almost lose him again. I put the water bottle to his lips and let him take a sip.

"What did you tell them, Diego?"

"I tried to stop," he says. "I tried. But . . ."

"What did you tell them?"

He looks at me through his swollen face.

"I told them where Tamoanchan is."

# CHAPTER NINETEEN

Together, Claudia and I help carry Diego out of the warehouse and out into Gastown. I have to hope we aren't going to be discovered. All it would take would be a shift change for the guards to throw our whole plan into disarray. Another two guards with the kind of weapons they carry could take us down in an instant. Claudia and I can't reach our weapons, laden as we are.

Diego seems to regain some of his strength as the cold wind hits him. But he keeps muttering about Tamoanchan and what he's spilled to the Gastown people. By now I've signaled to Rosie to bring in the *Osprey*. If everything went to plan, she set off some of the explosives I brought back from the helium plant on the opposite side of Gastown. The hope is it will draw attention there while we get Diego out on this side. Rosie's not going to be happy about the condition Diego's in. But there's no helping that.

I can't look away from the fact that all of this is my fault. I was the one who convinced Diego to come to Gastown. I sold him on the idea of gathering intelligence on the city when, after everything, they gathered intelligence from him. The most important intelligence of all.

All because I wanted my ship back.

And as much as I love my ship, as much as the *Cherub* is all that I have in the world, I find myself wondering if it was all worth it.

And there's still one thing missing.

"Diego," I say. I say it two more times before he seems to focus on me. "Diego, what happened to Miranda?"

It takes him a moment to respond. As if he's trying to place the name.

"She wasn't . . . I didn't see her. She wasn't with me when they took me."

"Did she get away?" I ask.

He shakes his head. "I don't know."

Damn, I think. We still don't know where she is. And even if she wasn't taken, she's somewhere in Gastown. And Gastown is about to be a very dangerous place. Even more than before.

"She'll be okay," Claudia says to me, over Diego's body. "If she got clear, she found a place to hide. If they got her, she would have been in there with him."

I cling to her words, wanting to believe them. But I'm not sure I do. Until I see Miranda with my own eyes, I won't believe any of this. I won't believe she's safe. I won't believe she's not dead.

Oh God, I think. Don't be dead, Miranda. Don't be dead.

Claudia gives me a look that makes me feel like I'm not completely in control of myself, but she doesn't say anything.

We half-carry, half-drag Diego over to where we told Rosie to meet us. It's a platform off the eastern side of Gastown. A commercial platform. The hope is that it's not occupied. That no one will be there at this time of night.

When we get there, the *Osprey* is already within sight. I get on the radio telling Rosie to find somewhere to dock. Diego's not going to be able to climb up the ladder. We're going to have to carry him inside.

Luckily, there's a little part of the dock that allows for Rosie to bring the *Osprey* in. A balloon is anchored there, giving the ship's envelope room to descend.

She opens the gondola door for us, and we carry Diego onboard. "They barely noticed me," she says. Then she sees Diego. "What the hell?"

"They were torturing him," I say.

"Oh my God."

"He's alive, though. He's beat-up, but he'll live. They weren't trying to kill him."

She gives me a look that makes me feel like the biggest asshole in the world. His body will escape with only scars, but his mind . . .

"It's worse than that," I say. "He told them where Tamoanchan is."

"What?"

"They put him through the gauntlet. He spilled. Any of us would have."

"Goddamn it."

"They'll be headed for the island."

Her face betrays her horror. "What do we do?"

"You take him and you make for Tamoanchan. But take a wide course. If the Gastown ships are headed there, you don't want to pass them. Not alone. And you need to keep your brother safe."

"But all those people . . ."

"You take care of Diego. Claudia and I will do what we can to stop the raiders."

Claudia gives me a look as if to say, What the hell are we going to do? but I silence her with my eyes. Or at least I think I do.

"The *Cherub* is fast. I think I can catch up to them."

"Then what are you going to do?" Rosie says.

"Whatever I can," I say. "If you get to Tamoanchan before they do, do what you can to get people out. Radio ahead if you can. Do what you can to evacuate."

"We'll never make it," she says.

I grab her and meet her eyes. "We're not going down without a fight. Any of us. Take your brother and get underway. Now."

She takes Diego, slinging his arm around her shoulder. "This is all your fault," she says. "We wouldn't even be here without you. You and your goddamned ship."

I don't say anything. What can I say?

"Godspeed," Claudia says into the silence.

Then we leave the gondola, and the *Osprey* sails away into the sky.

"Ben—" Claudia begins.

"I have to go after them," I say. "She's right. This is all my fault."

"They made their own decisions," Claudia says.

I can't meet Claudia's eyes. Not now.

"I have to go. I have to do what I can. They helped me get back the *Cherub*. I can't just leave them."

"And what about Miranda?" she says.

It's like a punch in my gut. Now that I have the *Cherub* back, Miranda is all I want. All I'm lacking in the world. But I can't afford to wait for her. I can't look for her. All those people are depending on me.

What can you do? says the voice in my head. But I know I have to try.

"Can you look for her?" I say. "I know I have no right to ask. But . . ."

"You don't want me with you?" she says.

"I do. You know I do. But . . . I owe her as well. I was supposed to look after her."

Claudia shakes her head. "It's more than that, isn't it?"

I wince. Then nod. "Yes."

"Okay," she says. "I'll look for her. Try to get her somewhere safe."

I put my good arm on her shoulder. "Thank you."

"When should I tell her you'll be back?"

I smile. It's a question we both don't want to answer.

Then I walk away.

✳    ✳    ✳

I head back toward the *Cherub* with my cap down low and my scarf up high. I'm turning about a block from the warehouse when I'm slammed against a corrugated metal wall and I feel a pistol nuzzled into the small of my back.

"Where did you take him?" asks my attacker.

My head is reeling from being slammed into the wall, and the pain in the rest of my body is joining in. Panic races through me. They've got me dead to rights. I can't move without the pistol going off and I'm in no shape for another fight.

Then the voice threads its way through the panic, and pain and fear and recognition hits almost as hard as my head into the wall.

"Miranda?" I say.

The gun moves away from my back. "Ben?"

Then I'm being turned around and Miranda is tugging my scarf down. I can't help smiling as I see her face. She holds her pistol in her hand. "Ben!"

I grab her and pull her to me, holding her as tight as I can. Already the Juice is fading and my muscles feel all watery. "Yeah. It's me. Thank fucking god, Miranda. I thought they got you."

"What . . . what did you do? Is Diego . . . ?"

"Walk with me," I say, and I pull her after me, after replacing the scarf around my face. "We got him out. Rosie took him."

"Thank goodness," she says. "I was going to try to get him out, but I wasn't sure I could take out all the guards."

I look at her and the gun she's still holding in her hand. "I thought you didn't like using that."

"Against Ferals," she says. "They don't have any choice in what happens to them. These assholes, though . . ."

It's such a Miranda thing to say that I start to laugh.

"What?" she says.

"It's just good to see you," I say.

"Where are we going?"

"Back to the *Cherub*."

"You got her back?"

I nod and a rush of warmth floods through me at the thought. I have my baby back. Then I remember what I'm about to do. "But there's a problem."

"What?"

"They tortured Diego. It looked bad. He told them where Tamoanchan was."

"Fuck," Miranda says. "What are we going to do?"

I want to smile again at her use of the word "we," but I keep it inside. "I'm going to go after them. Try to stop them somehow. I told Rosie to head straight back and let them know what's coming."

"I'm going with you," she says.

I think about telling her no. I think about how she would be safer in Gastown. But then I think of how beat-up I am and how I really want, maybe even need, her with me. "Okay," I say.

"Are you finally learning to listen to me?" she says.

"Stranger things have happened," I say.

We make it back to the *Cherub* but make sure to check our surroundings before getting too close. It's strangely unguarded. No alarm yet?

I don't wait to question our good luck. Instead I push Miranda ahead of me and onto my ship, quickly closing the door behind us. Then I start making the preparations to get up and in the air.

"What happened to the *Cherub*?" Miranda asks, looking around.

A pang shoots through me at the reminder of how my baby's been looted. "The Gastown raiders were using it. They did this."

"I'm sorry, Ben." She places her hand on my arm, and I'm sure I can feel its warmth through my sleeve.

"I have her back. That's all that matters," I say. I move to the controls, get the *Cherub* warmed up, start to bring her back into the sky.

Risking being overheard, I dial up Claudia's frequency and manage to get through. "I have Miranda," I say. "No need to look for her."

"Good," Claudia says. "But Ben. I've been monitoring the Gastown radio frequencies. The ships have already left. They're on their way to Tamoanchan already."

"Fuck," I say. That's probably why things seemed so quiet in the city. They already assembled their attack force.

I take a moment to look at the map to find the quickest route to Tamoanchan from Gastown, factoring in the weather conditions on the horizon and the assumption that there are several ships moving in formation. If the raiders stay true to form, they'll drop Ferals down on the island, which buys us some time. They'll want the Ferals to be alive and wriggling. Catch them too early and they'll expire before reaching Tamoanchan. So they'll need to stop on the coast and fish.

In the meantime, the *Cherub* will catch up to them.

"Ben, you're hurt." Miranda moves forward as I strip off my jacket and she catches sight of all the blood on me.

I try to smile but end up with a grimace. "It's just a scratch."

"Let me look at you."

"I'm okay," I say. "Claudia sewed up the gunshot."

"Gunshot?"

"The rest are from getting Diego out."

"Let me look at you." Her hand alights on my bare arm, and an electrical tingle runs through it at her touch.

"There's no time, Miranda," I say softly. "We need to leave."

She pulls away and nods. I turn back to the controls.

Miranda helps me fly. She's been on the *Cherub* long enough to know the basics. Soon we're speeding through the air, on the trail of the Gastown force.

"What happened to you?" I say. "We missed you at the rendezvous."

"I know," she says. Her left hand curls into a fist and hovers at her side. "I thought I was so clever."

"What happened, Miranda?"

She leans back against a counter, crossing her arms across her chest. Then she looks at her boots. "You know I was mad at you, right?"

I squirm a bit, then look away, out the window of the gondola. "I had that impression, yes."

"I was grateful for your help with breaking into the lab, but . . . it wasn't enough. And I got a glimpse of their data and that spooked me, so I headed back with Diego to the *Osprey*." She bites her bottom lip. A horrible habit—I cringe every time she does it, worrying she'll crack her lip, but it also does something to me. Inside. "I couldn't be around you. Not then. So I went with him to see what I could figure out."

"And what did you figure out?"

"They've been examining the virus, like we have, trying to understand its structure. I lifted as much as I could after taking a look at their journals. They had data on virus morphology, on its genome, on replication cycles. They had detailed analysis of mutations."

"So that I can understand, Miranda," I say.

She sighs. "They're working on the virus, trying to see how to engineer it. They want to, well, to mutate it. They don't have access to all the techniques they need to make it happen, but they've been trying."

I look away from the window. "What would that do?" My voice sounds incredibly small.

"You know how persistent the virus is, how effective it is. They want to use it as a delivery system. What if they were able to make it increase aggression, even more than it does now, but also are able to make the infected more susceptible to behavioral conditioning? The perfect troops. Or slaves. And they could use it as a weapon, infecting anyone, any group or settlement they targeted."

"Christ."

"It gets worse. They're also experimenting on the Ferals. I saw notes on behavioral conditioning and physical conditioning."

"Physical conditioning?"

"Yes. Muscular enhancement, increased aggression. I get the impression they see the Ferals as possible manpower, maybe even troops."

"Miranda," I say. "Down at the plant, I saw . . . a Feral. But it was big. Muscular. They were . . . they were feeding people to it."

"God."

"They're doing this. They're doing it down there. I saw others, Ferals in cages. Jesus, Miranda. They're monsters." I don't have to clarify that it's these scientists I'm talking about.

I think about everything Miranda's trying to do. How she's trying to fight the Bug. It was hard enough to do before, without having a bunch of mad scientists working on the other side.

"Ben," Miranda says. I turn to her for the first time in the conversation. My wound screams, but I ignore it. "Hey." She steps forward and puts a hand on the side of my face. "It's not all bad."

"Oh, isn't it?" I ask.

Her smile is small and slightly sad. "In trying to understand the virus, they had to break it down. Like we've been doing. I didn't get to look at the data in depth, but they have figures we don't have. With what they've done, we'd be able to accelerate our own understanding of the virus. Hell, I think we might get close to a detection system."

"What?"

"For all the evil they're doing with this data, we can use it to do some good. I think it'll advance our knowledge by about a year at least." She shakes her head, then smiles the biggest smile I've seen since I left Apple Pi. She fishes into her shirt pocket, right by her heart, and pulls out a small rectangular object. "This prize right here," she says, "is worth more than anything those Vikings are holding. If we can get this back to Sergei and Clay at Tamoanchan . . . Ben, we can make some real progress. Together with Alpha . . ."

I want to hug her, but I'm afraid it might be too much for me right now. Hell, I want to kiss her. While I was risking my life, and Rosie's, to get my ship back, she was risking hers to help save the human fucking race. And succeeding. Hell, I'd kiss Diego right now if I could. Then I get a flash of how he looked when we got him out.

"What went wrong?" I ask. "How did they get Diego?"

She shakes her head. Bites her lip again. "They were smarter than I thought," she says. "I underestimated them. They had a working camera. Several, probably, rigged up in the lab. I was okay—I guess I'm in the habit of keeping wrapped up in places like that. But Diego . . . you know how big he is. And part of his face was showing. They tracked him down, a whole Valhalla force, and there wasn't anything he could do.

"He . . . he told me to run, and so I did." She throws her arms up in frustration. "I didn't want to, but I knew I couldn't take them down. And they didn't know who I was. So I got away. They sent two people after me—they'd seen us together, after all, but I took them down and then kept moving. I planned on tracking Diego down and then rescuing him."

"Which is what you were trying to do when I ran into you," I say.

She nods. "That's about it."

Miranda's head drops, and I move forward and rub her arms, once again ignoring the pain at the movement. "What's the matter?" I ask.

"It's my fault," she said. "What happened to Diego. What's happening to Tamoanchan. I was the one who convinced him to go into that lab. I was the one who missed the cameras."

I pull her toward me then and hold her in my arms. With my good arm I stroke her hair. "It's not your fault," I say softly. "It's not your fault at all. It's mine. I was the one who brought us here. I was the one who convinced Diego to come in the first place. I wanted my ship and I didn't think about anything other than that. And now people are paying for that."

She pushes back from me, looks up into my eyes. "Diego made a choice to listen to you."

I shake my head. "I pushed him. And I took advantage of the shit he was in. Because of me. I didn't even know what he was going through back there, and yet it all worked to my advantage."

"You got him out," she says, but even she doesn't seem convinced.

"I did. But it's not enough." I drop my face into my hands. "The whole time I was after the *Cherub*, I kept thinking of it as all I had. And yet I was ignoring all the people, all the chances, all the fortune around me."

"Ben," Miranda says. "You didn't know."

"No, you're right," I say. "But I also didn't think. And of all the things I've learned from you, that might just be the most important."

She hugs me again, only stopping when I gasp a bit from the pain.

"So," I say, knowing I'm on treacherous ground. "Are you still mad at me?"

She sighs and shakes her head. "You know why I was mad, right?"

"I think so," I say.

"I know you see them as inhuman. Monsters. They've fallen over the edge and are lost. But I don't see them that way. They're lost, yes, but I feel like we can find them again. That we have to find them again."

"Miranda," I say. I want to quip. Maybe mouth-off. But I can't. This is too important. "I just . . . the kind of life I've led. I've had to see them that way. Or else I would likely be dead."

"Things are different now," she says. "You're with us. With me. And if we are . . . if this is going to continue to work, you're going to have to accept that."

Once again my thoughts become writhing snakes in my head. "So, what? I'm not supposed to shoot them if they're coming for you?"

"No, of course not. I hired you to protect me. You've always done a good job of that. I just need you to know that I don't take any pleasure in that. And I don't want you to either. Each Feral that dies is another person I won't be able to save. Do you understand?"

I nod, unable to find words. I don't know if I believe that she can save them, but she's going to try. Because that's what she does. When the world rains shit down on all of us, when others, like me, are moaning and looking for shelter, Miranda wades into it and tries to find a place where she can help.

And I'm going to help her.

"I missed you, Ben," she says.

I take her in my arms again. And there, for a moment, I forget about everything else. About my pain, about the Gastown ships, about Diego, even about the Ferals on the ground. For a moment, everything is all right. For a moment, the world is okay.

✷  ✷  ✷

It's as we're gaining ground that I realize I don't have a plan. "What am I going to do, Miranda?" I ask.

"What?" Miranda says.

"How are we going to stop a raider force?"

"You've always managed before."

I bang my fist against a table. "I've always been lucky. Against one or two ships at the most. Usually I just escape. The idea is always to get the *Cherub* out intact. Not to take down other ships. She's not built for combat."

"I always wondered about that," Miranda says. "You're so bent on guns, I'm surprised you didn't put at least a couple on the *Cherub*."

"She's too beautiful to ruin with guns," I say. Miranda gives me a strange look and then shakes her head. I realize too late what I've said. "Her defense is speed," I say quickly. "And in the air she can usually get away from anything she comes against. If I could run faster than Ferals on the ground, believe me, I'd do without the guns, too."

"Which still brings us back to how we're going to take on the other ships."

"They're going to be slow," I say, my mind chewing away at the problem. "And trailing Ferals. Which means hanging cables."

Miranda nods. "But not all of them. They would keep a ship or two as escorts to deal with any attacks."

"So we'll have to concentrate on those. Use our speed to tangle up their ships. And maybe take out those Ferals. If we can stop that, Tamoanchan has more of a chance."

Miranda chews on her lip again. "You're taking a risk here."

I close my eyes. "I know. But I need to. This happened because of me." I look Miranda in the eyes. "We can do this. I know we can."

"I'm glad you said 'we,'" she says, misunderstanding. I'd meant me and the *Cherub*.

"Actually," I say. "I was going to drop you off somewhere near the coast. I don't want to risk you getting hurt." I'd only just made the decision, but it seemed to be a good one.

"What?" Her eyes widen and her mouth sets into a hard line.

"I'm going to need to act quickly, and they're going to be firing at us—"

"I've been in situations like that with you in the past."

"Miranda—"

"And so, what? You're going to leave me on the ground? With Ferals?" It's a good point.

"Ben," she says. "If they get Tamoanchan, they get Alpha and they get Sergei and Clay. And there won't be anything to work toward. All of our work will be gone. This is important to me, too. I'm going with you."

"But what about the data in your pocket? Say we do lose Sergei and Clay (I ignore the look on her face as I say it), then you and that data are all that's left of our chance against the Bug."

"Ben," she says. She places a hand on my uninjured arm and slides it down to my hand, grasping it. "I know you're still getting used to this, to understanding it, but it's not all about survival. It's not all about the greater good. How many things have been done in the name of the greater good? I couldn't live with myself if I ran just to save some data."

"But it's not just data," I say.

She shakes her head. "It's about everyone. The lost, the injured, the victims. No matter whether they're infected or facing the raiders or hungry or sick or whatever. It's about Sergei and Clay as much as it's about Ferals. If I can save them, I need to try." She squeezes my hand. "Besides, you need me. You can barely stand straight.

"Look at it this way, then," she continues. "It's a matter of odds. Yours are better with me. Simple logic."

I want to tell her to go. I want to clamp down and shut her out. But I can't manage it.

She puts her other hand on my face. "It's about everyone. You, too."

I nod. "Okay, then," I say. "I guess that's settled."

"Damned straight."

So we get down to getting things ready. I have Miranda prepare some more pipe bombs and ready the remaining explosives I took from the helium plant. We assemble everything heavy we can find still aboard the ship. Then, for the first time in a long time, I say a small, silent prayer. It's not that I suddenly believe in God, or anything. It's just that I figure if there's any force for good in the world—be it a spirit or dead ancestors or Fate or whatever—I could use its help.

We hit the coast an hour later.

Ahead of us, already in formation, heavy with Ferals, we spot the Gastown ships.

※　　※　　※

They start out as blurs in the distance, lit up in the darkness. Five blobs that soon come into focus. Three of the ships dangle dark shapes below them. Ferals. This time, however, they're not on hooks. Which is bad news for us. I'd been hoping they would stick with their usual tactic because odds are, none of the Ferals would survive being stuck like that for as long as they have to travel. Tamoanchan is a long ways off the land. A dead, bleeding Feral is still dangerous, but not as dangerous as one that can run and flap around.

Instead, though, they have them in some kind of metal containers. I wonder how they rigged them up. I'm guessing they have some kind of quick-release mechanism to drop the Ferals down into Tamoanchan. Definitely not stupid, these assholes.

Then I have a scary thought. What if they haven't gone fishing like

I thought? What if they're using some of the monsters they're breeding down on the ground?

Supporting the Feral ships are two more. Whereas the three dirigibles carrying Ferals are light ships with semirigid hulls, the support ships are rigid zeppelins and carry armaments I can see from a distance.

We covered the distance in good time, but they've had time to fetch their Ferals and come up full. Now they'll be pushing hard for Tamoanchan.

It's okay, though. Because I'm faster.

We're running dark, all of our lights off, only our engine noise to give us away. With any luck, they won't see us until we're right on top of them.

I push the *Cherub* straight at them.

I imagine monsters inside the cages. Mutated Ferals, built for slaughter. Living bombs to drop on Tamoanchan, to cut through the populace, leaving a bloody trail behind. I can't help shivering.

It's another few minutes before the enemy ships notice us and the support ship to our right starts to turn toward us, bringing its guns to bear.

I push the *Cherub* up, trying to stay on top of the ship, hoping that will shield us from her armament.

"Ben," Miranda says, pointing.

The top of the other ship is protected by a mounted cannon. A cockpit protects the gunner from the environment. He starts shooting and we can hear the zip of the gunshots. Then the punching and cracking as several find their way into the *Cherub*.

"Damn."

I pull us away from the shots as best as I can, but the cockpit swivels with us.

"Get down," I yell at Miranda, but when I turn to her, I see she's already down with as much mass as possible between her and any bullets.

The raider is rising with us, and at a speed to rival the *Cherub*. I can't get on top of her where Miranda could drop a pipe bomb on them.

Then I look to my left and see the other support ship coming around at us. It makes a lot of sense—take us out quickly then continue on to their target. They're not expecting resistance. They probably think I'm a lone nut trying to take them on.

More bullets spatter into my ship and I wince.

These are Gastown ships, full of helium. If they had hydrogen we might figure out a way to ignite it, but the *Cherub* is the only hydrogen ship around.

Then I go cold.

The *Cherub* is a flying fireball. With all the explosives currently lining her belly, she's become a weapon.

A wave of light-headedness makes me grip the console tightly. The room starts spinning around me. No, Ben, the voice says. You just got her back. You can sail away right now. Take the ship away, get Miranda away and live on. With everything you want.

But I know I can't live like that. Can't live *with* that.

"Miranda," I say. "I need you to help me turn the *Cherub* into a bomb."

# CHAPTER TWENTY

"**W**hat the hell are you talking about?" she yells back.

"A bomb," I call, as I'm trying to avoid the pinching of the two approaching ships. I do the only thing that comes to mind. I push us straight for the middle ships. It might stop them from firing at us.

"Ben!"

"We have no weapons on the ship, so I need you to help me make the *Cherub* into a weapon." I spare her a quick look. "I can't do it without you."

"Oh, Ben," she says.

"It's the only thing I can think of to stop them. And we need to stop them."

"But your ship."

"Miranda. I need your help. I can't fly and get this done. I need you to take the explosives and place them around the *Cherub*. And bring me one of the detonators."

She just stares at me like her heart's breaking.

"Please, Miranda," I say softly. "We don't have much time."

"Okay," she says and runs off.

Bullets continue to strafe us as I bring us closer to the hookships. These are smaller, more delicate vessels. Not soft-shelled, but not nearly as well defended as the support ships.

Then they start moving in different directions. I curse but realize I'm dealing with experienced pilots. They're getting out of our way. For the first time ever, I chide myself for not mounting weapons on the *Cherub*. Sure, it would slow her down, but why not just a simple gun emplacement?

I turn the ship toward the nearest hookship and accelerate, as fast as I can, at its underside.

Miranda yells back to me from the cargo area. "What are you doing?" Panic in her voice.

"If this doesn't work, then I want to make sure the Ferals are taken out. They could do more damage than these ships."

My hands get sweaty as I carefully grip the steering yoke. It's a tricky thing, coming this close and not colliding with the other ship. But getting up close to it will also protect us from some of the fire we're getting.

Bullets rip into our underside and I revise my opinion.

We're barreling at the enemy hookship and I'm holding the *Cherub* steady. In a moment we'll either scrape ourselves against her underside or . . .

The top of our hull hits the cage with a clang that we can hear inside, and at the speed we're going, the metal box crumples and the Feral inside is smeared all over the *Cherub*'s envelope. I try not to think about all that Bugged-up blood on my baby, but I don't have time to worry about that because there's a ship above us and two others shooting at us.

For a moment I think about raising us and slamming into the other ship, but though the *Cherub*'s hull is rigid, she's not impervious.

Instead, I bring her up alongside the other ship, trying to use it as a shield. But while it protects us from one of the gunships, the other is coming in on an angle and bullets rake the *Cherub* like buckshot. Windows explode in a shower of glass and some of it cuts my face. The temperature in the gondola drops significantly, and I shiver even as I pull at the controls. The dial showing the pressure in the ballonets is showing several leaks.

My baby can't take much more of this.

The ship alongside us scrapes against the *Cherub* and she may as well be scraping against my skin.

One of the other hookships comes up on the other side, penning us in. I race for the opening, but another ship pulls down to block our way.

My father used to use the expression "like shooting fish in a barrel." I never understood what that meant. Until now.

More bullets rip into us, and I slow the *Cherub* down, matching the speed of the ships to either side.

I slam the switch for autopilot and then I run to Miranda in the cargo hold. "Done?" I ask.

"Pretty much," she says. "I just scattered them about where I thought they would have the most effect." She holds up a detonator. "How are we getting out, though?"

I move to my yellow raft and inflate it. Finally getting some use, I think. Then I head for the spare hydrogen tanks in the cargo bay. Sometimes the *Cherub* needs a little topping up. Then I wave Miranda over. "Quick, help me fill some of these ballonets." She helps me attach then fill the large, thick balloons. "They should help slow our descent."

All around us we can hear the whine and impact of the bullets from the enemy ships. I register hits on the engines as the noise of my baby changes from smooth to tortured.

Together we tie the ballonets securely to the raft. Then I hit the release for the cargo bay door. With a smile I can't feel, I wave my hand over the raft. "Your chariot," I say.

Miranda moves closer and wraps her arms around me. "Ben, I'm sorry. I know—"

I silence her then by kissing her. Her lips are warm and dry on mine and then wet, and I'm pulling her to me and I feel somehow liquid, and she's liquid, too. It's everything I've imagined it would be. And more. And my body starts to run away in excitement, but instead I pull her down on top of me, down into the raft, where I coil my boot and arm into the rope threaded around its side, and with my good arm I clutch Miranda to me.

Then I tip us out into the air.

Below, the sea waits to swallow us.

✳　　✳　　✳

We fall. Miranda screams and I want to, but I have no breath. No air. Everything is cold and loud and we spin around and around. One ballonet bursts almost immediately, but the others seem to hold. Above me I see the lights of the enemy ships. But not the *Cherub*. She's too dark.

Until she explodes into a fireball of light. It feels like the world ending. And maybe it is. The loudest sound I have ever heard blasts into us and fiery warmth, and then my breath really is gone and it's all I can do to hold onto the raft and then—

We smack hard into the water. I'm flung clear of the raft and Miranda slips from my fingers and—

COLD.

I can't breathe again, but this time it's because I'm sinking and my limbs are frozen and I know I'm going to die and I think it's okay because the *Cherub* is gone and what do I have to go back to.

And I think of Miranda. That's what I have to go back to. I need to help her. To protect her. And I need her. To help me. To protect me. Mostly from myself.

I thrash and kick and push my way back toward the air.

Always toward the air.

And at last I break the surface and suck in breath and I am so cold, but I need to stay awake. Alive. I need to find Miranda.

Light dances in the sky. Angels falling. The flaming fragments of their wings. Fires light the water, too. The burning wrecks of airships, once lighter than air, now just more flotsam and jetsam. I can't count the fires. There's an awful lot of wreckage, though. And I can't see any lights in the sky. Six ships, ripped apart and set alight.

Strangely, it's one of the most beautiful things I've ever seen.

I thrash in the water, trying to stay above the waves, looking frantically for Miranda.

Then I see it not too far away. The raft. The bright yellow of the rubber reflects the light of the fires and I swim for it, pulling myself into it.

Miranda is in it, her arms wrapped in the rope, and I smile and cough and laugh and cry and take her in my arms. She's cold and wet. We both are. But though I can't hear her breathe—my ears are shot—I can see it. And I huddle next to her and draw her toward me.

"Thank God," I say, in little more than a croak. "Thank God you're okay."

She gives me a weak smile and places her palm on my face, and for a moment we just lie next to each other, wet and shivering but together and alive.

Alive.

I think of the *Cherub*. I start to think of all the moments on that ship. All she did. All she gave me. But I push it all away. I can think of that later. Not now.

Now we need to stay alive.

I keep one hand on the revolver. I don't know if it will fire after being submerged, but I'll damn sure try if any of the Gastown people survived and come for us.

We might die yet, I think. If no one finds us. But right now, we're alive. And Miranda is next to me. And we'll figure out the next move. Together.

"Ben," Miranda says. "Are you okay?"

I pull her to me and kiss her as the lights dance around us.

# ACKNOWLEDGMENTS

t's easy to think of this novel as an airship, since it took so many people to get it off the ground. The world of *Falling Sky* was conceived at Clarion West in 2008, growing out of a short story I wrote there, and Paul Park was the first person to help me crystallize the idea. Mary Rosenblum helped to critique it and offered some insightful suggestions, one of which being that I should expand the then short story into a novel. Cory Doctorow also suggested some changes that helped solidify the themes of what would become the novel. I am indebted also to all my Clarion West classmates who helped refine this idea. Theresa DeLucci, Shane Hoversten, Eden Robins, Kira Walsh, Carol Ryles, Kristin Janz, Pritpaul Bains, Maggie Croft, Chris Reynaga, Caren Gussoff Sumption, Pam Rentz, Owen Salisbury, Douglas Lucas, Jim Stewart, Carlton Mellick III, Tracy Harford, and An Owomoyela—you aren't just my peers; you're my family.

Thanks are also due to my writing group, Altered Fluid, who helped to improve my writing over the last handful of years and offered support during the writing of this novel. Paul Berger, Matthew Kressel, Alaya Dawn Johnson, Devin Poore, K. Tempest Bradford, Kris Dikeman, Mercurio D. Rivera, E. C. Myers, Lilah Wild, Sam J. Miller, Greer Woodward, Danielle Friedman, Tom Crosshill, Rick Bowes and N. K. Jemisin— thank you for your example and your friendship and your honesty. I am so proud and grateful to be part of your group.

To Allyson Kohlmann and Nina Lourie—your encouragement, support, and love gave me lift and kept me aloft during much of this process. Thank you.

Very special thanks to my former agent and mechanic, Joe Monti, for giving me wonderful editorial feedback and ultimately for making this happen. Also to Barry Goldblatt, who helped see this through to the end.

Thanks, also, to Lou Anders, my editor, and all the hardworking people at Pyr (my air traffic control) who helped make this book what it is.

To Elisabeth Jamison—you have kept me sane throughout the process of launching this book. I have so much to thank you for but especially for climbing aboard and helping me steer. I can't imagine doing this without your love and support.

Finally, I'd like to thank my family for their support, especially my brother, Dev, my earliest comrade in the world of science fiction and fantasy. But most of all to my mother, Christine Khanna, who unfortunately didn't live to see this book published. My mother read me stories from a young age and encouraged me to read and to write all throughout my life, regardless of genre or medium or category. And when even I doubted that this day would ever come, when I couldn't believe it would happen, she always did. She was unwavering in her support and I miss her terribly. This is most of all for you, Mum.

# ABOUT THE AUTHOR

*Photo by Ellen B. Wright*

**R**ajan Khanna is a writer, narrator, and blogger who fell in love with airships at an early age. His short stories, narrations, and articles have appeared in various markets both in print and online. He currently lives in New York City. *Falling Sky* is his first novel. Visit him at his website www.rajankhanna.com, on Facebook www.facebook.com/rajankhanna, or on Twitter @rajanyk.